All Due Respect
the Anthology
edited by Chris Rhatigan

D1740134

Cover Image: Eric Beetner
Ebook Design: JW Manus

Table of Contents

INTRODUCTION

Alec Cizak founded *All Due Respect* in June 2010. The name came from a phrase frequently used in gangster movies that usually leads to a fight or a killing. Also, Cizak wanted to give one writer the stage as a way of conveying "all due respect."

The site has published, and will continue to publish, fiction about crime. Not solving crime. Not bemoaning crime. Cizak published one story per month. When I became editor in January 2012, I chose to publish two stories per month. Other than that, little has changed. The tight focus, consistency, and attention to quality over quantity are still the site's strengths.

If each issue is a shot of espresso, consider this collection a pot of black coffee. From Joe Clifford's "Day Tripper" to David Cranmer's "The Great Whydini," these are the stories that best represent *All Due Respect*. They're tough, no-bullshit tales about unsavory characters. Some are fun, some are excruciating, some are poetic.

Some are all three.

Chris Rhatigan
All Due Respect Editor

DAY TRIPPER

Joe Clifford

I brush the snow and sleet from my thinning hair. Wet, sticky clumps fall like rice pudding onto the shoulders of my Salvation Army jacket I've reinforced with duct tape. A pasty film coats my mouth, reminiscent of old drinking days, even though I gave up the bottle long ago. I'm pretty sure there's fungus growing in there. Tastes like cat ass. Probably caught an infection from the blood-sucking parasites at the hotel where I flop nightly on a thin, hard mattress, listening to the sex and violence next door, pushing her memory away.

I inhale the north winds deeply, heavy metal tinctures and silver polish punishing my lungs, and push open the doors to the under-lit lobby, which feels more like an emergency room than an employment agency.

I'm the first day-shifter in. It's barely 5 a.m. You have to get here early to land the good assignments. Schweitzer's packing plant. Forklift in the JC Penny warehouse. Janitorial duties at the hospital. Show up late, you get the shit jobs, stuck shoveling ditches on a dairy farm, fruitlessly stabbing tundra till your hands go numb and your testicles crawl back up into your abdomen.

I wince at Marjorie, the husky gal behind the desk. She has her big nose in one of those glossy celebrity magazines.

"Got the sign-in sheet?"

"Hrumph," she says. Marjorie doesn't even pay me the respect of looking up, just keeps staring at some anorexic movie star in a bikini, the one who named her kid after a piece of fruit. I don't know why Marjorie's doing that to herself. Fat bitch isn't squeezing into a two-piece if they cut her in half.

"Any idea when it'll be out?" My empty stomach grumbles and groans. It sounds like retarded hamsters fucking in my gut. I spent most of yesterday's measly payday trying to get even with the hotel. Can't ever seem to catch up, not with what they're paying me here. I have $2 in my pocket I'm saving for an emergency. Food doesn't qualify.

"Stop staring at me," Marjorie says, "you're making me nervous." Her gaze remains steadfast on this season's brightest summer fashions. She flaps a fat fist. "Go have some coffee."

I know not to push her buttons. Last time I gave Marjorie a hard time, I got stuck cleaning rat turds out of heating ventilators at the Piggy Wiggly.

In the break room, a closet barely big enough for one, Mr. Coffee rests between powdered creamer packets and a microwave that never gets wiped down. Starchy stalactites drip from its roof, overpowering the enclosed space with the concentrated aroma of burnt buttered popcorn and Dinty Moore. The coffee tastes like shit. But it's free. I need something to wake my ass up.

I don't sleep well. Can't turn my brain off. The whores screaming bloody murder all night don't help. Been a long time since I've had a woman. The hotel, the Hugo, is crawling with hookers, so access isn't the problem. I haven't been with anyone since Sheila. As long as there's hope for us, I cling to what still makes me feel human.

The last place you expect to end up is working day labor. Doesn't matter if you hold an MBA or used to own a house. When it's gone, it's gone. You do what you got to do. Because of the conditions I violated when I crossed state lines, I'm in the system, which means I can't renew my driver's license or land a legitimate job. I need to stay underground. For additional fees and a convenience charge, Labor Core makes that possible. Forget paycheck to paycheck, I'm day to day.

I poke the clumps of powdered creamer, but the coffee's too tepid to dissolve. Slurp another sip. The swill tastes like it's been filtered through a dirty old sock, somehow worse than the usual sludge. I lift the lid. On top of the moist grounds, a fat bloated cockroach stares back at me, spindly antennae curled like sweaty post-coital pubes. Damn thing's the size of my big toe, all waterlogged and alien looking. I stare into my Styrofoam cup. More than half is gone.

I chuck it in the trash and storm past Marjorie, who doesn't take her honking schnoz out of the magazine, and then I'm back out the door and up the block to the Marathon Station, brushing off the b-boys pushing rock, to shell out money I don't have for a real cup of coffee. Anything to get this taste out of my mouth.

When I return to Labor Core, a dozen guys are lined up. Like a Dust Bowl soup kitchen, bowlegged, gangly string beans shuffle in ill-fitting hand-me-downs and mismatched shoes. I make for the head of the line.

"Whoa," Big Ed says, grabbing my sleeve. Big Ed looks like Richard Kiel, Jaws from the old James Bond movies, scoliosis curving his spine more crooked than a convict riding a roller coaster.

"Just stepped outside," I tell him. "I was here first."

"That right?" Big Ed says, "Well, you wasn't when I got here. So step off."

The hobos stare, waiting for my next move. I glare at Marjorie, waiting for her to take my side. But she just sits there ogling airbrushed fantasies, stuffing her pie hole with fistfuls of miniature muffins from the vending machine.

Big Ed has me by half a foot. I can take this Midwestern yokel. The old me would do it, too. But it's not worth the trouble. The cops get involved, that warrant shows up. The only thing worse than this life is one locked in a cage. Then I can kiss any reconciliation with Sheila goodbye. Without hope of that, who knows what I might do.

After I sign up, I head back to the coffee room and fill

8

another cup of joe.

I find Big Ed. "No hard feelings," I say, handing him the coffee.

* * *

The only job left is an assignment nobody wants—moving furniture and other crap from storage pods to houses on the outskirts where the money lives. Up and down stairs all day, rich bitch housewives barking orders, tearing your back to shreds. Professional movers know how to lift with their knees, maximize space, compartmentalize. When you hire Labor Core, you're trying to save a few bucks by putting meth heads and morons who didn't graduate high school in charge of your most intimate possessions. Someone's bound to get pissed because of a dent in Aunt Agatha's cookie tray, and Labor Core's only too tickled to dock your already miniscule pay to recompense. Even worse, moving is a two-man job that requires a truck. And only one guy has one.

...

Jaspers is a holy roller and a gabber. Got stuck dusting a corn silo with him once. Eight hours listening to how every day is a gift (that's why it's called "the present") and pontificating on the fate of my mortal soul.

With a pair of bibbed overalls and a switch of twine for a belt, Jaspers should be frying butterballs at the county fair. He sports an unruly, stained gray beard, which shrouds most of a frost-burnt face, leaving visible only a pair of Charlie Manson crazy eyes.

Big flakes fall like tufts of eiderdown. If this were somebody else's life, I might even say the scene is pretty. We're packed up and on our way to the first house. We bounce along in his beat-up powder blue jalopy, seats so threadbare springs jab my ass. Jaspers dials in Christian talk radio. Cast thee out of Eden bullshit.

He hefts from his bib the assignment sheet, which contains all the addresses, holding it at arm's length, squinting. I don't even want to ask.

But I do anyway. "How many?" I'm hoping four, but know damn well it'll probably be five.

"Six," Jaspers says.

"Six?! Are they fucking nuts? We'll be doing this till midnight. Jesus Christ!"

"Please don't blaspheme in my truck."

I half-ass my sincerest apologies.

Neither of us mentions overtime because Labor Core doesn't work like that. They have to approve you for overtime pay, and they never do.

Traversing the western edge of Rochester, we enter the cookie-cutter subdivisions and gingerbread boxes where happy families live and every quaint street named after a tree and truncates in a delightful cul-de-sac. I'm not mocking it. Used to be me once upon a time.

We hammer out three houses in fewer than five and a half hours, skipping lunch and making good time. Best of all, our frenzied pace doesn't leave any time for holy rolling or chitchat. My luck starts to run out at the fourth house.

Hunched over, hauling a dresser up the stairs, I'm gingerly stepping backwards when Jaspers says, "It hurts to see you in so much pain."

"This is hell on my back."

"No, brother, I don't mean that kind of pain."

A hen pecks her beak over the railing. "Careful with that. That's a satinwood French Louis Highboy. Do you know what that's worth?"

More than I'll make this year, lady.

"You're dragging the bottom!" the hen bawks.

"Sorry, ma'am."

We've got a carpet runner so we're not scratching jack. Still, I lift higher, cayenne pepper scorching a million nerve endings throughout my lower lumbar.

It's closing in on six. This far north, daylight doesn't last long. We've loaded the last pod, securing its contents and covering with a tarp. Only one house remains, way on the other side of town, in the hoity hills of Diamond Lakes. To get there, we have to cut through downtown, a dumpy little strip lined with discount cigarette shacks and dollar stores, SROs like the Hugo.

Despite my protests, Jaspers stops at Taco Bell. With all the furniture, we won't fit under the drive-through. I say I'll wait outside. The snow has stopped, temperatures warming just enough to turn the parking lot into a giant slushie. Streetlights halo against the dimming horizon. Jaspers moans about eating alone.

When I don't order anything I have to confess I'm broke. Jaspers insists on paying for my meal, which I can reimburse him for at end of the day. Magnanimous. I get two 89-cent bean and cheese burritos. He excavates a pile of loose change from his overalls' bib pocket, painstakingly separating nickels and dimes from pokers chips and bits of lint, hair and gum wrapper, right to the penny. The black teenage girl taking our order looks at us with pity.

We sit down. No one else in the place. My arm sticks to a patch of gummy salsa. The whole restaurant smells like fart. Not much of a dining area, just a couple of tables. Feels like we're right on top of the cashier and manager, another black kid in his teens. Both of thom keep snickering at us like we've been written into their private joke.

"Why are you so angry?" Jaspers asks.

"Who says I'm angry?" I tear a hunk of soggy bean and cheese and nosh as fast as I can, swallowing the glob whole.

"It's worn all over you, brother."

"Stop saying that. We're not brothers."

"We are in the eyes of the Lord."

The heat is turned up too high, a choking heat that makes it hard to breathe, and along with the beeping and blipping of microwaves and fryers it instantly delivers a terrific headache.

"Can I ask you a personal question?"

"No."

"Do you believe in a higher power?"

"Thanks for the burritos." I hold one up; goopy thing limps over my fist like an old man's listless member. "I'm not interested in any conversions, okay? I just want to get my money."

"Why?"

"So I can pay for my hotel room."

"Why?"

"What are you, Jaspers? Six years old?"

"I'm trying to make a point."

"Then make it," I say, "and shut up about it."

I hear the disjointed crackle of the drive-through. Car wheels swish in the wet slop and artificial light stabs my eyeballs. This goddamn heat.

Jaspers ekes a grin, all halitosis and country yellow teeth, brow crinkling. "I just wonder why a guy like you is working day labor."

I chomp down and bean goo squirts out the sides.

"You play the part, but you seem a bit...educated...for Labor Core. If you don't mind me saying."

"Not that it's any of your business," I say, "but I'm looking for my wife." I wish someone would turn down this fucking thermometer. "Kind of got stranded here."

"Your wife lives in Rochester?"

"Not exactly."

"So she *sort of* lives here?"

"Hey," I call over his head to the two goofballs hot-dogging behind the counter. "You mind turning down the heat?"

"We can't hurt down the heat, sir," the boy says, giggling. "Corporate sets the temperature."

Fucking little asshole. My focus returns to Jaspers. "Her

parents do. Did. They're dead. I honestly don't know where she is."

"You don't know where your wife is?"

"She doesn't want me to know." I try swallowing. The goop wedges in my throat, gobs there like sick snotty phlegm, the fungus spreading. "I made some...mistakes."

At this Jasper's face beams. "We *all* make mistakes. That's why we need to let go, let God. *He* understands. He forgives us."

"What would you know about it? What mistakes have you made? Besides getting dressed this morning."

"I hurt a child," he responds without missing a beat. "I hurt a lot of them." Though he says this contritely, I swear I detect a perverse thrill, as if this is the conversation he's been hoping for all along. "I used to be a sick man," he says. "Battling the demon in the bottle, drowning my guilt in liquor. Like you."

"For the record, I don't drink."

"Maybe not now. But I've met my share of dry drunks. You got all the symptoms. Angry. Aggressive. Just waiting to boil over and lash out. Something will set you off."

"I'm nothing like you. I never did anything like that."

"But you hurt some of God's children just the same, didn't you?" His eyes twinkle with feigned kindness. "Ah, yes. I can see. You did."

I want to tell this sicko to piss off, but all these nights of not sleeping, this cardboard filler slop I'm shoveling down my gullet clogging my esophagus — this goddamn heat — I can't formulate the words.

"Go on," Jaspers says. "That's it, brother. Let it out."

It's only then I feel the tears roll down my cheeks.

Jaspers reaches across the table, cupping my hands in his. "I think the Lord has a plan for you, too."

...

Last thing I want to do is climb in this pervert's truck, but we have one more house, and I need the cash. I'd expected some Latter Day Saints bullshit, but not that. It inseminates the earworm back in my brain. And it won't come out. Coming home. Seeing her kneeling before him. The greasy satisfaction on his face. How could you? *Oh, you're a fine one to talk!* She ripped the sheets to cover her naked body, shrieking and flailing. *You ruined my life! I wish I'd never met you!* And on and on. He tried to slip his pants up, hoping to slink off. It was the cowardice that made me snap. I gripped the lamp on the nightstand like it was a baseball bat, cracking the base against the back of his well-groomed head, red horse cock still slick with her saliva flopping about as he spiraled to our imported Tabriz carpet; and then I was on top of him, hand around throat, slamming my fist into his mouth, smashing his head against the floor, nose breaking, skull fracturing, orbitals shattering, teeth cracking. *You're going to kill him!* She fought to tear me off. I spun and delivered a blow to her belly. The way she doubled over, the primal wail, even then it registered as more than just a punch.

How could I have known about the baby?

* * *

"You okay?" Jaspers asks as we pull up the long drive to the final house on the hill.

"Don't talk to me."

A gothic monolith with fake candles above the stairs, ornate handcrafted wreath hung on the door even though Christmas has long since passed. It's a greeting card, a fucking snow globe on a mantle. It's not real. None of this is real.

"Sometimes we need to share," Jaspers says. "I think you'll sleep better tonight."

"Shut the fuck up."

I clank the cast-iron doorknocker, an angel without any wings, as warm, homey tones fall invitingly from inside.

14

We've been at it over an hour, when the woman whose house it is insists we take a break. I'd gotten an eyeful when we'd walked in. I know the type. Long legs, manicured cuticles, flashing skin in all the tempting places, so pristine in need of a little sullying. She gives us the tour of the palace, pointing out newly acquired items, Italian this, Finnish that.

She casually mentions a husband out of town on business. I catch the way she looks at me, sundress twirling with each seductive step.

"Can I get you something to drink?" she asks.

"No, thank you, ma'am," Jaspers answers for us both. "We should get back to—"

"Sure," I say, "why the hell not?"

"I'll be right back." She sashays off, gliding to the swish of a high thread count.

I start getting a little tingle, a swell rising in a place I haven't for a while.

"What are you doing?" Jaspers whispers.

"Relax. One drink isn't going to kill anyone."

"I can't stand around and watch this."

"Then don't." I point outside. "Unpack the truck. Pile the shit on the porch. I'll find my way back."

"I don't think—"

"Jesus Christ, will you get out of my ass? Cruise down to the local schoolyard, get an eyeful. I don't care. Leave me alone!"

Jaspers slinks away.

She comes back in with the bottle and glasses. We both know where this is going.

There's no running anymore. I've been chasing a ghost all along.

* * *

When Jaspers returns, I've got her bent over the couch,

15

pretty little sundress bunched, head down, ass up, pants by my ankles, plowing her good. She likes what I'm giving, bellowing like a banshee. Falling off that wagon after so many years, you hit the ground hard. My head woozes exhilaration and ecstasy. I feel young again, strong again, like a man again.

At first I can't figure out why Jaspers is here or what he's saying. My head buzzes with blackhead flies. *Stop? Hurting her?* He starts pawing at me, tugging my arm, trying to pull me off. I look down and see blood. My first thought is the fucker's stabbed me. I search for the puncture wounds but can't find any. The blood is all over my cock and hands. Jaspers yanks me out of her, and emptiness returns to fill the void.

I face my assailant, who pantomimes like a drunken monkey, desperately trying to communicate God's great plan for me. I cold cock him. He tumbles backward. And I'm on top of him. Fistful of hair, slamming my knuckles against his country yellow teeth, smashing his head against on the linoleum, skull fracturing, orbitals shattering, nose breaking. When I'm through with him, he is a mash of purple pulp, and I could collapse from sheer exhaustion. But I won't. I'm finally seeing things clearly.

Back on my feet, I wipe away the blood and discover my pet. She has dropped to her hands and knees to commence her penance, ripped panties binding her ankles as she feebly tries to drag herself away, a filthy slug trailing slime.

"Where you going, baby?" I say, sweetly. "Get back here. I'm not done with you yet."

A DRINK NAMED FRED
Tom Hoisington

A grasshopper walks into a bar, and the bartender says, "Hey, you know we got a drink named after you?" And the grasshopper says, "You have a drink named Fred?"–ancient Buddhist koan

I walked into the Thirteenth Step Tavern twenty minutes after opening time. Sun slid in through the not-quite-all-the-way-closed plantation blinds. Ervin was the only other customer in the place. He was sitting at the bar, eating his usual mid-morning brunch of peanuts in the shell and Pabst Blue Ribbon. I pulled up a stool next to him, and Rebecca, the punky bartender with the nose ring and the alternating bubblegum-pink and raven-black hair, used the old can popper behind the bar to open me a Pabst of my own. She plunked it down in front of me and Ervin said: "Y'know, kid, I got a Gamblers Anonymous meeting this afternoon." Then he took a long pull on his beer, waiting for me to deliver the punch line.

"Betcha don't make it," I said.

His eyes smiled over the top of the can, and his lips curled away from its opening in a sly grin. He never got tired of that vaudeville bullshit, and he'd been doing it a long time; Ervin was going on twenty-four years as a daytime drunk. I was just starting my second week, having recently dropped out of grad school.

Am I racist if I feel the need to tell you Ervin was black, even if it has no bearing on the story?

Ervin was black.

Ervin was a Vietnam vet, too, but he confided in me once, just before closing time, that the old fatigue jacket he wore wasn't the one he'd worn over there. He'd lost his real jacket a long time ago. This one he'd bought at the Army-Navy Surplus. Then he'd cut his name-tag off his old canvas duffel bag and attached it above the left chest pocket of the new jacket to make it seem as if it were the one he'd worn over there.

Even when Ervin told me this, though, I didn't doubt that he'd actually been in Vietnam. He told the kind of stories that a guy trying to make himself look tough or trying to explain why he drank as a career just wouldn't tell. When Ervin told you a story about Vietnam, it was just for the sake of letting you know. He was just informing you that, at certain times, in particular regions of the world, this kind of shit went on. And that you should be advised. And prepared.

One time we were watching the TV at the Thirteenth Step, and HBO was having a free preview weekend — this was before I dropped out of grad school — and a movie about Vietnam came on. Black guys in Vietnam, no less. And one of the guys had a necklace of ears. And so I asked Ervin if he, or anyone he knew over there, had ever had a necklace of ears. Not to be a smart ass, just because that was some out-there shit, and Ervin talked about some out-there shit every now and again, and I wanted to know if this shit was real. And he didn't talk to me for a long time after that, like multiple weeks. I'd sit next to him still, but he'd just stare straight ahead, and eventually I'd give up and just hit on whatever tail walked through the door. But in the end he forgave me. I kept sitting next to him and one day he started giving me his Gamblers Anonymous straight line again.

But anyway, on this particular morning, Ervin and I were sitting there, drinking Pabst, and Rebecca was going back and forth from the front to the storeroom checking that morning's delivery, when Maggie's little fucker grandson walked in the front door.

Maggie Halloran owned the Thirteenth Step. Her husband had worked 30 years for the electric utility, retired, then realized his dream of opening a bar. Unfortunately, he then proceeded to die just a couple months later, leaving Maggie with somebody else's dream to look after. She said she didn't mind, and that it gave her something to do now that Sean—this is her husband—was gone, but you could tell that just being in the place wore on her. She was an old lady. She needed to be at home watching soap operas and drinking weak tea and eating dry cookies. She didn't need to be coming down here for a couple hours a day to check on the books or do payroll or just say "hi" to all the patrons. She didn't need to be coming down and hanging around with the likes of us.

Maggie'd been steady up my ass about school right up until the day I dropped out. Now she didn't seem to care anymore. She had come in just before noon on that first day, looked right at me, paused, and cocked her head a little, like she was doing one of those puzzles in the paper where eight things are different between two similar drawings, but, for the life of you, you just can't figure what they are.

"Why are you here?" she'd asked. There had been four of us in the bar at the time, but there was no doubt that she was talking to me. The other drunks, Maggie, and Rebecca all stared at me, expecting an answer.

"Just taking a sick day, Maggie," I lied. "Mental health."

"Bullshit," she said.

"That's the truth!"

"Bullshit. You've been talking about dropping out for months now. What did I tell you?"

"You said if I dropped out, I'd wind up here drinking beer in the mornings with all these other worthless winos."

None of the other drunks flinched. They seemed to think this was a fair assessment. Maggie kept staring at me. Finally, she pursed her lips, made a "psh" sound, waved a dismissive back of her hand to me, and took her ledger books back to the office. She had, apparently, written me off.

We tried to be good when Maggie was around. It was

19

pretty clear she hadn't intended to live out her golden years babysitting the herd at a neighborhood watering hole. Add that to the fact that she was raising her grandson, who was this dipshit, aspiring wannabe "gangsta" type, despite the fact he was translucent-white Irish and living in Portland, Oregon. He'd skip school and come in ordering beers for him and his friends, putting the bartender gals in a really awkward position. On the one hand, if they served him and Maggie found out about it, she would fire them on the spot. On the other, Maggie didn't have any other family and wasn't in great health—she was a lifetime smoker—so at any moment this fucking punk kid could wind up being the owner of the bar and their boss.

Catch 22, all the way. Usually the girls gave him and his knucklehead friends a couple cans of Pabst each and told them to scram. That worked, usually.

Sean, this kid's name was. Named after his grandfather, Maggie's dead husband. His mother was in county jail waiting to get arraigned on drug and solicitation charges, and probably some other shit as well. His dad, Maggie's son, got killed by an overly aggressive shop owner while he was trying to stick up a 7-11 with a rusty, unloaded revolver.

For his part, Sean would come in with red eyes sometimes, and you knew he was just warming up with the pot and booze until such time as he could get his hands on something more robust. You knew he was going to break her heart too, that he was already breaking her heart, and if you cared about her you hoped, for her own sake, that she died before this little pissant made whatever colossal mistake he was going to make to fuck up his life. You hoped she died first, even if it meant having to go and find another bar, which you really didn't want to do, because there was no way in fuck you were drinking at this bar after she was gone, giving all your money to that little fuck, when you knew he'd just put it all in a vein and sexually harass Rebecca and the girls.

Little fucker.

So anyway, on this particular day, this little maggot came in the door, holding it wide open so sunlight flooded the whole bar. No consideration. Not even 11:30 in the morning yet, and this little 16-or-17-(I forget)-year-old fucker just waltzed on in. He grabbed a stool at the far end of the bar from Ervin and me and fired up a smoke. When he saw us looking at him, he gave a little upward nod in acknowledgement. I can't speak for Ervin — he was behind me when this was happening — but the upward nod got a roll of the eyes from me.

When Rebecca came out from the storeroom, she saw the kid sitting there and started a little, but then walked down to his end of the bar. They talked quietly. We couldn't hear what they were saying, but the conversation got a lot more animated as it went along. Hands started waving. Fingers tapped the bar for emphasis. Eventually, Rebecca held up her index finger alone, and then turned it around and showed it to the kid again, as if that were the whole and total end of the argument.

He was going to get one. Just one.

She put a can of Pabst under the ancient beer-can popper and punched two holes in it — one to drink out of and one to let the air escape. She put it in front of him on the bar and walked back down to the storeroom, shaking her head the whole way. We watched her as she passed us, shaking her head and muttering, then turned back to look at Sean and tried to ask with our glances if he wasn't ashamed of himself for putting a working girl like her in a position like that. He was taking a long gulp of his beer, his throat muscles greedily pulling it down his esophagus.

Ervin and I turned back to the television — *NYPD Blue* reruns. The kid sat nursing his beer. He must not have had anywhere else to go if he wanted to hang around the Thirteenth Step. Slowly, the rest of the daytime crowd seeped in. The night crew guys from the factory that made hearing aids a few blocks down. Two or three strippers from 82nd Street Stars. A few old widower-retirees — or retirees who wished they were widowers — who used to work for the electric utilities, Maggie's husband's old cronies. The place would fill up in the late morning and early afternoons, if you can believe it. Daily. It was in the middle of that kind of neighborhood. The Upper East Side of Manhattan we were not.

In the time I'd been a regular there — both before and after dropping out of school — word had gotten around that I was a professor or a doctor or something. Most of the others didn't have a high school diploma, let alone any college, and they viewed me as some kind of oracle. They thought I knew how to function in the world, something they had never mastered. They'd bring papers and forms and questions up to my stool, irritating Ervin, and ask if I could help them make sense of it. Ask what they should do. Tax forms. Court summonses. Child support bills. I was called on to settle bar bets and arguments. I was asked for baseball stats from the sixties, which was well before I was born, and the winner for the Oscar for Best Picture in 1983. (I ran home and Googled it. I only lived about a block and a half away. When I returned with the answer about five minutes after they had asked, they looked at me as if I'd gone to commune with the gods.)

I don't mean for any of this to sound patronizing. I loved these people, found them charming. But I was always surprised at their world view, completely different from my own. The way they approached problems, often just ignoring them and hoping they would go away, mystified me. Knowledge was a valuable commodity with them. They had little of it, and admired anyone who could provide them with more. Public defense attorneys, bank tellers, accountants...They would even press the old electric utility guys on how to cut down on their power bills, how to roll back the meters on the sides of their rented houses. They wanted the inside dope. The skinny. They didn't want to be paying full price for all the electricity they used, like suckers. And, in my case, they wanted an encyclopedia, a compendium of knowledge they could offer these questions to. And since I'd been in grad school for a year and a quarter before dropping out, I — at the age of 24 — was the best candidate they had available for the job.

On this particular day, then, Shari, one of the strippers, was asking me about something a guy had said while she was giving him a "private dance" the night before. (Shari was her real name, not her stage name. At least I think it was.) Shari was a little pudgy — 82nd Street was not known for having the best talent in town. But the drink specials were good, and, in better financial times, I would stop in, just to check on how my friends from the bar were doing.

"A man of your education, at a place like that," Maggie would say the next day when she came in, and the girls mentioned having seen me the night before at work.

"They're not educating his dick," Ervin told her in my defense. "His dick ain't changing just because they're filling up his brain. His dick's still the same as the rest of ours."

Maggie noticeably flinched every time Ervin spat out the word "dick." Maggie didn't have a problem with cursing, but Ervin said what he said with a lot of conviction, and put all the emphasis of each sentence on the word "dick." Maybe Maggie was afraid he was right, and that no matter how much you educate a man, he's still going to act how he's going to act. Maybe she was thinking about her grandson and hoping he'd turn out better than we all knew he would.

Anyway, Shari came up to Ervin and me, and we spun around on our stools to field her question. She said she'd been grinding away on this guy, and his cell phone had rang. The guy had answered it, but motioned to Shari to keep going (what kind of motion would that have been?), and to the person on the other end of the line the guy had said: "Listen, if you buy half the fucking shares at 10, and the fucker goes down to five, and you buy the same number of shares that you bought at 10 while the fucker's still down at five, then you only need it to get back to seven-point-five to break even."

Shari wasn't stupid, or lacking in confidence. She'd strut around the bar in a tank top, her little pot belly pushing against the top button of her jeans. What she lacked in classically defined beauty she more than made up for in swagger, both here and at the strip club. She was one of their best earners because she was so self-assured. But lately, she'd been thinking about the big pile of bills under her bed and wondering if she shouldn't do something smarter with it, at least that's what she told me. And she'd been trying to read some investment books, like Suze Orman and shit, to get ideas on what she could do with the money, where she could keep it.

"So, is what this fucking guy saying right, Professor?" They all called me that, even though I told them I was nowhere near to it. They said it was a nickname, not an honorific. Not exactly in those words. "Can you actually do what he's talking about?"

"Well, Shari, I'm not an economist or a financial counselor," I had said. Before answering any of their questions, I always added a disclaimer. "But it sounds like what the guy is talking about is dollar cost averaging."

She grabbed a napkin and a pen from Rebecca and scribbled down the words. She wanted to look it up on the computers at the library later that day.

"I think the principle is sound," I said, trying to sound wise but not pedantic, and probably failing. "The only thing I'd warn you about is there's no guarantee 'the fucker' is going to go back up to seven and a half, especially if it already plunged and is now worth half what it used to be."

"Yeah, yeah, sure," she said, staring at the napkin where she'd written the words, marveling at it like she'd just been given the secret code to wealth and early retirement.

"Thanks Professor."

She went back to her booth with her friends, and Ervin and I turned back to Dennis Franz and Jimmy Smits. They were questioning a guy in the interrogation room, really laying into him. Those were some of our favorite scenes. We asked Rebecca to turn the volume up for us a little.

Eventually, Sean finished his beer, but he didn't get up to leave. After a while, though, Rebecca spotted him. She walked down to the end of the bar where he was sitting alone, picked up his beer, and tested the weight of it. She shook it from the top, letting the last few drops ricochet around the inside of the can, then dropped the empty into a bin behind the bar. She stood there looking at him, expectantly, arms crossed, not saying anything. After what seemed like a long time, the kid finally took the hint, if you could call it that, stood up, grabbed his coat off the stool — as he'd been sitting on it — and walked out the front door. Again, the kid opened the door way wider than he needed to and let in way more sunshine than was necessary.

The episode of *NYPD Blue* ended and another began — TBS or TNT or A&E had two of them back-to-back in the late mornings then. The other ones had *ER* and *West Wing*, but we liked *NYPD Blue*. On *West Wing* and *ER*, when somebody had a drug or alcohol problem, it was a real sensitive, touchy-feely type of thing, where you were really rooting for the person to get their shit together and start going to meetings. But on *NYPD Blue*, especially in the first season when David Caruso was still on, when Sipowicz was drunk, he was just a raging asshole. You could hardly get yourself to care whether he got into treatment or not, because, really, the guy deserved whatever ended up happening to him. This, to us, was closer to real life than the very-special-episode approach of the other shows. We knew lots of drunks, and they rarely inspired any kind of feelings in us. Most of them were leading just the kind of lives we thought they deserved.

When the second episode was over — and this was not a good one with drunk Sipowicz acting like an asshole, but rather a straight-forward procedural that spent more time on Martinez and Medavoy — Ervin wanted to get a sandwich from the butcher shop down the alley, Otto's. It was noon, and I'd heard his stomach growling all through the final twenty minutes of the show.

"C'mon, I'll get you something, too," he said. "You look like shit. You've been losing weight for fucking months now. Another couple weeks, and there won't be any of you left."

I looked down at myself. My belt was on its tightest notch, but still loose. The fabric of my waistband bunched up under it at odd intervals, taking up the slack in pants that had fit when I enrolled in classes four or five months ago.

"Yeah, okay," I said. "Maybe just a half one." I didn't want to take advantage of Ervin's generosity.

We slipped on our sunglasses just before sliding out the back door into the alley. At first, when we heard a voice, we didn't think the person was talking to us. People were always back in the alley smoking or taking cell-phone calls away from the noise of the jukebox or TVs or loud talk of the bar. We thought we were just walking through somebody else's conversation. But then the voice said something again, louder and insistent this time.

"Hey!"

We had already half started down the alley, and had to turn all the way around to see Sean, Maggie's grandson, emerging from behind the dumpster where he'd been hiding. In his right hand he held a small revolver at about waist level. His eyes were red, but wide open and all-the-way dilated, despite the brightness of the day. He looked pale and pasty and flop-sweaty, and like he wasn't enjoying his day very much.

"Give me some cash," he said, seemingly trying to be casual. I thought this was odd. You could tell he was new to mugging. I'd never had somebody pull a gun on me and then ask for just *some* of my cash, as if asking for a loan. It was a new approach.

"Sorry?" Ervin said, maybe still not fully believing the situation. For all the bullshit and awkward situations this dipshit kid put Maggie and the bartenders through, he'd given the customers a lot of room. Sometimes we'd catch him looking at us like he was trying to figure out if we were prey or predator, victims or criminals. He'd apparently made up his mind.

"I said give me your goddamn money." He hissed it low, eyes shooting to the door, wanting to be done and out of here and away from this before anyone else came into the situation.

"Son, don't you know not to rob poor people?" Ervin said, like a high-school sports coach questioning one of his player's technique. "You were nice and hid there behind that dumpster. You could have let us walk off and got the next person to come out. You know damn well me and this jackass don't have any goddamn money. Why would you want to hold a gun on us?"

"You got something," Sean said, scratching the left side of his face with a hand all grasped up, like a claw. "I want it. Give it to me. Now."

The sleeves of his over-sized coat fell all around his hands, threatening to engulf the gun, or at least get caught up in the hammer if he pulled the trigger. He looked like a kid in his dad's sports coat playing P.I. The visual seemed to occur to Ervin, too, because Ervin began to talk to Sean as if he were the kid's dad. Okay, not as if he were *Sean's* dad; Sean's dad was an armed robber himself, and a stupid one at that, much like his kid seemed to want to be. But a dad from a fifties-era sitcom. Ervin took a gentle but firm tone and slowly started walking toward the kid, foot by foot, step by step.

"Kid, why don't you give me that gun?" he asked.

"Back the fuck up," Sean said, but Ervin kept coming

slowly forward. Sean didn't back away to buy himself more room, and he didn't raise the gun or pull back the hammer to show the threat level rising. He just stood there, watching Ervin come on.

"Son, you don't want to do this, do you? You're going to break your grandmother's heart. Think about your dad. You're going to wind up in the grave next to his. Is that what you want?"

Sean stopped giving responses. He looked like an exhausted toddler in his car seat, fighting to stay awake because he'd told his parents he wasn't tired and wanted to prove the point. He looked like a washed-out kid who, more than anything, could use a solid meal and about twelve hours of sleep. I wasn't even scared of him, and I was a lot less familiar with these little urban dramas than Ervin was.

Ervin continued to close the distance between them, speaking softly and reassuringly. He talked to the kid like few people ever had, even Maggie, I was willing to bet. Ervin was patient and kind and understanding, and, as he took the last few steps and put his hand on top of the revolver, Sean let go of it, and his shoulders slumped, and Ervin was left with the gun in his hand at about shoulder level.

He quickly transferred it to his right hand, his strong hand, and leveled the barrel at the kid, saying, "Good, nice job, son. Now drop your pants for me."

Sean looked up from his defeated exhaustion, not believing what he'd just heard. I couldn't quite believe it myself.

"What?" Sean asked.

"I said drop your pants, son. Let's go."

"What the fuck for?" Sean asked, his teenage ballsiness and rebelliousness rushing back. He was trying to put his tough-guy mask back on, just a few moments to late.

"Because I'm a black man holding a gun on you and fucking telling you to. Why the fuck do you think?" Ervin said.

"You didn't do what I told you to when I had the fucking gun," Sean said, pouting, still trying to argue his way out of the situation by pointing out its unfairness.

"That's because you're a faggot and a pussy and I don't have to do what a faggot tells me to do, regardless of how many guns he has, because he ain't going to fucking use them," Ervin said. "Besides, if you're anything like your old man, you're probably so stupid as to not load the fucking thing. Did you load this fucking thing, bitch?"

Sean blinked, taken aback at how quickly Ervin's tone had turned from paternal care and concern to outright abuse and derision. "It's loaded," he said quietly, in defense of his own intelligence.

"Then I guess you better drop your pants, huh?" Ervin said.

The kid quickly went to work on the top of his baggy jeans, undoing first the belt then the button and zipper. When he pushed down his pants and then his boxers, I was thankful that his over-sized shirt still hung low enough to cover up his goods while he faced us.

"Good, now turn around," Ervin said.

"What the fuck for?" the kid said, getting less defiant and more openly scared with each step. I eyed the back door of the Thirteenth Step. Anybody walking into this situation now wouldn't know that Sean had started it, and might have a hard time believing the facts of the case, given where it had wound up. Ervin didn't seem to care that it was broad daylight, and that a person, or delivery truck, could enter the alley at any minute. He seemed totally focused on Sean.

"Turn around there and put your hands on the dumpster," Ervin said.

Sean relented and did what he was told.

"Stick your hips out. Point that skinny white ass toward us."

Sean did it, and as he bent further over, his shirt started

to crawl up the back of his legs. Eventually, we could see the bottom of his ass.

"Now spread 'em," Ervin said. Sean started to inch his hands apart on the dumpster.

"Your feet, fucker. You know what this is," Ervin said.

"Aw, man, c'mon..." Sean started to say, but then Ervin pulled back the hammer, and Sean spread his legs. Ervin was much more effective at using the gun as a prop for emphasis than Sean had been.

"You wanna go first, Prof?" Ervin asked me after he was finally satisfied with Sean's pose.

"What the fuck are you talking about, Erv?" I said. "What the fuck are you doing?"

"Aw, I'm just fucking with him," Ervin said, then walked up behind Sean and inserted the short barrel of the gun up between Sean's ass cheeks.

Sean grunted in what sounded like surprise more than pain. Ervin wasn't pushing hard against the kid's sphincter, and there wasn't any blood. But the barrel had to be cold, and the psychic damage to some half-developed wannabe man like Sean, there was just no telling. It probably would have been better, in his estimation, to just beat the hell out of him so he could show his war wounds to his friends. Now he had to carry this around with him, this secret. That he had pulled a gun on two of the drunks from his grandmother's bar, that they had got it away from him with sweet talk, and that they had then shoved it up his ass. Literally.

"You said this gun was loaded?" Ervin asked him. Ervin stood at full height with his arm reached low to get the angle he wanted for this maneuver.

"Yeah," said Sean, his voice strained. Maybe Ervin was pushing harder than I thought.

"I don't want you coming in and bothering my bartenders anymore," Ervin said. "You hear me." It wasn't a question.

"Yeah," said Sean again. That one word may have been his entire vocabulary with a gun up his ass.

"The next time you come in like a big man, ordering those girls around, trying to get them a five-grand fine from Liquor Control, I'm going to turn to my friend here and say, 'Hey, isn't that the kid that we took his gun away from him and shoved it up his ass?'"

Sean grunted in understanding.

"And you know we'll be there. We're always fucking there. And if I hear you being an asshole to your grandmother, I might just say the same thing. There's no telling what might set me off, get me talking about this to everybody. So you know what I'd do around here from now on if I were you?"

Sean didn't answer.

"Tread. Fucking. Lightly."

Ervin pulled the gun out of the kid's ass, but kept holding it on him as he backed away. Sean grabbed his boxers and jeans, pulled them up, and turned around to look at us. His eyes were red and the tracks of tears only made it halfway down his face, where they'd fallen off, since he'd been bent over. He did up his pants and wiped at his eyes and nose with his sleeve. He was still looking at the gun fearfully.

"Go on, get the fuck out of here," Ervin said.

Now that the expectation was that we weren't going to shoot him, I expected Sean to try to put his tough-guy act back on. Tell us to fuck off. Tell us we were broken-down drunk old assholes who didn't matter anyway. But he didn't. He just turned and walked away from us, toward the end of the alley that was farthest away from his house, away from everything. I wondered where he was going. Ervin waited until the kid turned the corner out of the alley, then said to me:

"C'mon, let's go get that sandwich."

Then he tucked the small revolver in the pocket of his

olive-green fatigue coat and said: "I got to wash my hands."

"What the fuck was that, man?" I asked him. I wanted to know what had inspired him to do that, how he'd ever even thought of putting a gun up somebody's ass. At the same time, I didn't want to piss him off. This was a new side of Ervin I was seeing and I didn't know what he was capable of.

"I bet I can get three-hundred bucks for this at the pawn shop," Ervin said, fingering the butt of the gun in his coat pocket.

"Erv," I said.

"You remember how you asked me about necklaces full of ears that one time?"

"Yeah," I said.

"Well, we didn't wear necklaces full of ears. We just wore two or three of them. On our dog tags. And not while we were on base or in the cities or shit. Just when we were on patrol. Just when we were in the villages, so they knew not to fuck with us."

I nodded. What do you say to that?

"You'd have done it too," he said, looking up. "You're no better than me. Than we were. You'd have been right there, doing the same shit to get by as everybody else."

I was flattered that he thought I was that kind of man, the kind of man he had fought alongside in Vietnam, but he didn't seem to think it was a compliment.

© 2013, Tom Hoisington

EVEN SVEN
Mike Toomey

The phone rang.

"Hello?"

"You know who this is?"

"Keep talking, I'll see if I can figure it out."

"I'm a guy you used to know."

"Okay."

"You still working?"

Pause.

"I said — "

"I know."

Pause.

"Do you know if you're still working or not?"

Pause.

"Yeah. I mean, I got a job-job but if the right thing were to come along, yeah, I take work if it comes my way."

"You know who this is?"

"I might. Way back, right? Long time."

"Long time indeed. You wanna meet me tomorrow?"

"Where?"

"That diner still there? On Alvont?"

"It's a Starbucks now."

"The fuck. I guess I oughta try a Starbuck anyway. How about 10:30?"

"A.M. or P.M.?"

"A.M., asshole. It's a meeting not a job. You know who I am yet?"

"I got an idea. You still got that mustache?"

"I didn't have a mustache."

The phone went dead.

Usually you get a call like that it's someone who got

grabbed up on something and are trying to trade their way out of a jackpot. Usually the number comes up restricted because it's coming from some police precinct. Usually you take the call then throw your phone in the trash because it is burnt.

But I thought I knew the voice. And it was from the past. I thought it was the kind of guy who wouldn't try to trade his way out of a jam — and hadn't. I wasn't really looking for work, but if it was the guy I thought it was, it would be worth meeting him, anyway.

The meet was 10:30; I got to Alvont Street at 9 and parked across the street. He rolled up at 10:15 by himself. He got out of the car, looked over his shoulder and went inside.

There was something wrong with his leg. Bad wrong. He walked like he didn't have a knee. He would plant his left foot and then whip his right leg forward by jerking his hip. Took him forever to just get in the door.

He was the guy I remembered. Older now — thirty years will age anyone, I guess. His name was Jimmy something but he was occasionally called Sven. I never called him that but I'd heard it a few times. Last I'd heard he was doing twenty-five to life on an armed robbery that got fucked. Last time I saw him he'd been a young man and I'd been a kid; now he looked like a grandfather.

I waited ten more minutes before I followed him in.

"Glad you could make it."

"I thought you said you didn't have a mustache."

"I said I didn't have a mustache then, I got a mustache now."

"Looks good."

"You sound like the guys inside."

"I was kidding."

"I know. Take a seat..."

There was a long pause and we just kinda looked at each other. Eventually, I guess I sat down across from him.

"So this is Starbucks."

"Yeah."

"How's the coffee?"

"Probably better than what you're used to."

"Probably. Probably. How's your old man doing?"

"My father died like eight years ago."

"That's too bad."

"But I think you mean my uncle."

"Big Wahlid? That was your uncle? I thought you were his kid? I thought Big Wahlid and Little Wahlid were like some Arab father-son team."

"Nope, he was my uncle. My father would have discouraged me from doing what I did."

"Well, how's your uncle, then?"

"He's dead too."

"There's a lot of that going around."

I went up and ordered us two house blends, partially because I knew he wouldn't know what venti meant.

He took it black and winced when he sipped it, underestimating how hot it was.

"That is good coffee."

"Oughta be, for what they charge."

"Glad I'm not paying."

We both sipped our cups. I waited until he got to it.

"You remember Danny Weslet?"

"Tall guy? With the bad teeth?"

What I actually remembered about Danny Weslet were his hands. He had girl's hands. They were white and soft and his nails were always cut into perfect crescent moons. He didn't take any special care of them, as far as I knew; they just were like that naturally.

"Yeah. That's the guy. Though I heard he got his teeth fixed."

"What about him?"

"I got a meeting with him Friday night."

"Like this meeting?"

"Similar. But at night."

"What are you looking for?"

"Answers."

"I mean from me."

"Oh. No heavy-lifting. Mostly driving and standing around looking like you're tough. I don't get around so well anymore and I can't be chasing this guy through the woods..."

"I'm not gonna chase him through the woods either."

"Nobody's asking you to chase anybody. I'm just saying I show up there with half a leg, Weslet's gonna start wondering about a foot-race. At least if you're standing there he might think twice. You can stand there, right?"

"I can do that."

"Good."

The other thing I knew about Weslet was this: he did six years on the same rap that put Sven away for twenty-seven. I hadn't seen or heard of either of them since they went in. My uncle, Big Wahlid, had been killed shortly thereafter and I wound up with no connection to the people he worked for so I had to get a real job. I had completely lost touch with that life until the phone rang that night.

A lot of it was just sitting in a car. We drove out 412 late Friday afternoon to this town just inside the border. We took his car but I drove; he said it bothered his leg to drive so much.

"What happened with that?"

"This White Supremacist did it in the joint."

"Did you try telling him you're white?"

"Yeah, he didn't seem to care."

"What were you standing up for the rights of your disenfranchised minority brothers?"

"Nothing that noble. I bumped him on the way back from the food line so he had two of his buddies hold my foot on a bench while he jumped on my knee."

"The doctors did a good job of fixing it."

"Yeah. The prison doctor and the prison barber are the

same guy."

"He give you that haircut too?"

We ended up parking down the end of this road in the woods. The houses were far enough apart that you would have to really want some sugar to walk over to your neighbor's place. The house was number 18 but I don't remember the street name. It was dark when we got there but not night yet, so we just sat in the car watching the house. He pulled a six pack from behind the seat while we waited. He said any more than three beers a piece and we'd run the risk of the cops finding two moes passed out tomorrow morning.

"What's it like inside?"

"The joint?"

"No, a woman. Yeah, the joint."

"It's bad, but it's not bad in the way that you think."

"It's not all dudes jumping on your knee?"

"No. It's not. I mean, don't get me wrong; that shit can happen and it does happen but it's the little things inside that ruin your life."

"Like what?"

"Like, for example, I went in there determined to establish a routine. I was like I'll do these same things at the same time every day and that routine will be the thing that sustains my sanity in here. I'm in there and I'm sticking to this regiment: up, fifty push-ups, breakfast, read for an hour, run a mile in the yard, lunch...you know, like that."

"Uh-huh."

"So the guard can't tell you not to do push-ups before breakfast but he'll just stand there every morning and watch until one day you don't want to give him the satisfaction and so you skip it. It doesn't sound like much but when it's all you have, giving it up just...cuts. Humans are creatures of habit so when you rob them of those habits you strip us of our humanity. I don't know."

A woman opened the door of number 18 and stood in

the frame holding the storm door ajar with her hip. A man met her there and kissed her on the cheek. She got in the car and drove off. He went back inside. He was older but the man was definitely Danny Weslet.

I looked at Sven after the car had disappeared.

"Not yet."

"How'd you get out?"

"I dug a tunnel."

I just glared at him.

"No. I got that cancer of the prick. They decided it was too expensive to treat it if I was a ward of the fine state of Missoura, so they sprung me so I could deal with it myself."

"You dealing with it?"

"I am dealing with it."

"Must be hell."

"Hell is when you have to watch some wrong shit happen and can't do shit about it."

"What?"

"Nothing. It's time."

We crossed the street and made our way up the lawn. I thought it was odd that we didn't have masks or anything.

"Should I have a gun?"

"Do you have a gun?"

"No. Do you?"

Weslet opened the door. He didn't recognize us at first; I'm not sure he ever recognized me. He looked the same, still youthful-looking and tall. His teeth were fixed but in a way that you could tell they'd been fixed and his hands still looked like a surgeon's.

"Can I help you?"

"Don't you remember me, Danny? I remember you."

You could see the moment of realization in Weslet's eyes. You could see the pupils dilate as he tried to slam the door shut. Too late, Sven's gimpy foot was already in.

"Listen, Jim, I don't know what they told you. I did my time. They had me on a lesser charge; the DA threw out the gun thing because she knew it wouldn't stick. I did my six and kept my mouth shut. Jim, c'mon. You don't have to..."

"Where's your phone, Danny?"

"I don't know. The other room?"

Sven took out his own phone and dialed a number. Sven took the phone when Weslet's pocket started bleating.

Weslet never tried to run and Sven never touched him. Weslet just led us to a room in the back with a desk, a computer and a small TV. Weslet talked a little, bargaining. Sven would answer occasionally in the way you would answer a small child. Neither of them gave any indication that I was there.

"C'mon, Jim. It was a long time ago. I'm a different guy now. That was a long time ago."

"Yeah, it was. A long time."

"Jim —"

"Go get your boy."

"What?"

"Your boy. Tell him to come down here."

"Jim? No, he doesn't need to see this. Just do it and go. He's not...he doesn't need to..."

"Danny, go get your boy before I go get him myself."

Slowly, Weslet got up and exited the room. He walked so close to Sven that I thought he was going to take a swing at him. Instead he just whispered, "Jim." But Sven didn't even look at him.

"Is he gonna run?"

"No."

We waited what seemed to be an eternity. The house was bigger than it seemed from the outside but it wasn't this big.

"You sure?"

I heard him before I saw him. Like Darth Vader. It sounded like the kid was having an asthma attack. That wasn't it.

The kid was in a puffer wheel-chair. He was pitched to

one side and drooling on himself. His hands were pressed against his chest; curled at the wrist. There was a clear, accordion-like tube attached to the back of the chair that was helping him breathe.

"Jesus Christ."

The kid and his chair took up the whole room once they got in it. He was maybe twenty, probably younger. It was hard to tell. Weslet was crying now, or had been when he had been out of the room. His eyes were red-rimmed and you could tell he knew.

"Jim. Please. Not in front of my boy."

Sven took a pair of handcuffs out of his jacket and pointed Weslet towards the chair. Weslet got on his knees. Sven latched one of the cuffs between the rubber spokes of the wheel and had Weslet put the other around his wrist.

"You can hold his hand."

That was the end of his humanity.

"Jim."

Weslet took the boy's palsied hand in his own and stroked it. He was whispering to him, softly so we could hear the sound of it but not the words.

Sven opened a pocket knife and cut the tube that was pumping air into the boy. The accordion kept moving but the air just hissed out; the hose flapping where it had been torn.

Sven jerked his neck toward the door then grabbed me by the collar when I didn't follow. I wanted to say something. Tell Weslet that I hadn't known that this was going to happen. Hadn't known what he was going to do. What we had done. Outside I puked in the grass while Sven dragged his ruined leg into the car.

He drove us back to St. Louis, neither of us saying a word.

© 2012, Mike Toomey

7 SECONDS
Erin Cole

Pam lived a sheltered life, like most of us, ferrets in the cage of a civilized society. She thought life was about work, about the mundane responsibilities of buying milk, taking her car to the repair shop, and recycling. It was about trying to lose weight and lower her cholesterol, about watching *Walking Dead*, babysitting her niece, and trying to get that promotion that kept falling through her hands like wet noodles. But seven seconds can change just about everything, especially when they are occurring at the speed of fucking terror.

For Pam, one second proved to be the difference between normalcy and hell. It intruded into her mundane world much like a stick in the ribs when her ex-coworker, Stan, the one who was fired last week, the one who was rude to customers and surfed porn on his computer, walked into the office with a semi-automatic gun.

Though it seemed obvious to say, Pam didn't realize then that life was actually about staying alive. It was about keeping your guts inside your skin, ducking your brain matter from the drill of zipping bullets, and biting down on your screams when a friend split open in front of you. Life, *as Pam would soon learn*, was sometimes, simply, about not dying.

The First Second

The blast from Stan's gun cut into Pam's ears as though it were actually shards of glass. She had heard gunfire on the television, in the theater, even music, but never in real life, never standing just ten coffee-break paces away.

Deafening didn't describe it. She likened it to the arms of

a giant, snatching her by the shoulders and shaking her person from its bones. It reached a hand into her throat and pulled out a voice she didn't recognize — that of a cowering, sniffling child she thought she had lost long ago.

The Second Second

Pam didn't dive to the floor, that instinct to escape danger. Instead, fear raped her of muscle and shoved her down on her knees, kicked her in the gut, and spat on her head. That is how she would describe it later — fear, the goddamn bully that rammed her face in the Berber carpet and made fun of her undies showing, the thin, faded stained ones she didn't want anyone to see.

Fear had reduced her to a crawling thing, a blubbering shell of pathetic weakness. In complete mercy to a prick who knew of no mercy. A prick who walked out last week shouting, "Fuck you!" He had pointed at her and others, "And fuck you! And you! And you! Fuck you all!" He slammed through the front doors — *Thank God he's gone*, everyone had agreed.

But Stan wasn't gone...not in that sense. Stan was just getting started. He bought more bullets, listened to Eminem, Tool, and Ozzy Osborne, dressed himself in ammo and black leather, and made promises to people he hated in the mirror. Stan was gelling a new mold for himself, birthing the monster he always knew he was. But this didn't occur out of coercion; it came forth willingly, almost pleadingly, and he petted it.

The Third Second

You are going to die! Pam's thoughts bawled. She cranked her head to the side as a body flew past her. Not one running or diving to the floor. This one, his name was Tim Reynolds (he was their accountant), soared through midair with a shower of bright, red, chunky blood spraying from the back of his head. Blood that looked more like pureed mushroom marinara. He landed with limbs splayed limp, as though asleep. Slumped by the deformities of death. *He's dead! Stan killed Tim! Tim is dead!* More bawling thoughts, all crammed into her head like bees in a hive.

The Fourth Second

Shock is a rapid occurrence in susceptible minds, those who are already vulnerable to the voices of the dark, those who don't carefully plan for the future or analyze the past, but for someone like Pam, it just didn't happen. It belonged in Wall Street executives, parents of twins, church-goers learning of born-again atheists, and dim-witted sluts in horror movies — not in Pam, not when she was at work, going about her day filing monthly reports.

But, shock did break Pam, broke her into several unrecognizable parts: there was Scared Pam, I'm So Fucking Stupid I Didn't See This Coming Pam, Still Single Pam, I'm Going to Key Stan's Fucking Car Pam, and Tormented Frail Pam. These parts of her self were strangers, and she hated them all. Angry Pam would have been her next self had she not seen a sharp shadow descend over her. The shadow of Bad Stan, with his big, fancy, black automatic gun. Stan who liked plump tits and asses to go with them, Stan who always parked crooked, stole food from the fridge, never returned customer phone calls, and hoarded all the office supplies. Yeah, that Stan — Piece of Fucking Shit Stan with a Loaded Fucking Gun Stan.

The Fifth Second

Stan's shadow might as well have been the devil's. He towered over Pam with searing hate in his eyes. She realized then that she didn't really know Stan and never had. But he didn't know her either; otherwise, he wouldn't be pointing his devil-gun at her. People made fun of her too — still, she wasn't about to go out and purchase a pawn shop gun and shoot their brains out for it. She wanted to tell him that, shove it down his throat until he gagged for pity. People are mean and that's just a part of life. But here she was, living that fucking part of life. The last of the ink to her story: *Homely Woman Shot Dead Before She Could Make Something of Herself.*

At that moment, Pam wanted to be evil like Stan. His gaze had infected her, and she spat at him with the fiery, nasty hate of a demon child.

The Sixth Second

Stan smiled — maybe he liked her now, now that she had proved to him that she could be vile too. But no, of course not. Life was never effortless like that; it was a merciless, cutthroat motherfucker like Stan, Selfish Stan, The Only Evil Allowed in the World Stan, and he raised his gun and pointed it at her face, his finger curling over the trigger.

Pam's body flinched under the pressure of impending death. A blast cracked through the air, further puncturing the tender drums of her ears with invisible splinters of glass. She anticipated the burn of a bullet nailing her to the floor in a pool of ache. But what she realized next melted over her — gooey, chocolate icing on warm brownies or the heat of stepping into a hot tub with a cute guy. It was Stan, sinking to the floor with a blood-soaked hole in the middle of his forehead. Evil Stan, Selfish Stan, Perverted Piece of Shit Stan with his Big Fancy Black Gun Stan. Dead Stan.

The Seventh Second

Pam stood, dumbfounded beneath the yellowing corkboard ceiling of the Metroplex Plaza, and took in the architectural revulsion around her: the moaning survivors aghast with horror, the unlucky chosen stilled by the unthinkable, and the lunatic who had orchestrated it all, his expression softer in death than it had ever been in life. There was only one Pam now, I Am Alive Pam.

One Hour A.S. (*After. Stan.*)

There were many questions, several police, lots of spinning, red, white lights, most of it just a robotic blur of 'yes,' 'no,' 'I don't know,' 'maybe.' After a long, draining hour, I'm Still Alive Pam walked out of the Metroplex Plaza. A cruel, white-cold sun tucked itself behind the pines. She spotted more police surrounding Dead Stan's car, which had been parked directly in front of her rental. They stepped away carrying boxes of his things. Probably more ammunition and some pathetic note about how sorry or how not sorry he was and blah, blah, blah.

A ring hummed in her purse. She pulled out her phone (the repair shop) and answered.

"Hello?" It still wasn't her voice.

"It's Strifer's Auto Shop, just letting you know that your car is ready."

"Uh-huh."

He paused on the line, maybe thinking she had simply forgotten about her car, which she had, but it wasn't for simple reasons. It was because she had blood speckled over her hands and face; blood that didn't belong to her, dark, red, evil blood that shriveled up dry against her skin. It was because she had images, fresh, hot memories and feelings that squirmed in her head and gut in a slimy, scaly life of its own.

"We'll be open until 9 p.m."

"'Kay." She hung up.

Life was mundane again. Mundane and tinted with fuckedupness.

The police were still sifting through Dead Stan's things. Pam had to walk by his car to get to hers. Gripping the long rental key in her fingers, she ran the tip down the length of Dead Stan's car as she passed by, starting at the gas tank and stopping at the hood. It grated under her fingers and screeched a quiet bird's tune in her ear. Her numbness ebbed slightly. Revengeful, Devious Pam smiled to herself, thinking how pissed Alive Stan would have been.

RATCHET

Stephen D. Rogers

"So you're Ratchet."

I nodded. "J-O-H. Double N. I. You can dot the I with a little heart if it makes you happy."

"Johnni. Can't say I've ever seen a man spell it that way before."

"Now you have."

He shrugged and then chuckled as though he wasn't accustomed to laughter. "You're probably wondering why I asked you to come in and meet with me today. Being summoned to the principal's office and all."

"You have a problem."

He smoothed his wash-and-wear tie. "I told my assistant that you were with the Board of Education. It's best that she—and everybody else for that matter—never knows the truth."

"What seems to be the problem?"

Rocking back in his executive chair, he spread his arms. "No doubt you're aware of the school shootings that have plagued this country for the last few years."

"Actually, the problem is neither new nor confined to this country. Back in 1927, 45 were killed and 58 injured at the Bath Elementary School, Bath, Michigan. And in 1996, three years before Columbine, 18 were killed at the Dunblane Primary School, Dunblane, Scotland."

His eyes narrowed. "You know why I asked you here."

"No, I just like to read."

"Is that so?" He stared at me for a moment before continuing. "There is a student who concerns me."

"In what way?"

"He fits what passes for the profile. Unfortunately, while

47

several of his teachers have spoken to me about this student, he is far too smart to publicize his intentions, whatever they may be."

"You do realize the profile could match a sizeable percentage of your student population."

"If I could suspend him with cause, I would, but I can't. I spoke to some people and sought you out because I fear for the safety of my staff and students."

"And you're hoping..."

"The problem goes away." He moved a granite penholder from one side of his desk to the other.

"Just like that."

"The person I talked to said you'd be able to help. She said you'd been successful negotiating her child-support situation."

"How will I be paid?"

He relaxed. "As an educational consultant. There's enough in the budget to cover what you charged the person with whom I talked. Of course we'll need completed I-9 and CORI forms on file."

"I'm sure you can take care of those." I stood. "Is that a copy of the student's file?"

"No one must know I gave you this."

I tucked the manila folder under my arm. "I'll try not to drop it at the crime scene."

He winced. "If at all possible, I'd like to see this resolved peacefully."

"Of course you would. That's why they made you principal."

In my car, I reviewed the file to make sure I had everything I needed. William Jackson. 132 Hadley Ave. I was good to go.

Where I went was Hadley Avenue, speaking to the neighbors as someone who was thinking of moving to the area. No, the house I was looking at wasn't on the market yet, but I had this friend who works at a real estate office.

I learned enough from people with too much time on their hands — or people who were simply starved for adult conversation — to gain a fairly complete picture of the family. Two working parents, three children (William in the middle), and a dog that barked when the wind shifted direction.

For the most part, the street was quiet, with very few loud parties. Sometimes the kids played outside too late during the summer, but that was as to be expected. At least out on the street, you could see what they were doing.

Emergency telephone numbers from William's file led me to the employers of his parents, which led me to his parents, which led to more information gathered on the sly. "If your boy works at the Galleria, you must not be the mother of my son's friend. Sorry about that. From across the room, you looked a lot like her."

Since the neighbors told me William didn't come home after school, I headed for the Galleria to await his appearance.

"Billy starts at three, but the bus drops him off about fifteen minutes before that. He hangs around out back."

I was sitting outside at the picnic table, brushing up on my knowledge of musical development during the Tang Dynasty, when a teenage boy came through the door labeled: "Employees Only / No Deliveries 11–1 p.m."

He stopped when he saw me.

Closing the book, I asked if he was William Jackson.

"Who wants to know?"

"Me." I nodded toward the bench on the opposite site of the table. "Why don't you take a load off?"

William hesitated for only a second. Then a walk that started off tentative became a strut until he reached me and straddled the bench. "And who are you?"

"Look at me, William." I parted two fingers to point at my eyes. "You could say I'm no stranger to violence. But I never had any illusions. The people I killed, they're just

49

dead. They don't respect me or regret anything they might have done. Nobody thinks I'm cool now, or wants to let me inside their circle."

William blinked.

"Violence won't cleanse you of the various pains you're experiencing. Instead of solving your problems, it will only hurt a lot of people, most of them innocent, and obliterate your precious individuality. You feel powerless now? Just wait until the media turns you into a freak."

Except for that involuntary blink, William hadn't moved a muscle.

"I could kill you right here and get away with it, because that's what I do, but I sense in you the power to succeed. Do you really want to beat all the people who taunt you? Rise above them. You do that and you've won."

Closing my book, I stood. "Did you pick up what I was laying down?"

"Yes, sir."

"Good. You'll do just fine."

I'd forgotten that the first known Chinese opera troupe was called Pearl Garden. I wouldn't forget that again.

LET'S MAKE A DEAL
Scotch Rutherford

The glitz bus ran twice a day, Anaheim to the Neon City. It was a four and a half hour trek, and at $69.95 round trip with comps included, it was a real steal. There was always a sixty-minute window between the arrival of the junket dropping off, and the one picking up. Most of the clientele were elderly, and filed into the coach a half hour early, so it was always within ten minutes of the top of the hour that the westbound driver received the cash on delivery.

Leon Diggs watched as a non-descript elderly gentleman loaded the black rollaway bag into the side luggage compartment of the coach. The old man walked away as the driver snapped the luggage bay shut. As the driver entered the coach, he felt the cold steel pressed hard against the back of his head near the brainstem.

"Hit the release switch for the luggage bay, or you'll be staring at your brains on that dash."

The driver hit the switch, and Leon nodded to his partner Jesse; both were wearing trucker hats and sunglasses. Jesse grabbed the rollaway bag and checked it; black on the outside, green on the inside. He didn't count it, but to him it looked like forty grand. Leon kept the barrel on the driver as he backed away.

"Don't turn around."

Then he and Jesse made their escape. But even after he knew they were gone, the driver didn't reach for the phone, or call for help. He didn't dial the PD or anyone else; he didn't have to.

* * *

Leon sat comfortably in his Lazy Boy recliner in front of the TV watching *Let's Make a Deal* as he cleaned his father's Navy issue Colt .45, nursing a cold Bud Lite. He watched Wayne Brady call on a platinum blonde in a devil costume.

"Now you've got $400 right now, or you can let it ride on what's behind door number two."

"I think I'll take the 400 bucks, Wayne."

"Stupid cunt," Leon grunted.

His father had been a longtime fan of the show since back when Monty Hall had the helm, and they'd never missed an episode. Five out of ten times people would take the money.

"Anyone with a pair of balls knows they've got a 50/50 chance, so it's worth a shot," his old man would say. Half the time they'd end up with a lifetime supply of Turtle Wax, the other half would win a new car, or a Carnival cruise.

"Let's see what's behind door number two," Brady said.

"It's a full-size custom Airstream RV, complete with a five-day, four-night stay at The Sunset by The Sea—south coast Florida's premier luxury RV park," rattled off the announcer to the blonde devil's dismay.

"A Florida trailer park by the sea—that's one way of finding oil," Leon chuckled to himself.

"Baby, that's where we need to live. It's a decent place to raise a family," Luanne said.

She was prego. Only eight weeks, but on her tiny frame it was already starting to show. It had happened the night he'd finally hit her button—three days later, she was late. Leon had been her first. They'd hit it off right away, when her step dad, Leon's cousin Jesse, had introduced them. At the time she was far from legal, but Leon had done the right thing; he'd put it in her ass all the way up to her sixteenth birthday.

"Rent's due in three days. Teddy upped it to twelve hundred," Luanne said.

Teddy Bixby had doubled the rent park-wide at the

King's Court Mobile Home Park. For most people it wasn't worth it to pay through the nose for a park-owned trailer on a poorly maintained lot. People were packing up daily, and the park numbers were down to a single-digit retention rate. This had weighed in heavy on Leon's mind. Not to mention that his Chevy S10 pickup had been repossessed and he'd been stuck driving Luanne's shit box Dodge Neon. Luanne was a sweet kid, but sometimes she didn't know when to shut the fuck up.

"Shut up, will ya? I told you I got it covered. Fuckin' inbreeder," Leon said.

"Fuck you, you fucking piece of shit," she snarled, slapping his wrist, almost knocking the .45 out of his hand.

Luanne had indiscreetly given her cousin a blowjob on his eighteenth birthday.

"I told you that wadd'nt even sex — I can't believe you brought that up."

It was time to go.

* * *

It felt good to get out of the house. Leon's trailer didn't have AC, and August in The Neon City was no joke. The fresh produce section at Albertson's was a nice escape. His shopping cart glided smoothly between isles of fresh fruit, until it ran into the bottom of an expensive sole of Italian design.

"Leon, what's crackin' homes?"

Frets Findlay was a grifter and a knee-capper who worked for the designer dope man himself, Max Castle. Leon made like he didn't know, but he knew.

"Who the fuck are you?"

"Tough guy, huh," barked a foul-breathed chicone with a clean shaven head, four inches from Leon's face, as he knuckled onto the side of the shopping cart. He had cold, dark eyes, like a shark's, sporting jailhouse ink, and looked fresh out of Warm Springs.

"Chill Diablo, Leon's just a little confused," Findlay said, leaning in over the front of Leon's shopping cart. "You owe a certain associate of my employer some money. Does the name Ray Copperhead mean anything to you?"

"Copperhead's dead," Leon said.

"But your debt ain't. It dies when you do, not him. Max handles all Ray's action now—and don't even start with that Max who stuff. And Leon, you can forget about those bullshit two points—it's now five percent. You got five days before we come around looking for payment," Findlay said, as he backed away from the cart.

"Maricon," Diablo barked four inches from Leon's ear, rattling his cart.

"That's what being a gambling junkie will get you, before two broken knees," his old man would say. Leon was glad his old man wouldn't be around to see that.

* * *

Luanne figured winning the bingo tourney at the Holy Christ Church in Henderson was the best way out of their financial problems. At least, for the ones she knew about. Leon had other plans. Luanne was a devout member of the church congregation, and was a lot more comfortable committing sin in God's house rather than inside a casino, or out on the street. Leon was indifferent.

Luanne sat directly behind her lucky treasure trolls, amidst a sea of blue hairs, pounding her daubers to paper, sometimes three sheets a game, for nearly four hours, until she watched some tweaker beat her and the geezers for just under two grand. Leon had seen enough and was already outside. He thought about Findlay, and how he'd gotten the name "Frets" clocking roulette wheels, until the boys got wise. This was back in the 80s, before it was all corporations—so he walked away with his record

54

untouched, and a broken hand. Then Leon thought about all the other goldbrickers that ran a gambit on the so-called above-board houses that shafted the everyday sucker, and how all those grifters had gaffed the slots and the table games and gotten away with it. There were more than a few that had dodged Gaming Control, and the Leviathan Black Book. But none of them, none of them had taken a shot at bingo.

"How 'bout I just end your miserable life right now," Leon said, jamming his father's Korean War issue Colt .45 against the tweaker's frail ribcage.

The guy was a three-time loser, and more crooked than any cop in Clark County, so no mask was needed.

"Hand it over."

"What the fuck man, I just won this fair and square."

"Fuck it," Leon said, as he cocked the hammer.

"Okay, okay — listen, I got the 411 on a serious fuckin' score, man."

"I'm listening."

"There's this gambling junket out of Anaheim —"

The tweaker laid it all out. Leon lowered the .45 and listened.

"Now that's a good fuckin' tip on a score. C'mon man, let me keep half."

"Fuck you. Hand it over, you junkie piece of shit," Leon said pressing the barrel of the .45 against the tweaker's sternum. Leon took the bankroll, and slipped it into his pocket, still holding the pistol firm. "Now hand over your stash."

* * *

That night they ate dinner in silence. Luanne was still worried about the rent, and Leon was yet to share the news of his new found wealth. He waited until she was in the bedroom, with the door shut, and the light out, before he stepped outside, took out his cell and dialed up Luanne's old man, his cousin Jesse. They arranged to meet at Terrible's Town Bowling Alley and Casino off Boulder Highway.

"Forty grand—are you sure?"

"That's the average. Sometime's there's more."

"They're running powder out of a fuckin' junket—are you sure?"

Jesse watched Leon's ball roll down the lane, almost veering off into the gutter, before righting itself.

"No, but that shit bag tweaker I rolled told me how it's gonna go down. The way I see it, if a lone geezer puts a single rollaway bag in the luggage bay of the outgoing junket fifty minutes before it boards, then we move on it," Leon said, nailing a strike.

"Well shit, it's worth a case I guess. But right now, I need some of that high elevation you promised."

"I got your lift ticket right here, cuz," Leon said, slapping his pants pocket. "So where's my snow bunny? I'm not tryin' to hit the slopes without getting my cock sucked."

"Hey, can I bowl a frame?" chirped an adorable teeny bopper in skin-tight jeans, and what looked like a belly shirt spray painted over her perky breasts.

"See, what'd I tell you? Hey cutie, where's your friend?" Jesse asked.

"She got grounded," the teeny bopper replied.

"Grounded?"

"Yeah, she still in high school," she said talking in that homey slang, the way most white girls her age did.

"Oh, but you're past that, right?" Leon asked, ogling her c-cup bust.

"Actually, I dropped out. And Jes," she said, turning to him, "If it's all the same to you, I kept her half, so I'm down to blow his horn while you tailgate me," she said, before her lips curled into a shit-eating grin.

"Here that?" Jesse said. "She's down to play bumper cars."

56

"In that case, we'll flip to see who gets to rear-end her first."

* * *

Jesse met Leon at The Eiffel Tower Experience, in front of The Paris hotel, half a block down from a place they called The Four Corners, where the Flamingo met the strip. Jesse pulled up in a Toyota Prius he'd stole out of long-term parking at McCarran Airport.

"Put these on," Jesse said, as they waited at the light, handing Leon a trucker hat and a pair of wraparound shades.

The vast front lot at The Mandalay Bay Hotel always had heavy traffic rushing in and out, especially midday, when congestion was high. Once they found The Glitz Bus junkets, Jesse pulled into a space with a great vantage point of both the glowing chrome shuttles from behind tinted glass.

"Here we go," Leon said, glancing at his watch "It's ten past."

They watched the elderly courier step out of the incoming junket, and walk the black rollaway bag up to the luggage bay of the outgoing shuttle.

"That's our cue," Leon said, re-tucking the .45 under his untucked tee shirt. Jesse pulled up close enough to make a quick escape, as Leon dashed out the passenger side to make his move on the driver. The junket driver snapped the luggage bay shut as Leon power walked in his direction. When he stepped back on the coach, Leon followed, jamming the .45 against the back of the driver's head.

Jesse heard the loud snap of the luggage bay release, and quickly moved in to snatch up the rollaway bag. He checked it for cash, and gave Leon the nod.

"Easy money," Jesse said, as Leon dove into the passenger side.

"This is a great tune," Leon said, as Jesse peeled his trucker hat, and gunned the yellow light.

They both were surprised at how smoothly the whole thing had gotten off, as they tore out of the lot onto Vegas Boulevard South, to the FM sounds of Molly Hatchet's "Flirtin' With Disaster."

Jesse dropped Leon off at The Last Chance car lot at the crossroads, where Blue Diamond crossed the 15, then drove off to ditch the Prius. Leon picked out a pristine cream-colored '68 Continental. It was puff, and the dealer wanted 100 yards.

"Make it 95 hundred. All I've got is cash."

Leon picked up Jesse a couple miles down the road, a few blocks from where he buried the Prius.

"68 Continental," Jesse said, and remarked on the suicide door, before it slammed shut behind him, the way a car door should. "This thing rides smooth. You should have gotten a Caddy, though. They've got a better cruise."

"Don't start with me," Leon said.

"What are you doin'?"

"Gotta make a call," Leon said, pulling to the curb. "No cell phones."

He pulled out a powder white business card from the bottom of his pants pocket, lifted the receiver, and punched in the numbers.

"Hello."

"It's Leon."

"Oh, hello Leon. You better not be calling about an extension."

"Nah, I got the whole thing."

"The whole five percent?"

"No. The whole thing. The principle and the interest."

There was a pause on the other end.

"Oh yeah? How soon?"

"As soon as you want it."

"You know The Key Club on the north side?"

"Yep."

"Eight o'clock."

Leon and Jesse snorted some dust and took a long ride through the desert to kill time. But no matter how smooth the cruise, or how high he got, Leon just couldn't take the edge off. Not to mention he'd been backed up since the day before.

"You look like you're wound pretty tight. You want me to go in with you?"

"Nah, I got it covered," Leon said, pulling the .45 from his waistband, and dumping it in the glove box. "Just leave it running. I'll be back in twenty minutes."

* * *

He recognized the doorman when he walked in. "Diablo, right? I'm here to see Frets."

"Turn around."

Diablo patted him up and down, and Leon thought he spent a little too much time frisking his ass.

"Looks good to me," Diablo said, tipping his head to the right. "In there."

Leon walked past three topless dancers gyrating mindlessly to electronic, meeting Frets Findlay on the opposite side of the tri-corner stage. He sat coolly in a leather upholstered booth, with bling around his neck and ice on his fingers, sucking an oyster off a half shell.

"Leon, my man. Whatchu got for me?" he said with a smug grin. Bronze tanned with a high forehead, Findlay had the kind off off-white look that could've passed him off for anything, with beady black eyes that narrowed when he smiled. Leon figured him for Filipino.

"I'm impressed Leon," Findlay said, counting the kale, as Leon laid the scratch on the table. "Looks like it's all here," he said, digging back into his plate of half shells, without looking up.

Leon held out his hand. Findlay raised an eyebrow when he glanced up at it.

"So this is it — I'm square, right?"

"You certainly are," Findlay said with a snicker, and shook Leon's hand. "Come back any time. Your credit's always good here," Findlay said, as Leon headed for the door.

* * *

Paying Findlay off should have been a relief, but Jesse could see Leon was still backed up like the Hoover Dam, as he slumped into the passenger side.

"I know what you need," Jesse said, as he pulled away from the curb.

That night Jesse hired the same teeny bopper he and Leon had double tapped the night before, but this time she brought a friend. They hit the Motel 6 by the airport, and set up pretty maids in a row, snorting line after line until they ran out of coke; passing the teen pros back and forth between them.

* * *

It wasn't until the next morning that Leon realized he'd started to come down. His eyes were heavy, and the fatigue from being up two nights running had set in, as he stumbled from the car back to his trailer on lot 142. As he struggled with the lock, he realized his appetite was back, and he was ready to move his bowels. He tossed the rollaway bag with what was left of his half of the forty grand in the stand-up closet by the door, and headed for the porcelain throne.

No sooner had he gotten his pants around his ankles and pressed his ass to the seat, the bathroom door was flung open.

"You were out all night."

"Yeah."

Here we go, Leon thought. Since she'd been pregnant, Luanne practically never left the house, and never dressed past a pair of panties under one of Leon's undershirts. Her eyes kept a serious pitch, but her mouth curled into a disarming grin.

"You won a jackpot didn't you?"

Leon's was tongue tied.

"I knew it. You gonna drive us to Florida in your new car with all that cash you got in the closet, aren't you?"

"That's the plan. And who knows, maybe we'll make it official — maybe I'll start screwing you straight."

To that tune Luanne peeled Leon's undershirt, letting her perky D-cups breathe, before she got down on her knees, taking Leon's length into her mouth. Soon after that Leon felt the ultimate release. As soon as he felt regular — he went, and at the same time he came; her little head bobbing furiously under his palm. And she swallowed it all down as Leon moaned. Then he reached for the TP.

Hours later, Leon awoke in his recliner to more of the same. Then Luanne zipped up his pants, wiped her chin, and brought him a cold beer.

"Take this over to Teddy," Leon said, pulling the wad from his pants. "We're gonna need another month to sort things out before we go."

Luanne took the cash, slipped on a pair of flip flops, and left to pay the rent without any questions.

Leon waited for the front door to slam before he cracked open his beer. For once, the place was quiet, and so were his thoughts. He'd only managed one sip of his Bud Light, before *Let's Make a Deal* came on. He put down the beer, and picked up the phone.

"I need your half of the money."

"You're still high, aren't you?" Jesse said.

"Look, you trusted me before."

"Jesus fucking Christ—"

61

"Look, Findlay's tapped into you know who — we can triple our money. The stuff's so primo, it's gotta be cut three times before sale."

There was silence on the other end.

"Did I lose you?" Leon said.

"I'll be over in the morning. No guarantees though."

After Luanne made dinner, Leon took a ride. He drove Boulder Highway, until he found the closest roadside payphone.

"Hello."

"It's Leon. I want to make a deal. I'm interested in a diamond."

"You're interested in a diamond?"

"Yeah."

"I've got half karats, one karats — what are you looking for?"

"One karat."

"One karat — okay, the price is 3-4."

"All I've got is 2-53."

"It's flawless — the price is 3-4."

"You said I've got good credit."

"After 24 hours — you've got some balls — you — "

He could hear someone call to Findlay in the background, then a slight rumble as the mouthpiece of the receiver was muffled. Leon waited.

"Leon?"

"Yeah."

"Hey, 2-53 is fine. Remember where you met me the other day?"

"Yeah."

"Be there same time tomorrow. It's a go. Okay buddy, see you then."

Buddy? Leon wondered why Findlay had become so chummy. 2-53 was wiretap code for 25 and three zeros. And as much as he wanted to put a ring on Luanne's finger, the diamonds were Max Castle's premium synthetic mother of pearl; so in essence, the best cubic zirconia money could buy. Now all he needed was Jesse to come through with the money.

* * *

It was early Monday morning when Leon heard the loud knock at the door, and his heart jumped out of his chest. Then he glanced at the alarm clock; it was 8:35. It couldn't be the cops, the dawn patrol always showed up before 6 a.m. He slid on a pair of pants, and pulled the .45 from the night stand, and made his way to the door. When he looked through the peep hole, he saw three ruggedly built cholos he'd never seen before. Leon cocked the .45, holding it at the ready, parallel to his thigh, pointed at the deck. Before he could ask, the guy closest to the door held out a jumbo Ziploc of powder, stating his business without a word. Luanne appeared in the bedroom doorway, looking like she usually did.

"Go put on some clothes, hon. We've got company."

Leon uncocked the .45, and slid it into his waistband, then pulled his untucked tee over it, obscuring the weapon.

"You guys friends of Findlay's?" Leon said, with the door open about halfway.

"Yeah man," replied the guy with the jumbo Ziploc.

"I wasn't supposed to meet him 'til tonight," Leon said.

"He goin' out of town, so he told us to come early. Catch you before you left for the day. You still interested?"

Leon thought about it.

"Yeah. I don't have all the money just yet, but you're welcome to wait inside."

* * *

The guy with the powder introduced himself as Octavio, as he perched a pair of red lens sunglasses over a head full

63

of sun-browned black hair tied back in corn rows. He didn't offer the names of his two associates. One looked stoic behind big framed sunglasses that hugged his face like a windshield, the other had crazy eyes when he half-smiled, revealing a mouth full of gold teeth.

Leon offered Octavio a seat on the sofa closest to his Lazy Boy recliner as he sat down. The other two took seats without being offered. Leon heard the hum of a phone on vibrate, then fished around in his pocket for his cell.

"Must be yours," he said, as Octavio pressed his Blackberry firmly against his ear.

As he listened intently to the party on the other end, Octavio gestured with a chin bob to the guy with the gold teeth, as Leon glanced out the window in the opposite direction. The guy with the gold teeth asked to use Leon's bathroom, and Leon pointed him toward the back.

"When can we expect your friend?" Octavio asked.

"He said morning, so I assume any time now."

"Look what I found," Gold Teeth said, with the barrel of his 9mm tight against Luanne's cheek.

Leon felt his heart jump, then a driving pressure in his temple, as Sunglasses jabbed his 9mm up against it, and cocked the hammer.

"Whatchu got?" he said, patting Leon down before pulling the .45 from his waistband.

Then he and Gold Teeth zip-tied Leon's ankles and wrists to his Lazy Boy recliner.

"I'm only gonna ask you once, you little white cunt," Octavio said to Leon with a steel trap glare, before glancing over at Luanne. "Where's our money?"

"My cousin—"

"Your cousin got more of that same bullshit. We ain't after no bullshit. They sweatin' my boy over at the bank right now over your bullshit."

The little tweaker must've tipped the junkets off. Should've let the little junkie keep his stash, Leon thought.

"Now look, if you got someone you can call, if you got some of the real deal stashed somewhere — you better let us know right now."

"Look, we put down a score — I didn't know it was fake. I know better than to pay you guys back with phony bills. C'mon, you gotta believe me — I didn't know," Leon said.

"But you know what's gonna happen next, don't you?" Octavio said, as Sunglasses peeled a 9 from his waistband. Luanne shrieked as she watched him blast both Leon's kneecaps.

"Shut the fuck up bitch," Gold Teeth said, ripping Luanne's head back, gripping a handful of her hair. Then he pulled the 9mm away from her temple, uncocked it, and slid it back into his pants. Then he reached around, and undid Luanne's jeans. But when he fished his hands into her panties, she grabbed his arm and bit it. Then he grabbed her by the throat and punched her so hard he knocked out her front row of teeth.

"Where's our fuckin' money?!" Octavio blasted six inches from Leon's face. Leon was going out of his mind the pain was so intense.

As Luanne spit blood, hugging the floor, Gold Teeth grabbed a fistful of her hair, yanked it back and said, "Now you can't bite me."

What happened next was hard for Leon to watch. Before they'd even started their gruesome violation, Luanne had pissed herself. The look on her face was a look of horror that slowly paled to blue, as Sunglasses grunted with pleasure. When she started to shriek in pain, Gold Teeth started face-fucking her.

Leon sat helplessly, strapped to the recliner, with two shattered knees, bleeding copiously through his jeans. His face tightened, and his eyes clamped shut. He would've given anything in that moment, even the chance to trade places with her. And if there had been any doubt before, he knew then that he loved her.

Sunglasses moaned as he came, cursing "fucking" back and forth between "whore" and "cunt," as though he had Turrets.

"Okay, that's enough," Octavio said. "Yo, we don't need dude's boy jumpin' our shit. Somebody post outside."

Sunglasses did up his pants, and walked out the door, as Gold Teeth took his place at the mound, pushing his way inside.

Two shots rang out and everybody froze — nobody knew who dropped the hammer. The sound of tires spinning and the roar of a high performance engine in first gear gave way to a loud knock at the door.

"Leon," yelled Jesse's familiar voice, "How many?"

Gold Teeth kept his gun on Luanne, and Octavio put his gun on Leon, who didn't dare speak. Then both men opened fire on the door as it swung open. Jesse aimed for the gold teeth, as he squeezed the trigger eye level with the top step, below both men's line of fire. Then he tipped the barrel to the left, and shot Octavio dead. He ran over to the recliner, and cut Leon's zip ties. But when he hovered over Luanne's tiny, violated body, as she convulsed on the floor, he caught two 9mm slugs in the head and dropped.

Leon watched the shooter with gold teeth gurgle his last breath, closing his crazy eyes, but the damage was done. He pulled himself to the floor, screaming in pain when his bloody knees rubbed raw, dragging his weight using his elbows, all the way over to Luanne. He found her shirt on the floor, and slid it on her, then pulled up her jeans, and zipped up the front of her pants. She was trembling, and wasn't able to speak. He put her hand in his, and squeezed until his knees went numb. Then the whole scene became like a lucid dream, until the picture went flat and everything faded to white, as Leon let go.

© 2011, Scotch Rutherford

WHEELS ON THE BUS
Patricia Abbott

Trixie's traveling by bus from Providence to Norfolk. She's not sure how this happened — who came up with the exact scheme for instance. It could've been her, but her ideas usually center on drinking, dancing, partying — not on things like long distance travel. An amazing thought pops into her head: No one on earth knows her whereabouts right now. If the bus slides into a ditch — which is possible, since the rain is falling hard — her parents will be shocked to get a call from a hospital or police station. Especially on a night when they assume — if they think about her at all, which she doubts — that she's grinding her teeth in her dormitory bed. Sending her to a Christian college after problematic high school issues did not slow her down for long. An underbelly of rebels with parents having similar ideas was easy to track down. She spotted a few at orientation even.

"They can make me sign their stupid pledge, but they can't make me keep it," she told her roommate, as she lit a Marlboro. The desk lamp threw up a shadow of Sandra reading her Bible on the wall. "What do you think?" Trixie asked, addressing the shadow. "Do you even hear me?"

It's easy to get talked into something like this bus trip, to make an excuse to the part of her brain that demands one. Or perhaps, it was she who did the talking — some plan she just can't remember. But right now, she's definitely on this bus — and heading south — if she read the sign correctly. Nicholas sleeps restlessly on the seat beside her, head against the window, breath fogging the glass. The ghostly image of a name — is it Bonnie? — lurks behind his smudges, disappearing in a whoosh as the bus passes through Philly, where some strange Greek building sits high up on a hill.

God, Nicholas sleeps with his mouth wide open. Ugh. Is this the boy who could sink a basketball from half-court? Was it Nick who made the girls squeal when he danced at a coffeehouse in Little Compton last week? Stuff like that—so important when you live in a dorm and eat cafeteria food—is insignificant already. She's moving out of that cloistered life, with its small rewards and petty concerns, at sixty miles an hour. It was probably her idea—this escape from the drudgery of chapel, classes, pledges not to smoke. It sounds like her. She took the bull by the horn as her dad always says to her brother, who hasn't left his room since he found out he has magic hands.

Trixie barely knows Nicholas, but they were at a party last night where issues like the war, bourgeoisie values, civil rights, university investments in the war machine, led to the idea of taking a stand. All of them were in on it at first—escaping from this institution—living on the road. They toasted it even, raising their arms in unison. Curtis read aloud to them from a document written in some place out in Michigan. But everyone else—like Tina, Sharon, Paul, and Curtis too—went off to class or the cafeteria this morning, whereas Nick and she remain committed, or perhaps trapped by, what she now sees is a meaningless gesture. She'd bet a dollar that Nick is failing his courses. Little prick.

She lights a cigarette, and as she begins to let go of the lighter's flame, a hand from the seat in front grabs her wrist. No—grab is too strong a word—the guy encircles it with his fingers. In the light, she sees his full beard, long hair, John Lennon glasses. Next to him, a guitar case rests, neck up. Immediately, this is what she wants for herself. A life filled with music and travel. She visualizes this guy on a stage with her banging a tambourine. Hadn't Mimi Farina played one at that coffeehouse in Peabody?

"Gotta light?"

He holds onto her wrist while she nods and presses the thumbwheel hard.

A second later, they each exhale a stream of smoke.

"Sleeping Beauty?" he says, looking at Nick.

Nicholas looks ridiculous. He could be an ex-Marine with his buttoned-up collar and pressed khakis, his loafers so shiny and new. She thinks of telling this guy that Nick's no one she knows at all—an anonymous seat mate. And he practically is that by now. He shifts uneasily beside her, perhaps sensing her disapproval.

"Hey, come up here—where we can talk."

Standing, the bearded guy moves the guitar case to the rack above. It seems impolite not to take the seat, so she does. The guy takes up more room than the boy beside her—something about his shoulders. Nick's probably running home to Norfolk to his parents' house since he's flunking out of school. Isn't that where he lives? Maybe it was his idea for her to come along—to deflect his parents' disappointment by having a stranger in the house.

Is any of this true? Her head is pounding as she tries to remember.

"Where you headed?"

Exactly. Where?

"The end of the route," she says, stubbing out her cigarette. It's just making her more nauseated anyway. She remembers then that she gets bus sick. Her mother had to drive her to high school.

"Miami, huh," he says.

She's startled—not knowing the bus goes all the way to Miami.

"Looks like you forgot your swimsuit." He has a nice voice, deep and friendly. "Know what I just did?" She shakes her head. "Took a bus from Baltimore to the Canadian border and then chickened out."

She frowns, not getting it.

He reaches in his pocket and pulls out a piece of paper, turning on the overhead light.

"Draft notice," he says, poking at it with a thick index

finger. "I'm in deep shit now. I'll be wading through rice paddies in a couple months. Sucking Agent Orange down like this nicotine." He turns it over in his large hands. "Serves me right for graduating from U.M.B.C. Could have slowed it down — gotten another year. By then, the war will be over probably."

"You should've gone through with it. The Canada thing, I mean."

Her voice sounds certain, but she doesn't really know much about it — has trouble concentrating on anything really since she discovered Sharon's supply of paregoric. Trixie presses it against her gums when she can get away with it, saying it's for toothaches — what Sharon claims anyway — says she needs it for the pain from tightening her braces. No one yet has drawn attention to the fact she wears no braces. The stolen bottle is one of the few things she's brought along. Even now, she longs to unscrew the top.

He nods. "Yeah, you're right. And I'm thinking of heading back north. Have the address of some place in Canada. A dodger shelter." He pulls another paper out of his pocket. "Not sure how to get there from the border and I can't ask them — the border guards, I mean." He laughs nervously. "Can you picture that? Say, officer can you tell me where you hide your American friends?"

"You'll figure it out." She sounds too certain, and, of course, it's because she really is not certain at all. And doesn't give a fuck. Can he see that on her face? "Maybe get on a bus. They must have buses like this one in Canada. I could come with you," she says suddenly.

He laughs, but then sees she's serious. "Why would you wanna to do that?"

"This trip," she gestures around her, "was just a way to leave where I was." Was that it? She thinks about throwing out some of the arguments she heard last night but feels too fuzzy to try it. "I get bored," she explains, mostly to herself.

"What about him?" He nods toward Nicholas.

"He's going home to Norfolk," she says. "Hey, isn't William Shatner from Canada?"

"William who?"

"Captain Kirk on *Star Trek*," she said. "You know — the TV show."

"I don't...hey, the bus is stopping," he says, peering out the window. "We're in Wilmington. Good a place to turn around as any." Stepping past her, he removes his guitar case and a knapsack from the overhead rack? "You coming — "

"Trixie." She looks behind her. "Sure, I'm coming." She turns to her still sleeping seat mate. "Live well and prosper, Nicholas." Nicholas does not wake up. "What's your name?" she asks the man who's carrying her bag now. "Hey, did you tell me your name?"

"Bill."

"Trixie," she says.

Bill looks like the kind of guy who can get her paregoric, the kind of guy who knows the ropes. "Wait a sec while I get my other bag," she tells him, reaching over Nicholas to grab his duffle bag. It might have something cool inside it. She wonders what her parents will think when she calls them from Canada. Do Canadian phone booths even take American money? Do they speak English, or is it French? It didn't matter much. She would learn to speak their language.

© 2013, Patricia Abbott

HOODWINKED
Nigel Bird

John Campion was always going to do well for himself. Everyone knew it.

Day he packed up and left for college, we didn't reckon on seeing him ever again, not if them tutors could get him to tell stories the way he did down at the tavern. Like he'd swallowed the blarney stone and digested the whole darned thing. Couldn't burp without embellishing facts and when he puked he threw up a thesaurus.

"Truth be stranger than fiction," he'd say before he started. The words "I ever tell you about..." always got us in a huddle.

Never had to pay for a beer his whole life far as I know.

* * *

Turned out we was wrong about never seeing him again.

It was Easter.

He showed up on the mountain without sending word to man nor beast. Carried the rucksack he left with and a bag of books to give to everyone. Signed the copies. JC's very own novel.

Wasn't alone neither. Had a woman with him. Film director. Wore her hair long and her smile wide, just as I like them.

Word got round about the movie they was planning to make. Based on that novel of his it was. Had the place buzzing like a saw. Biggest news in the hills since McGregor turned on his wife and kids and swallowed the barrels of his gun.

JC and Eve stayed for a couple of weeks. Chatted to just about everyone.

Eve was nice. Kind of lady you'd like to get into the sack. A little modern maybe, a head full of crazy notions, but it didn't stop me or nobody else taking a crack at her.

We was all spraying the wrong tree anyhow. Only had eyes for the female variety, so JC said.

* * *

They came back six months later, heading up a party of caravans and trucks that carried an army of crew.

Had everything a man could want right there with them, down to the kitchens and the food.

Right off they set to auditioning folk.

My brother Paul got himself a part. All he had to do was pretend to fill cars at the gas station. Could have trained a chimp to do that. Wasn't even going to get to say nothing, which was probably for the best.

Meant I had to stay home and look after the birds, set them flying for anyone who'd pay to watch.

First thing Paul did with his dough was to head on in to town. Came back with a brand new pair of jeans and a mobile phone. Looked mighty fine, I told him, but wouldn't be no good to a hungry man.

Had a fancy camera in it.

Ask me a phone's a phone. No need to go putting things together that don't fit.

* * *

Lead actor was Johnny 'Cupcake' Owens.

Night he showed up, pretty much all of the females in the county got themselves hysterical.

Even old Mamma Creek left the house for a look — first time she'd left her porch since Jacob passed away the year before. He was got by the cancer. A seven-year-old girl managed to lift him from his bed when the tumor was through with him.

Almost as light as one of my birds he must have been.

Biggest I've got is Philly.

Ten pounds is all she weighs. Sits on my glove like she weren't nothing.

Finest monkey-eating, ball-sucking eagle in the country, that's for sure.

* * *

I drove Marlene and the kids down to see Cupcake. She'd have broken my nose if I hadn't. Queued for an hour to get his autograph and shit.

Hardly recognized him up there on the platform. Didn't look anything like Commander Scott in that Warzone movie. Like someone had taken his ass and shaved off a few inches here and there. Felt good knowing I could take him without breaking sweat.

That wife of his looked pissed off by it all.

Three months gone she was. Got the feeling she wasn't going to like being out of the city, not one bit.

* * *

For the next couple of months you couldn't move for bumping into one of them actors or key-grips or whoever.

Not that I was complaining.

Got so I was wearing them birds out. Flew the falcons three times a day. Almost killed them.

Kept the bank happy with all the trade we was doing.

Paul was having a ball. Couldn't get enough of being under the lights.

Got so he didn't take off the make-up after his shots. Wore it like a badge. He'd a been better off in a dress, you ask me, even with a beard longer than Santa's. But it was nice to see him happy. Like he'd found something to be proud of.

* * *

Maybe his taste for the high-life was what did for him.

Even if it was, doesn't make it right.

A few weeks before the end-of-filming, Paul came back like he'd won the Oscar for best pumper of gas.

Pulled out his phone and showed me.

Johnny Cupcake's white ass shining like the moon. Nothing wrong with that. Except it was framed between the legs of one of the Creek twins.

Couldn't be sure if it was Amy or Mary he was screwing from the angle, not that it mattered much either way. Certainly wasn't Mrs. Cupcake and she definitely wasn't old enough for a knee-wobbler behind an oak tree with an older guy.

* * *

Plan made sense, pretty much.

Send the photo on to Johnny, make sure he knew it was real. Ask for a bag of cash to keep it from the press and give him the phone in return.

Didn't want to be greedy, neither. Not so much to make him think too hard, not so little to leave us short.

$20 thousand we decided, a fart in a warehouse to a star like Cake.

Enough for us to set up a little concern of our own. A hunting and fishing shop to go alongside the Birds Of Prey Experience.

* * *

I dropped Paul off just down from the pond where they was to meet.

Pulled off nice and smooth and never looked back.

Cake might be rich, but he was also careful. Didn't want no one getting wind of any of it.

Smoked near a half pack of tobacco waiting for that brother of mine to show.

Ruby closed the diner and came and sat for a while. Told me how she was going to change the menu soon as the film came out. Name the burgers after the stars. Was even thinking of changing the name of the establishment.

I said she should hold her horses. Wait till the film was really a film before she did any such thing. Besides, Skin and Bone didn't seem the right kind of handle for a place you go and eat, but what the fuck did I know?

We changed the subject and climbed into the back seat for a little hot-loving. Sure does know how to please a man does Rosy Ford.

After we was done, I drove her home and circled back.

Still no sign of Paul.

Got it into my head that he'd run off on me, him holding all the cards like he did.

Did my best to find the bastard. Fumed over it for days. Practically had a heart attack just thinking about it.

* * *

By the time they found him the film crew were long gone, leaving nothing behind but a couple of broken hearts and a whole load of dreams for folk to cling to.

Paul didn't even look human after two weeks in the water. Only knew it was him on account of what was left of the tattoos he wore on his arms.

Something had been taking bites out of him. Nibbled away his privates. Had to bury him that way, like he weren't even a man no more, just a sexless slab of fish-food.

How the hell was I going to let the scum get away with that?

* * *

I followed the news of Johnny Cupcake for months. Weren't difficult. What with him being a star and his wife giving birth to a baby girl and all. They were in every magazine on the stand.

Spent my time training the birds. Put them through their paces.

Spent most of my time working Philly. Getting her to do a few new tricks to keep her mind off losing her favorite owner.

When it was time, I packed everything I needed and headed over to California to get me some of that revenge I was owed.

* * *

Johnny, Betty and Baby Oregon lived on a huge chunk of land, in a house bigger than my school.

Found myself a vantage point. Weren't difficult on account of the land being in a valley. Trees on the slopes made hiding easy.

Philly was glad to get out the back of the van. I gave her a little fly when the sun went down then tethered her up for the night.

Me, I didn't sleep much. Too many things rattling in my head. I'd tried to work a way to keep the bird safe, but I guessed that was something I had to leave in the hands of the gods.

Guess Betty hadn't slept too well either. Her and Oregon were up at the crack of dawn and out on the lawn by mid-morning.

Cupcake wasn't quite so eager. Didn't see him till past

noon. Idle sloth was still in his dressing gown. Way he looked I didn't reckon there was even enough going on to get Mamma Creek excited.

I watched it all through my binoculars.

Soon as they set the baby in the pram, I took Philly from her stump.

Felt the strength of her claws on the back of my hand through the leather of the glove.

Gave her back a stroke, the feathers soft and smooth. Like I was saying goodbye.

She wasn't going to budge an inch till I took off her hood, like she was royalty perched there on my arm.

I thought about it. Considered putting her back in the cage and heading home.

Didn't though. Instead I pulled off the hood and threw her into the air.

She was straight up there feeling for currents, waiting to ride the air so's she could save on her energy. A thing of beauty, she was, circling above me like she expected me to get out a chunk of meat and the lure.

When she ran out of patience, she headed out over the valley.

I watched her all the way.

That span of hers, bigger than a man, threw a shadow onto the ground like she was a bomber plane ready to drop.

Over the fence she went, right by the security hut and the man at the gate. I watched her shadow pass over the roof and saw her closing in.

By the time she swooped, there was nothing anyone could do.

She was going straight for the baby just like she'd been trained.

Cost me plenty replacing them plastic dolls we'd practiced on, but I didn't mind.

Only thing I didn't know was how good a grip she was going to get. Could take her real high with a good connect, might not even get her off the ground if her claws didn't stick.

I held my breath as Philly closed in. Right between the parents she went and hit the target. Bull's eye.

I could see them throwing their arms about and screaming, running about like headless chickens, but Philly was too high to notice.

Must have been a hundred feet in the air when the grip gave.

Oregon accelerated downwards like she was in a hurry to get back to her folks.

Philly took off with the blanket dangling like a flag, not that it was going to be much use to her out in the wilds.

I'd seen enough. Didn't even wait for the kid to hit the ground.

Got behind the wheel and drove off with my eyes pointing straight ahead.

Sure, I didn't feel good about what I'd done. No mother should have to grieve the way she was going to and no kid taken before their time. But there was nothing I could do. I needed paying back. My ma and pa and Paul needed paying back.

I guess after what happened we was just about even.

* * *

Ma only cries if she's peeling onions. Didn't so much as sniffle even when we discovered those McGregor kids all blown to pieces, but that night, when Paul appeared on the screen, I could feel her body sobbing like she was a car doing kangaroos.

Her hand looked like a glove of bones shaking at the end of her arm.

I tried to take hold.

She slapped me hard.

Didn't hurt none, at least not on the outside, but it was

enough to let me know that she was ashamed of herself.

* * *

All those days of filming and he was only in a couple of scenes.

Give him his due though. He served those customers like he'd been doing it all his life.

He stood tall. Like he might just walk out of the screen at any moment. Was worth all the dressing up and fancy talk we had to sit through before the movie.

Johnny Cupcake sat on the front row. Didn't move a muscle the entire show. Not even when Paul stared right into the fucker's eyes.

When the lights came up and we were waiting on the speeches, he passed a note over to one of them Creek twins. Reckon it were Mary, but couldn't be sure.

Eve stood up on stage and called Johnny up.

The whole crowd stood and whooped and clapped like they was dying seals. Couldn't blame them neither. Folk from the mountain don't get out much, not like that.

He thanked everyone and said a few things about how we'd changed his life forever. Then he winked down at someone near the front.

To see him, aged twenty years in only two, you had to wonder what had been going on in the man's life. I confess, I was glowing inside.

One thing for sure, he weren't going to be getting any of those action parts no more.

Soon as it was over, I got myself ready to leave.

Ma though, she weren't having any. She was off down those steps waving her stick, making sure she got to him first.

Couldn't remember the last time she'd moved so quick.

Mounted the stage like an athlete.

Straight over to him she went, pointing and shouting.

Might have been easier to understand if she'd been wearing her teeth.

She jabbed her arm out suddenly, real impolite.

Johnny Cupcake didn't even flinch.

Took the pen she waved.

Signed everything she put in front of him.

SUGAR AND SPICE

Andrez Bergen

Rankine lifted his head off the floor and peered at his gut, at the blood pumping out of the big hole in his shirtfront, running down the sides and creating a huge puddle on the carpet.

"Crap," he muttered. "That's going to be a bugger to patch."

Wasn't supposed to be like this, no way. Three days ago, Mitch reckoned it'd be a blow-over, easy street romp — if not exactly sugar and spice and everything nice, then something marginally sweet.

The shop was down an unpopular arcade, in the city on Bourke Street, not much pedestrian traffic, and the nearest cop house three blocks away.

Basics, security-wise: a camera that probably didn't work, just for show to scare the amateurs, and a newly installed magnetic tag security detector straddling the doorway. Probably bought on eBay, but they heard it go off when some kid tried something, so they knew that baby was no Trojan Horse.

The bloke behind the counter seemed to actually be two people sharing the same beard, receding hairline, and dress-sense (bordering on offensive suburban hippy).

There were no nametags to double-check who was who and they were always too busy reading shit to pay attention to customers' questions — which Mitch said worked to their advantage since they wouldn't know what was going on till it was too late.

The big attraction? This was no diamond merchant, not a bank, nor a service station/convenience store. It wasn't even a dodgy school kiosk, their usual port-of-criminal-call.

This was a comic book store, a minor affair specializing in new releases from America and a wad of collectibles. No manga at all, which was one of the reasons Rankine had never heard of the place.

The thing was, they had a copy of *Action Comics* #1 up on the wall.

This meant nothing to Rankine, who coveted an early, uncensored printing of Katsura Masakazu's *Video Girl Ai* manga, since later printings changed the art to cover up the nudity.

Mitch courteously filled in the massive gaps in his American comic know-how: the issue that gave Superman his big break, published in the U.S. in 1938 for just ten cents. Over seventy years later, a rare copy was sold online for $2.16 million.

"You know Nick Ratatouille?" Mitch went on.

"Maybe." Rankine had been out front of the folks' place, sitting on his bum on the nature-strip, fixing an elusive puncture on the tyre of his painstakingly rebuilt 1974 Malvern Star chopper, trying not to get tangled up in Mitch's plans.

Mitch had a tendency to lead partners astray — namely arrest or injury, or both — even if he always got off scot-free. Still, this was one question Rankine believed he could tackle without a lure or a slap. "Isn't he the muscle for Occitan and the boys over on Catalan Crescent?"

"Right on. He heard from a mate who heard from another mate that it was sold by Nicolas Cage."

"You reckon the comic in that shop is the same one he owned?"

"No, you moron — but if that one got two mill, there's every chance the one on the wall in this dive will get half that, at least. A million, R, that we can split down the middle. You could get your bloody Malvern Star gold-plated if you want."

That'd been the clincher. Not the gold plating but the

swandooly. Rankine went along with it all, even forking out the dosh for the ski masks from an army disposals shop on Elizabeth Street and a couple of BB guns he got FedEx'd from Japan that were replica full-scale Enfield revolvers.

Knocking over a comic book store would be a breeze. Nothing could go wrong.

So they'd skipped out on high school on a Monday—he'd forged the letters from their mums as usual—and got out of their uniforms in the toilets at South Yarra Station before heading into town on a Frankston Line train at 2:10 p.m.

Got off at Flinders Street before three, after some typical bloody delays, and waltzed straight to the arcade. Flicked through some brand new Marvel comics that bored Rankine silly, waiting till no one else was in the shop, and then pulled on the balaclavas and pointed their faux firearms at the bird behind the counter.

"Give us the fucking comic, dickhead!" Mitch screamed in too loud a voice.

"Sure, kid, sure, don't get your knickers in a knot," Old Beard-and-Bald assured him, hands clutching air. "Which one?"

"Clark Kent up there, on the wall." Mitch waved the gun in a general direction over the clerk's head. "Move it!"

"You mean...are you talking about this?" The man pointed to *Action Comics* #1, a primitive-looking Superman lifting a green car above his head and smashing it.

"Sure. Hand it over."

"You boys do realize it's a repro?"

Rankine leaned forward. "A what?"

"Reproduction. This isn't the real thing—why on earth would we have it sitting right here in our shop? That'd be lunacy."

Rankine couldn't be sure, but he sussed the old hippy was lying. Mitch, however, was in a rage, shoving his pop gun forward.

"Bullshit!" he shouted, so incensed he'd lost control of his drool.

Rankine observed this spittle traveling across air from his partner's mouth; saw it settle down on the desktop and sit there, bubbly and offensive.

That was when Beard-and-Bald got angry. He stared at the saliva, and then dropped his right hand—

Fretting some, Mitch waggled his toy. "Don't move!"

—and the man stood up straight with an Uzi submachine gun stuck in his mitt. Rankine had a sneaking suspicion this baby hadn't been purchased via mail order from Tokyo; conjecture confirmed when the thing start dishing out real 9mm bullets.

"Nobody spits in my shop! No fucker steals my comics!" Beard-and-Bald raved as he raked the small area, destroying much of the merchandise before he found his real targets.

Mitch, Rankine could see from his place spread-eagled on his back, was dead as a dodo, folded up against the wall with brains wallpapering a bunch of DC comics in a rack.

He returned attention to his stomach, felt dizzy, tried to pull together the flaps of skin there—same technique as sticking together the flaps of rubber with the puncture the other day.

Now, if only he had his tyre sealant glue.

© 2013, Andrez Bergen

HABEUS CORPUS

Benedict J. Jones

By the time I got there they'd already taken three of his fingers. Hammer and chisel, me I'd have preferred bolt cutters, but then I've been known to be a soft touch. Sometimes. At least they had cauterised the wounds with an iron so he hadn't passed out from blood loss. He didn't look too clever though.

When I got the call, I was propping up a bar in Angel while talking to a woman with dyed red hair and legs that were longer then her dress. The intruding chirp of my mobile was as unwelcome as a razor's kiss on a cold morning but when I saw the caller ID I knew I'd have to take it. I excused myself from the pouting red head and stepped out.

"Boss?" I flipped the collar on my Burberry and wished I'd brought an umbrella.

"They've got him."

"What d'you want me to do?"

"What you do best. Supervise."

He disconnected the call and left me looking for a cab on a rain-slicked Upper Street.

They had him in the underground parking area of a half-constructed apartment block in Silvertown. We'd used the place before when we needed to have a quiet word with someone. I tapped in the security code and walked across the harshly lit bare concrete. The kid was tied to an office chair with wire and two of the lads, Kyle and Carl, were going at his hand with the hammer and chisel, the chair on a sheet of clear plastic. They let up on the meat carpentry as I approached. Kyle and Carl looked like they were brothers, cousins at least. They weren't, just birds of a feather; gym-bulked bodies, perma-tans from the electric beach, and a penchant for dark clothes and violence. They'd kicked the shit out of the kid tied to the chair; broke nose, eye puffed shut, bloody mouth looking short of a few pearlies, not to mention his hand.

I strolled over and surveyed the damage. I whistled.

"He told you yet?"

A shaking of heads, the lads looked sheepish.

"Go on, take a breather."

They walked away, probably going to compare triceps and tips on which whey protein is best for building knuckle mass. I slid my Burberry off, took out my Marlboros. I lit two and stuffed one into matey boy's mouth. I took a good tug on my cigarette and watched the kid. He managed to pull in a lungful of smoke and the filter clung to the sticky blood of his torn lips.

"Wha'sh thish then? Good cop time?" He laughed to himself. It sounded hollow, like he was already dead. I picked up the hammer that Carl had left and I rapped him over the knee.

"Nah I reckon you've had enough, son, you want to spill it."

He spat the cigarette out.

"Go fuck yourself!"

Proper hard case. How're you meant to respond to that? After I took the remaining finger and his thumb he still wouldn't talk. I pulled his jeans down and let him feel the chisel. Then he spilled it.

* * *

"Boss, we've got a problem."

"I don't like problems."

"I know."

"I take it he didn't tell you where?"

"Sort of...Reckons he was off his face and can't

remember the name of the place. Says he'll know it when he sees it."

"You believe him?"

"Yeah."

"Yeah?"

"He wouldn't hold anything back, boss. We'll throw him in the car and go find this place."

"I just want my boy back."

"I know, boss. I know."

The boss terminated the call and I looked over at Carl and Kyle.

"Get him cleaned up. We're going for a drive."

After they'd hosed the kid off, Carl splashed bleach on the floor while Kyle went to get their BMW X5, black, of course. It had smoked windows which was all for the good as I secured the kids hands with a zip tie and pushed him into the back. Carl got in next to the kid, Kyle drove and I rode shotgun—except I had a 9mm Walther in the pocket of my Burberry.

We hit the motorway and I watched the kid in the rear view mirror as the orange lights slipped by as bright streams beyond the windows. The kid had his eyes shut as though asleep. No way could he have been sleeping. We'd tossed some codine down his neck but his hand should have been screaming at him. I tapped the radio on and got some of the bass heavy shit that Carl and Kyle listen to and tuned it to a station relaying the Tottenham game.

* * *

When we reached the outskirts of Gravesend, I gave Carl a look and the kid got a slap. His eyes snapped open, wide and pink, the color of a bloodshot sky.

"What's your name, kid?"

"Jamie."

"Well, Jamie, you want to come up with something?"

He looked out of the window.

"Straight on and take your second left." I nodded to Kyle.

"Second right then straight on, take your right at the tower block." Jamie had his eyes closed and was speaking from memory.

I looked around. Kyle had pulled up on a grass verge outside a block of flats.

"This doesn't look like the place you told me about, Jamie."

"It's not. This is where we started."

"What were you on?"

"Speedballs—coke and H, before that just the horse."

"Dirty little junkie!" spat Kyle.

"You including your boss's kid in with that?" Carl sank his fist into the kid's solar plexus before I could stop him. Jamie struggled to catch his breath.

"Come on," I said. "I told you there was an easy way out of this. There's a hard way as well—a way that'll make what happened to you earlier seem like a steak and a blowjob on your birthday—savvy?"

He caught his breath and nodded without looking at me then he spoke.

"We jacked a car up at the Asda."

"Which way, Jamie?" I asked.

"Go left then right and straight on."

The Asda car park was emptying but the shop was still brightly lit.

"So..." I shifted around in my seat to look Jamie in the face.

"We spotted a woman putting her shopping in her car, silver Volvo. I gripped her up and Danny showed her an old needle. Told her he had the germ and if she kicked up a scene he'd stick her."

Carl was looking at the kid in disgust.

"We took the ride and we headed east." We moved off.

We went on like that until we hit the motorway and headed out into the Kent marshes. It was closing in on ten o'clock.

"So what happened, Jamie?"

He caught my eyes in the rear view mirror for a moment before he spoke.

"Just wanted to get away from it all. Take ourselves off, just us and the gear."

"Like a junkie Withnail and I?" Everyone looked at me in confusion and I just nodded for Jamie to continue.

"And that's what we did."

"If that was all that happened, we wouldn't be here, would we?"

"Billy was hitting it hard. Must've been a scud batch. When I came to he was all blue and wide eyed."

"Then?"

"He was my mate. I treated him proper, better than his dad would've."

I saw Carl cock his fist and threw him an eye. He lowered his fist.

Kyle pulled up at a fork in the road.

"Which road, Jamie?"

"The chalet we broke into is down the left road. Billy's down the other one."

We took the right fork. There were fewer lights now and we flew through the darkness like a black arrow.

"Church up ahead," said Kyle.

"This the one, Jamie?"

"Yeah." He nodded and his chin dipped down to his chest.

"Park further up and we can walk back down." Kyle pulled in at the far end of the wall of the churchyard. I chambered a round into the Walther and slid it back into my pocket.

"Bring a torch and a crowbar." I said to Carl. I climbed out and Kyle pulled Jamie out onto the road.

"You carried him here yourself?"

"He was my mate." The kid left it at that as though it explained how a junkie got his needle mate over a seven-foot-high wall. No way was I going over the wall. Carl snapped the lock off the gate to the churchyard with the crowbar. I kept the torch off and we headed up the path toward a church that looked like it belonged on the set of a Hammer horror film.

"Where?"

"In the main bit of the graveyard."

We skirted the church and I kept one hand on the Walther in my pocket as we walked. Among the weathered stone markers and marble crosses sat a small, dome-topped mausoleum.

"He's in there."

"Stay here and I'll take a look see," I said to the lads as I held the heavy Maglite in my left hand. I left Jamie with his twin guardians and threaded my way through the tombstones and graves. I slipped the safety off the Walther without taking it out of my pocket as I headed toward the death house. Stepping between a pair of small pillars, I pushed open the tomb's metal door and switched on the Maglite.

The torch beam played around the shadowy interior of the mausoleum. Billy Cochran was laid out in one corner. He was as white and cold as the marble upon which he lay. In the weak light and shadow he reminded me of a photograph I had seen of Che Guevara after he'd been shot down — the one that reminded everyone of Jesus. There were no obvious signs of violence on the emaciated body. I played the torch across the rest of the area and then slipped the safety back on the Walther. My hands were shaking so I sparked a Marlboro as I walked back to the waiting trio.

"It's him. Let's take Jamie back to the car and call the boss."

Carl and Kyle got Jamie into the back seat and then got

in themselves. I lit another cigarette and made the call.

"Yes?"

"We've found him, boss."

"Is he..."

"I'm sorry, Mister Cochran."

The line was silent for a moment.

"Where?"

I rattled off the address of the church.

"I'll be there in an hour."

"Boss, I can deal with this."

"No. I'm doing this for my boy. One hour."

The call was cut. I stared at my phone. I couldn't imagine the boss leaving his fortified mansion in Hayes. But then blood is blood. Carl was looking at me and I gestured for him to drop the window.

"He's coming."

"What? The boss?"

I nodded.

"Listen, I want you to drive the kid around. Being parked up here might draw attention we don't need. I'll call you when it's time to come back."

"Are we gonna..." He gestured toward the back of the car, at Jamie, with his head.

"I'd have thought so," I replied.

"Where are you going?"

"Going to walk into the village and see if I can catch last orders."

Carl nodded and put the window back up. I buttoned up my Burberry and headed down the lane into the village. A fog began to come down and made the lights of the village appear dim and dirty.

* * *

"Large brandy." the red-faced landlord gave me a look that said he didn't know me and shouldn't have to serve me.

I gave him one back that told him he didn't need the trouble. He turned to the optics and got me the drink. I looked around the pub—two old boys in flat caps with pints of bitter, a sad looking dog and a middle-aged woman with too much flesh on display.

"Anything else?" asked the landlord.

"No thanks." I passed him a tenner. If this was the good life in the country then they could keep it. I took a bite out of the brandy and thought about the red head I'd left at the bar in Angel. She had had the kind of figure that would've warmed me up as well as the brandy I was drinking.

The landlord rang the bell for last orders and I grabbed another brandy. My phone rang as I raised the glass to my lips. The landlord tutted and continued to polish the beer taps.

"I'm here."

"I'll be there in five, boss." I nodded to the sad-looking dog, downed my brandy and headed back out into the night.

The boss's Jaguar was parked close to the gate of the churchyard. As I approached, the driver's door opened. The man who emerged wore an open-necked shirt and blazer straight off Saville row, which were at odds with the severe military cut of his hair. The well-tailored blazer failed to disguise the bulge beneath the driver's left armpit. I kept my hands away from my sides as I approached.

"Hello, Connor."

He nodded in response. Connor had served two tours in Helmand before he came to work for Mister Cochran. His skin was still dark and his eyes seemed marked by the harshness of the land in which he had served.

The back door opened and the boss climbed out.

"You want me to call the others back?"

"Not yet. I want to see Billy first." He headed off into the churchyard. Connor reached into the car and grabbed up a torch and a roll of black fabric.

"What's that?" I asked.

"Body bag." He replied flatly as he locked up the Jag. "You carrying?"

"Yeah. You?"

"'Course." He looked around.

"Relax, Connor. Just us here."

"If the Fletchers knew the boss was out here or the Hasan brothers or the fucking Russians."

"I know, Connor. But they don't. No one knows we're out here."

The ex-soldier grunted and adjusted the pistol in his shoulder rig.

"Are you two fucking coming?" hissed the boss from out of the shadows, and we hurried through the gate after him.

When we reached the mausoleum, we stopped.

"In there?" asked the boss.

"Yes. He's in there."

"Connor, you stay here. Form a perimeter or something."

I stayed behind Cochran and lit the way for him with a Maglite. When we were inside, I kept my lips together like a frigid girls legs. The boss didn't say a word at first. He just stared at the body.

"That's it then. Stupid little bastard...You got a fag?"

I fumbled for my Marlboros. The boss slipped it between his lips and I lit it for him. As the flame sparked movement blurred in the corner of my eye. I turned in time to see Billy sit up, a silenced pistol aimed straight at his father. The muzzle flash blinded me for a second. I felt the boss fall against me and then what felt like a punch hit me in the ribs and dropped me to my knees. I blinked the muzzle flash away and as my vision returned I took in the boss lying on the floor next to me, half his head gone. I looked sideways at Billy as I struggled to take a breath.

"Toss your piece," he said in a voice that sounded as though his throat had been cut.

I took the Walther out between my thumb and index finger and threw it into the shadows. Shoe leather slapped on stone and Connor stepped through the doorway. Two more muzzle flashes and the ex-soldier fell back onto the floor.

"Shit..." I felt my side and my hand came away dark with blood that appeared black in the half-light thrown by the torch. I sat back and picked up the cigarette that I had lit for the boss. I stole a drag and bit down the pain.

I heard more footsteps at the door. Billy's arm kept the pistol aimed straight. Jamie appeared and grinned down at me. He dropped two heads into my lap. Carl and Kyle wouldn't have been happy — their orange perma-tans had been replaced by the pale marble pallor of death. I took another pull on the cigarette.

"I hope you boys are getting well paid for this."

Billy smiled and lowered the gun. Then he spoke again in that cutthroat voice.

"The Hasans reckon they're getting a bargain. Hundred grand for the head of the mighty Jimmy Cochran. 'Course when they come to the payoff, they'll be getting a little surprise as well."

Billy stood up — pale, naked, risen. He walked past me and clapped Jamie on the shoulder.

"Be all ours, Jame. Whole fucking city."

I took a last tug on the Marlboro, burnt down to the filter. I flicked it away into the dark.

"Go on then." I started to cough and for a moment I couldn't stop, when I finally caught my breath again I continued. "Get it done. Two in the head like your dad please."

Billy leaned down and I could smell the scent of death all over him.

"Not for you. We need you."

Then I was lifted by hands that seemed too strong for a pair of junk hounds.

"What for?" I asked when they got me stood up.

"What you do best. Supervise, ease the transition." I saw the glint in Billy's eye and realized he's as bad as his old man. Jamie took my weight and helped me toward the door.

"Get you patched up old man. Course you try anything and I'll take a lot more than a couple of fingers."

I laughed and that just ended up with me coughing again.

DISABILITY, INC.

Garnett Elliott

Stanley met Chas in the waiting room of Dr. Zaleski's office. Stanley was feeling more than a little conspicuous, what with his level three sex offender ankle bracelet and the fact that his hands were cuffed — in front of him, at least. Chas didn't seem to mind. He had a big bandage wrapped around his head and looked pretty goofy, too. Zaleski's waiting room was always full of characters, on account he was the only private shrink in Yuba City.

"What's Dr. Z going to do for you?" Chas said, leaning close so the rest of the riff-raff couldn't overhear.

"He's gonna get this bracelet off of me. And clear my name. Because the truth is, I'm not really a chester."

Chas grinned like he'd heard this before. "You're not?"

"Hell no. I like 'em young, don't get me wrong, but around sixteen or thereabouts. You know, almost legal."

"Sixteen's still a minor."

"By the letter of the law, maybe. But Dr. Z's got this big gray book, lays out all the different ways people can be fucked in the head. And the book says, you got to be liking them thirteen or younger in order to be considered a true ped-o-file. And I like 'em sixteen."

"That seems pretty straightforward."

"Yup. Also, Dr. Z says it's not my fault I like teenagers, seeing as how my own teenaged years were so screwy. My momma raised me in a tool shed. Kept me separate from all my brothers and sisters."

Stanley didn't add that was because his momma had caught him messing in un-Christian ways with his brothers and sisters, but that hardly seemed the point.

"What's Dr. Z doin' for you?"

Chas gestured at the bandage. "I'm going on disability. You read about what happened to me in the paper? At the Pack 'Em Inn Steakhouse?"

Stanley didn't read too much, but he did recall hearing something about the restaurant. He snapped his fingers. "You're that guy, the one got hit by a — what was it? A sled?"

"That's right. The owners strung a bunch of antiques from the ceiling, trying to make the place look snazzy. Well, my table had a hundred and fifty pound hardwood toboggan suspended over it — "

"'Ta-boggin'?"

"That's a sled. Anyways, one of the wires snapped and the thing hit the side of my skull. And here I am."

Stanley scratched at his chin. He had to raise both hands to do it, because of the cuffs. "I thought I heard you came out of that fine. That the sled hit at a funny angle and only glanced off your skull."

"That's what those idiots in the E.R. told everyone," Chas said, "but that's not the truth. I've been emotionally traumatized. Dr. Z's helping me with the specifics. Did you know I can't sit in a restaurant anymore? No kidding, I'll freak out if I try it."

"Damn."

"Worst thing is, ever since the accident, I haven't been able to get it up. Dr. Z says it's part of my 'psychic scarring.' He says if my lawsuit against the Pack 'Em Inn fails, I got plenty of ammo for those tight-assed bastards at Social Security."

"Man, that sounds nice." Stanley tried not to sigh. All he wanted to do was win his freedom, get some of his self-respect back. But old Chas here had the keys to the Promised Land. It just didn't seem fair, how some people got punished for their natural urges, while others had the good luck to have a hundred-and-fifty-pound, hardwood toboggan fall on their head.

The door to Dr. Z's office opened. A fat woman in a leg-brace and a crutch under her left armpit came stumping out. She'd looked depressed as hell before she'd gone back for her appointment. All listless and droopy, like maybe she'd shoot herself in the parking lot. But now her eyes blazed with hope. She two-stepped over to the cashier's window and slapped down her co-pay, beaming at the world.

Dr. Z had that kind of power.

He leaned his handsome face out into the waiting room. Curly black hair shot through with streaks of silver. Long, gray sideburns and a strong Pollack's nose. His gaze wandered over the hopefuls sitting at attention.

"You want to come back now, Stan?"

Did he ever.

* * *

Two months later, Chas came over to visit Stanley's place with a bucket of KFC wings and a case of Coors Light. They gnawed chicken-bones on the dusty back porch, pausing only to guzzle or fart.

"How's it feel to be a free man?" Chas said, smearing away hot sauce with the back of his hand.

"S'alright." Stanley pointed to the ankle where the bracelet used to be. "Got busted down to a level one. Unsupervised probation, which is as close to 'free' as I'm gonna get. Feels better, though. How about you?"

"Getting a check every month. Dr. Z went toe-to-toe with D.E.S. for me."

"Man's a miracle worker."

"Sure is."

Stanley chucked an empty can at an emaciated chicken who'd wandered too close to the porch. It sailed right over the bird's head. The chicken kept pecking at the ground like nothing had happened. Chas laughed and rooted around in the bucket, but when he looked up at Stanley again his eyes were sad.

"I got to tell you, though, the disabled life ain't what I thought it'd be," he said.

"Yeah?"

"First off, I don't get that much. Enough for rent and cable TV, a little food. Cheap food. And cheap-ass cable, too. None of the premium channels with naked women and such." He looked wistful. "I thought having all that time on my hands would be like, you know, the ultimate freedom. Lots of things I could do. But all I end up doing is watching daytime TV and jerking off."

"I thought you said couldn't get it up no more?"

"Nah, that's passed. I guess that psychic wound's healed over."

Stanley thought about asking him if he could eat in restaurants again, but held off. When disability was the one thing a man had going for him, you didn't want to question it too much. "I figure my life ain't so great, either."

"You don't own this double-wide, do you?"

"Nope. Belongs to the old lady that answered the door. Ma Pootie. 'Cept she's not really my ma. See, when I moved out here I had to go around to all the neighbors and explain I'm a sex offender. But Ma Pootie, instead of gettin' mad, offered to take me in. Said I could do handyman's jobs for her."

Chas raised his eyebrows. "What kind of 'handyman's' jobs'?"

"It's nothing like that."

"Where the fuck do you sleep here, anyways? When I came in it was all stacked boxes and bird cages."

Stanley nodded at the battered Tuff Shed on the edge of the property. A dead cottonwood draped its skeletal branches over the roof, which had rusted through in a couple places.

Chas shook his head. "Back in the tool shed again, huh?"

"It's not so bad, 'cept for the heat. And the black widows."

"Jesus, when I start feeling down on myself I know where to come."

"That why you paid a visit? So you can feel superior?"

"Don't get bitchy about it. Shit, I come over here with free Coors and chicken—"

"No one told you to come over."

"—which you wolf down and don't even offer to pay for, like any goddamn decent person." He waved at the bucket of bones. "On my income, this is a major purchase. I've shot my wad for the month."

Stanley felt hot blood surge to his temples. "Don't you be calling me cheap, you goddamn faker."

"Kid-toucher."

Stanley shot up and balled his fists.

The door to the porch rattled open. An old woman wearing a padded housecoat stepped out. Two parakeets perched on the narrow slope of her left shoulder, while an African Gray rode the hump on her right. She glanced at the empty beer cans strewn across the porch and her thin mouth curled down at the corners.

"Thought I heard some hollerin' out here," she said.

Stanley unclenched his fists. "No, Ma Pootie."

"That's good. Because there's an important person wants to talk to you on the phone. Dr. Zaleski."

The African Gray squawked and shit a fresh white streak down her shoulder.

* * *

Dr. Z wanted to meet at the Big Tiki Miniature Golf course. Stanley had no idea why. During the phone conversation he let slip Chas was over on a visit, and Dr. Z said that was a good thing.

"Invite him along," he said.

"What's this all about, Doc?"

"An exciting opportunity. I'll explain later."

He hung up.

Of course Chas wanted to go. They took his new F-150, as Stanley had been without a vehicle for months.

The Big Tiki itself wasn't looking so hot. Sun-faded, covered in spots with graffiti, the fifteen foot fiberglass idol cast stern eyes over the clubhouse and the four acres of worn Astroturf behind it. There were a decent number of cars parked for a Tuesday evening.

"I don't see Dr. Z's Lexus," Stanley said, surveying the lot.

"We must be early."

"We could play a couple holes. I used to come here as a kid, but I don't remember it being this busy."

Chas chuckled. "It's doing business, alright."

They argued about who was going to pay for clubs and a caddy of balls, until Stanley finally gave in. He saw what Chas had meant about 'business' once they got out onto the greens. Cholos were everywhere. Old school gangsters, wearing hair nets and untucked Dickies dress shirts with black slacks. The farther out from the clubhouse, the more furtive they got. By the thirteenth hole, plastic baggies were being slipped from pockets, money flashed, and dope changing hands. Stanley watched with disapproval.

"This used to be a family kind of place," he said.

"Fucking wetbacks."

A big cholo caught them staring and glared back. Stanley and Chas took a sudden interest in knocking their balls through a series of arched flamingo legs.

Dr. Z came strolling up five minutes later.

He wore wraparound sunglasses, despite the failing light, and a Stetson pulled low over his forehead. T-shirt and jeans. Pale bands of flesh showed where his silver rings and watch should have been. But even with the dressing down, a presence surrounded him like a giant soap bubble. Several of the cholos recognized him, shook his hand, and he responded with quips of fluid Spanish. It took him awhile to work his way to the thirteenth hole.

"Christ," he said, removing the hat to scratch his head, "so much for being inconspicuous."

Stanley offered his putter. "You want to give it a shot, Doc?"

"No thank you, boys. I'll just watch and talk while you play." He settled his hands into his pockets. "Now, I don't want you two to feel like I'm rushing things here, being all business. But time's a valuable commodity, so I'm not going to waste yours or mine with a lot of small talk."

"We appreciate that, Dr. Z," Chas said.

"Well, here it is then. Do either of you gentlemen have criminal records? Beyond those unfair allegations against you, Stanley."

"I got a DUI, about four years back," Stanley said. "Plus some credit shit, but that was all handled in civil court."

"I had a string of B and E's when I was in my early twenties," Chas said.

"B and E's, that's good." Dr. Z licked his lips. "That could come in handy."

The sodium lamps were blinking into life overhead. Smaller floodlights on the ground flicked on, bathing the flamingos, the giant windmills, in cones of red, blue, and green. Dr. Z cast a triple shadow.

"Why you want to know about our records?" Stanley asked. "When you said you had an 'exciting opportunity,' I thought you meant selling Amway or something."

"No, no." Dr. Z took off his sunglasses. His eyes underneath had lost some of their intensity. He had those puffy little bags going on, and dark circles, too. "I guess you could figure, looking after the emotional needs of an entire community like Yuba City can wear on a man."

"I don't know how you do it," Chas said.

"I'd go off my fucking rocker," Stanley added.

"Well, it's not come to that. Yet. Some of my patients, though...you familiar with the old widow, Mrs. Groyle? She

103

first saw me about eight years ago, right after her husband died. Bad case of depression. It's grown worse over time, and I've tried everything. Therapy, medication, ECT—that means shock treatments."

"They still do those?" Chas said.

"Sometimes. Nothing's worked, though. Mrs. Groyle has lapsed into a vegetative state. She leaves her house to see me, and that's about it."

"Why doesn't she just off herself?" Stanley said.

"That's the problem. She's made four attempts already. I've taken away her husband's guns, her knives, and controlled her access to medications, but she's a diabetic. Insulin-dependent. That means she's got to inject herself every day, and she knows an overdose of insulin can be lethal."

Chas snorted. "How's that a problem? If she kills herself, you don't have to treat her anymore. Case closed."

"Not quite. She's under my care, so her family can sue for malpractice. And they will. You wouldn't believe how litigious people have become."

"Oh, I would," Chas said, "I would."

"She'll keep trying until she succeeds. Or she'll just give up and stop injecting herself. Either way, she dies. I don't need the legal hassles and I don't need any more dings against my license." He spread his broad hands. "So I'm stuck."

"What you want us to do, Doc?" Stanley said.

The shadows had lengthened under the Stetson's brim. Zaleski's face, what was still visible in the lurid glow of the colored lights, grew still.

"I think I know what he's getting at," Chas said.

* * *

They staked out Mrs. Groyle's house from the F-150's roomy cab.

104

Chas had parked across the street, hidden in the shadows of a plum-tree grove. He wore a black Toby Keith t-shirt and black baseball cap, with crankcase oil smeared over his face. Every now and then he'd lift the old Bushnell scope he'd brought along and peer at the house.

"He didn't have to threaten us like that," Stanley said.

"He didn't threaten so much as give us incentive. Like he said, he's got to write letters to keep my disability checks coming and the police off your back. He can't very well do that if he's been sued out of business."

Stanley hated to concede the point, but there it was.

They waited another thirty minutes. An over-ripe plum hit the truck's hood with a soft plop. Birds called. Stanley finished off the last two cans of Silver Bullet from the cooler they'd brought along.

"Fuck it," Chas said at last, tossing the Bushnell onto the dashboard. "Let's go and get her done."

"I thought you said we'd wait 'til nightfall."

"How many people you seen? This place's deserted. Maybe two cars have passed the whole time."

Chas was already slipping out of the cab, so Stanley did likewise. His shoes squished into the grove's soft loam. Hunkered over, Chas padded from tree to tree like a rural commando. Stanley followed. Just the other side of the road lay an Okies-era farmhouse in peeling yellow paint. Weeds had overrun the front yard. A huge oleander bush screened the neighbor's trailer to the left.

Chas pointed and made a twirling motion with his fingers.

They circled around to the rear of the house. The grass had grown even more wooly-bully back there. Stanley checked for dog turds and didn't find any, which he took as a good sign. There was an enclosed porch with rusted screen mesh and a flimsy door.

"We get through that," Chas said, pointing, "and I bet you ten bucks the interior door's not even locked."

"I'll try it."

Stanley wrapped his fingers around the handle and pulled. He'd lost most of his muscle tone since he'd stopped working in the feed lot, but Ma Pootie always had him moving heavy boxes, so he had a little strength left. The door groaned. He slipped another hand over his right, braced his left foot up against the frame, and yanked.

The door came sailing off its hinges. He had to jump backwards to avoid losing his balance.

Inside, the narrow porch had been heaped with bundles of yellowed newspaper. An antique barometer hung askew. Stanley tried the knob on the adjoining door. As predicted, it turned with no resistance.

Warm air and the smell of old mayonnaise came wafting out.

"The fuck's that?" he whispered to Chas, who had a hand over his nose.

"Maybe she's already dead."

The door opened onto a small kitchen. Every available surface was stacked with china plates, paper plates, forks, spoons, cups, mugs, bowls, crusted TV dinners, napkins, soup cans, milk cartons, wrappers, and pieces of rotting fruit. The table had no space to actually eat. Water the color of strong coffee filled both sinks, with an inch of grayish scum riding the surface.

Stanley felt the beer in his stomach turn sour.

"Holy fuck," Chas said, forgetting to whisper.

The floor was worse. Same stuff as on the counters, but also hair, magazines, and old clothes. A sort of trail had been worn through the debris that wound from the hall, circled the table, and led to the refrigerator.

A part of Stanley's memory recalled his Aunt Flo's house, and he instinctively began hopping. Left foot, right foot. Aunt Flo had been a pill-head.

"Why you dancing like that?" Chas said. But just as he said it a two-inch cockroach bolted from a nearby mound and crawled up his pant leg. Chas screamed. He shook his foot and slapped his pants. A mass of feelers seemed to poke from everywhere at once.

"Keep moving," Stanley said.

They danced down the hall, following the trail. Stanley half-expected Mrs. Groyle to come popping up with a shotgun, what with all this advance warning they were giving her, but it didn't happen. The trail led through an open doorway and into the bedroom. The first thing Stanley noticed was how clean it was. Clean compared to the Kitchen of Horrors, anyway. No crap on the floor. A nightstand with a syringe and a couple medicine bottles, shoved up against a queen-sized bed —

A woman lay on the bed.

He recognized her from Dr. Z's waiting room. She rested atop the sheets in a floral-print nightgown, hands folded across her chest. Greasy-gray hair. But she wasn't asleep. Her eyes were open and regarding the two of them with languid calm.

"Ah—" Stanley said, and looked away. What was he supposed to say? *We're here to do for you, ma'am?* It was awkward. Chas didn't seem too bothered, though. He snatched the pillow out from under her head and started smothering her with it, just like that. She put up no fight.

"You going to watch," Chas said, pressing his weight against the pillow with both elbows, "or you going to make yourself useful?"

"Doing what?"

"I don't know. Find something to hit her with, just in case."

The woman moaned a muffled "Thank you" from under the pillow, and continued her non-struggle.

Stanley hunted for a heavy object. He found a porcelain doll on the dresser, but it didn't have enough heft. It occurred to him they should be wearing gloves. His fingerprints were all over the back doors. Funny, how Chas had thought to bring beer and an old rifle scope, but forgot something as basic as gloves. He figured they better get a rag and wipe everything down.

"You hear that?" Chas said, still hunched over Mrs. Groyle.

"Hear what?"

"That scratching. From the front of the house."

Stanley listened. After a moment, he caught it: the unmistakable sound of a key fitting a lock.

"Shit," he said.

Chas held a finger to his lips. Underneath him, Mrs. Groyle's chest had stopped moving up and down.

A door creaked open. "Claire?" rasped a man's voice. "Claire baby, it's me. The wife's gone down to Family Dollar." Footsteps shuffled. "Jesus, you really should pick this place up a little. Ruins the am-biance, you know what I mean?"

Stanley heard the footsteps come closer. He looked at Chas, who had frozen in place next to the bed. His eyes were wide. They should be doing something, he knew. Like hiding behind the door, getting ready to pounce. Anything but just standing there.

"I've been waitin'," baby," called the cigarette-voice. "Your honey-dripper's all ready to go." Something swished and hit the floor in the hallway, just outside the door. Stanley tensed. Before he could snatch up the porcelain doll, a scraggly, white-haired old man flounced into the room. He wore only an undershirt and black socks. His erect cock jutted from beneath his paunch.

"Claire, sweetie—"

The old man stopped.

His eyes flicked from Stanley to Chas, then rested on the inert form of his would-be lover. Some of the stiffness left his dick.

"You two ain't supposed to be here," he said.

"It's not—" Stanley began, but all the air whuffed out of

him as the old guy's fist connected with his gut. Stanley doubled over. Mr. Honey-Dripper used the opportunity to wheel and go scrambling from the room.

"Stop him!" screamed Chas, shaking like he'd been the one hit. "He's going to get the cops."

Stanley realized his partner wasn't so good in a pinch.

He ran out into the hallway, his stomach cramping. Reached the front room just in time to see a wrinkled white butt disappear out the door. He leapt after it, almost tripping on a stack of unopened boxes. Goddamn house was like an obstacle course. Out on the lawn, the old guy veered right and dove into the giant oleander bush. Stanley figured he was making for the trailer next door.

He charged the bush. Leaves parted. His head and upper body broke through, but a stout branch snagged his legs. He fell forward. The ground came up and clipped his teeth. Twisting, he craned his head around to see his right ankle caught in a crotch between two branches.

"Chas," he hollered. "Get your ass over here."

He thrashed his foot around, trying to free it. The weathered trailer lay only ten feet away, and the door hung wide open. As he struggled, he heard a frantic scratching noise coming from inside. Then the old man's voice called out:

"Prince, kill."

Ninety pounds of black-furred German shepherd exploded from the trailer doorway, its muzzle already dripping, yellowed canines bared as it machine-gunned barks. Stanley flailed, threw his forearms up in front of his face. The dog subtracted the distance between them in two bounds, clamped its jaws over his wrist and bit deep. Hot blood spurted. Stanley pounded at the Shepherd's nose with his good hand. Frenzied, the beast let go his wrist and tore into the veins and soft flesh of his throat.

Stanley's howls turned to gurgles.

He fought on anyway, for what could have been

minutes or just a string of drawn-out seconds. His vision dimmed. The dog smacked and chewed. At some point he heard footfalls echo across the street, and some point later an engine turned over.

He called out for Chas one more time.

The last thing he glimpsed before the lights went dark: the F-150 roaring out of the plum grove, black-faced Chas hunched over the wheel, not looking back.

* * *

Sheriff Joe Strawbridge paid a visit to Dr. Z's office the next day.

He brought with him two pulled-pork sandwiches on fresh torta rolls, and two tall Styrofoam cups of sweet tea. Dr. Z didn't waste any time tearing into his half of the lunch.

"You, ah, find out what happened?" he said, between bites.

Strawbridge lowered his cup. "Damndest thing. Dog was actually eating the guy, time we got there." He belched. "I figure the whole mess was a theft gone bad. Neighbor gave a fair description of Charles Stankworth, also got the first four digits of his truck's plate when he high-tailed it. Probably in Mexico by now."

"I never would have pegged Chas for murder."

"Attempted murder, you mean."

"Mrs. Groyle — ?"

"She pulled through, yeah. Only unconscious. You should've seen the look on her face, when she came 'round to the paramedics. I swear she was disappointed."

A vein swelled along Dr. Z's left temple. He coughed and pounded his chest.

"You okay, Doc?"

"Just pork grease."

"A weird thing I realized yesterday. Three of these people are, or were, patients of yours. What's the odds of

110

that?"

"Yuba City's a small community."

"Yeah, true." Strawbridge locked eyes with him. "Other weird coincidence, I got a couple people saying they saw you, Stanley, and Chas over at the Big Tiki Tuesday night, talking."

"I bumped into them."

"You did, huh?"

"Yes."

The crystal clock on the desk ticked loud. It had been bestowed to Dr. Z by the Yuba City Chamber of Commerce. The vein bulging along his temple did a snake's dance.

Strawbridge looked away. "Of course," he said, flushing. "Sometimes I forget how popular you are. And I hate to bring this up, seeing as how one of your clients just got killed, but I was wondering about that work-related disability claim I put in. You hear anything back from the state?"

"Good news," Dr. Z said, reaching across the desk to pat his shoulder. "Nothing but good news for you, Joe."

© 2010, Garnett Elliott

METHAMPHETAMINE AND A SHOTGUN
Alec Cizak

With respect to Chester Himes.

Debbie had been over earlier. She laid out a couple of rails. They topped off the crank with a joint she rolled with papers decorated like the American flag. After burning down Old Glory, they got busy on Ethan's bed. He only came once. It took him half an hour to get there, thanks to the dope. Debbie seemed happy enough. She put her clothes on and left without telling him where she was going.

Ethan sat up, his back propped by a cracked wall in his one room apartment. There was no kitchen. There were no windows that weren't holding broken glass together with tape and cardboard. Aside from the bed, there was only a folding table with two metal chairs by the door. That was where they had gotten high. Normally, Ethan would provide the drugs. His source had been buckled by the pigs. The only possession he had at that point was a Remington 12-guage. A cop had traded it to him for some crank.

"We use these to take down fuckers on PCP," the johnny had said. "You shoot somebody nice and close, their head'll bust open like a hamster in a microwave."

Ethan was aware of everything relevant, which was nothing. Meth and heroin brought him to the same place, but in different ways. Smack allowed him to quietly accept mortality. It was like an angel, gently rubbing his shoulders, whispering, "Someday you're going to die, and that's okay." Crank, on the other hand, made him feel as though possession of this knowledge hoisted him above common people who couldn't face the reality that their lives, at the end of the day, would mean nothing.

While he was riding a wave of superiority, he felt the

undertow of worry, rising up from the depths of his mind, forming a hand, then a claw, and wrapping its tough, leathery fingers around his skull. "I think I'm thirsty," he said. What he thought, however, was:

Why did Debbie leave so goddamn soon?

The claw grew larger and scooped him off the bed. The effort to move muscles and bones in his body was easier than slicing through a lightly melted stick of butter. Walking across the room, he understood that his feet were heavier than the Earth and that they bounced off of the floor as though it were made up of a million titties, waiting to cradle him if he chose to fall. He stopped at the table and looked at the shotgun. There were three shells next to it.

* * *

They met him on the elevator. Luckily, Ethan was alone. They started on his shins and elbows. He could feel their little feet scampering up and down and in circles. They were too cowardly to show themselves in the physical world. He was certain they were millipedes. When he started using meth he scratched them, opening up his skin and marking himself as an addict. Now he was wiser. They wanted him to tear himself apart. They were sent by the enemy. He tolerated the itching the way he put up with roaches and mice in his apartment.

In the lobby, the mailman was stuffing clouds into thin metal boxes. Ethan bit down on his lower lip to keep from asking the guy just who the hell he thought he was, doing God's work without God's permission. Before he could get to the street, he broke out in hysterical laughter. "I'm God," he reminded himself.

The postman backed against the wall, his hands raised. "Anything you say, man."

Ethan pushed the glass doors leading outside open. He was still chuckling over his own mistaken identity. The palm trees lining both sides of the street waved to him.

It was Saturday afternoon in Koreatown. Children played on thin strips of grass between the apartment buildings and sidewalks. Their parents sat on steps talking. Plotting, Ethan thought. "Your kids are smarter than you," he said. He pointed at the adults and every one of them jumped up and backwards. They ran to their sons and daughters.

"Don't even think about it!"

The adults stopped. They put their hands up. "Please," they said. They whimpered, cried, sobbed into the grass that danced to the same rhythm as the palm trees. They got on their knees and worshipped Ethan.

"That's more like it," he said. He headed up Ardmore, towards Third Street. There was a consumer temple on the corner of Kingsley and Third, just one block over. The way the sidewalk moved under Ethan's feet, he began to suspect the whole thing had been planned—his thirst, his paranoia about Debbie. Why was she in such a hurry to leave? he wondered again. When he turned onto Third, he saw the Kipling Hotel. A relic from the time before the world had been blessed by his presence. He crossed the street. Cars stopped for him. The people inside them pointed at him. Some grabbed their cell phones. Some made phone calls. Some even took pictures.

"They know I'm God," said Ethan.

The front door to the Kipling swung open and a man in a suit and tie stepped out and put his hand in his pocket. Ethan wondered why anybody would be dressed like that on a Saturday. He watched the man pull out a set of keys and drop them on the ground. Then he saw her, sitting inside the SUV the man eventually unlocked and climbed into.

Debbie was in the passenger seat. She was in the back, as well. And sitting right next to her was Debbie. Even in the rear, where normal people put groceries and bowling balls, two more Debbies sat, facing the opposite direction. In the driver's side, the man was desperately trying to get the key into the ignition.

"You sonofabitch," Ethan said. He drew back and pointed a giant, angry finger at the windshield. The glass exploded into a star-shower of crystals. The interior of the car filled like a bath tub with red, boiling lava.

Somewhere, someone screamed, "Oh my God!"

Ethan nodded. Proud to be so easily recognized. He saw the harsh orange and green announcing the 7-11 across the street from the Kipling. There would be liquids in the money temple that would wash away the snakes of worry burrowing permanent homes just under his skin. He remembered root beer, a substance that worked on his temporary shell like gasoline in an engine.

"Debbie's there, too," he said to himself. "I'm sure she is."

Cars screeched in the parking lot, peeling up pavement like a banana skin, to get out of his way. Ethan put his free hand out and motioned for everyone to calm down. "Relax," he said, "you have my permission to be here." Two homeless guys standing outside and opening the door for customers in hopes of getting spare change ran away as fast as they could.

Ethan laughed. "I hope you folks realize that kissing my ass won't help you. Not ultimately." He entered the convenience store.

The first thing he noticed was that Singh, the attendant on duty, was talking on the phone. He looked nervous. Ethan realized the short man, usually his friend, was hiding something. "Who's on the other end?" He pointed at Singh.

Singh dropped the phone and put his hands up.

Ethan could hear the voice coming from the receiver: "Sir? Sir?"

It was Debbie.

"You tagging my girl behind my back?"

"What?" Singh looked desperately at the only other

115

customer in the store.

It was a kid with a skateboard and Big Gulp overflowing with neon green bubbles. He held his arms out, pretending to be Jesus. "Mister, you're in big trouble," he said.

Ethan looked at the skater. "You fucking her too?"

"Who?"

"Debbie."

"No man. I ain't doing nobody named Debbie."

Ethan nodded. He stepped back. The kid dropped the cup and ran out the door.

Singh moved slowly to the other side of the counter.

"Where do you think you're going?"

Singh's white hair snaked around like it had been hooked up to electricity. The fluorescent lights bounced off his otherwise bald head with a basketball rhythm.

"Shame on you," Ethan said. His voice sounded like a vicious thunderclap. His judgment was so severe the blood of the devil spilled all over the cigarette rack behind the counter. "I said I'd get to the bottom of this." He walked to the coolers and opened one of the doors. "I haven't been wrong so far." The rush of cold air made him think he had been reborn in an arctic region. He closed his eyes and saw himself on an iceberg, drifting over the ocean. The night sky in front of him bled blue into purple into black and stars pierced the curtain like the gaze of a million dead people, curious to see if he would put the last piece of the puzzle together.

Ethan opened his eyes, found a bottle of Barq's root beer and walked back to the counter. He looked around for the cashier. "I'm a fair man," he said. He dropped two wrinkled dollar bills on the counter. They smelled like a farm he had visited with his mother when he was eight. Manure and pigs and horses and chickens, all rolled up together to manufacture a super-stench that never quite left his senses. Then he heard the sirens.

"I'm no fool," he said. The song shrieking through the

air was anything but beautiful. Besides, he thought, I'm only interested in Debbie.

The front door opened and a skinny man in a uniform stepped inside. His hands were shaking. "S-s-sir," he said.

Ethan realized the new customer was holding a pistol. A .40 caliber semi-automatic. The tiny finger was pointed right at him. His face scrunched up. Ethan wondered if his eyes would collapse into his mouth. The gall, he thought. "You don't judge me," he said. Then he pointed right back at the johnny.

The officer jumped through the glass windows protecting the store from the laughing wind. As shards spun in magic circles, Ethan briefly saw a hole in the universe open up. A huge eye, all pupil and no color, stared back. Even gods have fathers, he thought.

He stepped over the cop, who was now wrapped up in a sticky red blanket, and walked back towards Ardmore. Crowds of people had gathered across Third Street, all of them looking as if they might run away, on command. Ethan smiled. There were more sirens scraping the summer blue off the atmosphere. They would have to come for him, he decided. He was going home to enjoy his root beer and the rest of his buzz. With all the competition out of the way, Debbie would no doubt return. If she was smart, she would apologize.

As he approached his apartment building on the corner of Fourth and Ardmore, he realized the sirens belonged to the police. Lots of them. The air was filled from pocket to pocket with the annoying scream of emergency vehicles providing the illusion that something could be done to prevent the final tragedy. Ethan shook his head. He pitied everyone around him. "I'll help you," he said, "all of you." Then he remembered:

He was out of shells.

© 2010, Alec Cizak

DEVIATION JONES: A TRILOGY
Christopher Grant

Part 1: Who's That Lady?

She's hotter than Pam Grier on a hundred-degree day. Sorry, Pam, but she is.

The first thing you'd notice about her is her afro. Black with pink and gold running through it somehow. Not highlights. Just born that way, I guess. Her purple sunglasses hiding eyes that no doubt burn with her untamed fire. The bikini top she wears hints at chocolate breasts topped with chocolate-chip nipples. The low-rise jeans hang just below the purple waistband of a thong resting on her hips. When she bends over, you can see ass-crack heaven.

Thing is, this woman, her name's Deviation Jones.

And she's an assassin of some repute.

The rifle in her hands is right now aimed at the hover-parade coming around the corner.

The City celebrates the latest debacle known as the presidential election.

Funny that this president, just like the last one, didn't actually win. The same thing has happened ever since The City took over the counting duties twelve years ago.

But it's always been this way, hasn't it? Just trading trash for shit.

Deviation rests her eye on the scope and says, "Adjust," and the scope does as it's told, honing in on the front of the car carrying the new president.

The goal is to get him out of the protective bubble that surrounds him. Literal bubble, too; it's made out of pure latex. How appropriate that the guy that's gonna fuck us for the next four years is being protected by a condom.

Her finger touches the trigger and the bolt hits the hood, penetrating it and connecting with the engine block, effectively killing the car. It's a literal bolt, just like the literal bubble, fired at something like the speed of sound that flies through the air, through the hood, through the engine block.

At that rate of speed, no one saw it and thus Deviation doesn't have to run for her fucking life. She can, instead, set up for the kill shot. A bolt right through the president's skull, bursting through the cranium, hitting the brainpan. Squish.

Just then, as the new car pulls up and they ready the president to make his move, the door of the roof entrance behind Deviation opens and a black-shaded behemoth comes through.

"Fuck me," Deviation says.

We'd love to do just that, Deviation, believe us. But it looks like you might have something else to take care of first.

Part 2: How To Get Off a Roof the Simplest Way Possible

The guy's, what, like three-fifty, well over six-and-a-half feet tall. The seams on the dark suit that he wears are screaming as they attempt to hold together. The sunglasses on his face are tiny.

Deviation Jones, she's got that gun of hers and she raises it now, sighting on the behemoth. She doesn't have the chance to say, "Adjust," before the gun's barrel is in his ham hock of a hand. He snaps the barrel in half and tosses the gun aside.

"Shit," Deviation says. No kidding, babe.

The guy's other hand comes *this* close to punching a hole through her head. Or at least her considerable afro. Instead, he smashes right through the ledge behind Deviation and now he's stuck.

That's one way to get off a roof the simplest way possible.

Unfortunately, it's not that simple, and Deviation, lady, you should have just run the fuck through that door.

The blob flexes his muscles, doing a curl, and busts through the brick and mortar, causing all kinds of debris to tumble to the street, sixty-some stories below. We'd hate to be the guy that doesn't have his umbrella handy down there.

Now it's a race up there, sixty-some stories above the street, both of them going for the door. Come on, girl, you can make it if you try.

The Punch does it.

Punch: a drug of choice, not of habit, can be snorted or ingested. Punch Gives You Pep (cue smiling blonde beautiful bikini-clad woman). Use only as directed.

Deviation's through the door ten seconds before the behemoth and down to the fortieth floor before he even clears the fiftieth.

She's in the hallway of the twenty-ninth floor, looking for another exit, when he catches up with her. You're not the only one with Punch onboard, baby. Grab a weapon and get ready to rock.

Deviation smashes the glass on the In Case Of Emergency box with her bare fist. Damn that stings. She grabs the fire axe and a wide stance and waits for the goon to make the first move. He does the same, except grabbing a fire axe. One to a hallway, sorry, pal.

They circle each other. The suspense is terrible. We hope it lasts.

A door behind Deviation opens up and this dweeb in a bowtie steps right into the fist of the behemoth, who was thinking the distraction would catch Deviation off-guard. Silly behemoth, tricks are for kids.

Deviation swings the ax and buries it in the blob's side. The impact of the blow rattles her purple sunglasses, sending them askew across her nose. She has trouble yanking the axe free, stuck in the gristle, muscle and bone the way it is. Finally, it comes loose with a torrent of blood and she takes another hack, catching him in the neck. Jugular. Done. He chokes on his own blood.

Deviation adjusts her sunglasses and drops the ax. Then she gets the idea to drag the dweeb over and set the axe in his hands. Waste not, want not.

Part 3: The Boss

The undulating hips of the topless four-armed dancer make a man want to do naughty things to her indeed. Her breasts swaying back and forth ain't half-bad, either.

She gyrates and swivels and shakes and erections pop up everywhere around the room. Thank god for pants.

The air is thick with opium smoke and you could get high without even trying. Those who have partaken laze about without cares or fears.

There is a horn of some kind blowing from somewhere but Deviation Jones cannot see it as she steps into the tent.

There are vid-screens all over the place showing the president's car breaking down in the middle of his celebratory hover-parade.

Oh, so that's how they transfer someone from one hovercar to another. Good to know.

In the middle of this circus sits one of the fattest men she's ever laid her eyes on. Go on a diet, buddy.

The dancer approaches Deviation and, with one of her hands, pulls her forward for a kiss. Deviation lets herself go for a moment. Who can blame her?

"He's still sucking down air," the corpulent one says leering at the two women. The dancer moves away from Deviation and shakes her generous ass in Fatty's face.

"Not my fault," Deviation says. You tell him, baby. "I hit the engine block and just as they..."

"I don't care what happened," the fat man says, starting to lose his patience. "All I know is that he's still alive. And, if he's still alive, that means the rest of us are living on borrowed time. Especially you."

"So what the fuck am I supposed to do?" Deviation asks the obvious question.

"Duck," the fat man says.

Four guns materialize out of nowhere, hanging in midair momentarily. The dancer plucks them with her four hands and trains them on Deviation, then squeezes the triggers all at the same time.

Somehow, Deviation avoids getting hit but her pleather jacket isn't so lucky, taking two in the left sleeve, down by the wrist, the bullets going through cleanly. The four-armed topless bitch wouldn't know high fashion if it came up and slapped her across the face and now she's gone and murdered it.

The other two bullets perforate the spleens of two of the lazing opium addicts. The rest don't even seem to notice. Can't understand why not. Oh, yeah, the opium.

Deviation doesn't waste a second and, at the risk of being shot point-blank, grabs the dancer by the head and snaps her neck. The dancer screams, nearly deafening anyone within a couple blocks. Seriously, her voice breaks windows up to five hundred feet away. Her four arms beat wildly at the carpet and it takes her body over a minute to register that this is death. Bye-bye.

Guess who's next?

The fat man can't get out of his chair. How'd he get into it in the first place?

Deviation smiles as she pulls the knife from her boot.

"Now, I did a job," Deviation says.

"You didn't complete it," the fat man says, sweat rolling down into the folds around his chin. Er, chins. Gotta hand it to him — even when faced with death, even when his voice squeaks higher than a soprano's, he's got balls.

"Who was the goon?" Deviation says.

The silence says it all. The silence is followed by the scream of a fat man. A fat man who doesn't have balls anymore, if the scrotum that Deviation tosses aside is anything to judge by.

Good for you, girl. Proves money isn't everything.

THE LAST AMBASSADOR TO PUSHMATA
Gary Clifton

Gilberto's mama was a whore—white chick with more tattoos than teeth even before skin ink became fashionable. With a face ugly as a monitor lizard, she was living proof a guy with a hard-on instantly became partly blind. His daddy was a Mexican as far as she recalled, but damned if she could recall more than is first name: Gilberto. Mama didn't dick around adding any "junior" to little Gilberto's moniker.

Behind an assload of juvvie busts and an adult year in TDC, Gilbert made twenty years on the crappy streets of east Dallas. Then the bouncer at Ripside Topless tossed him out on his ass, after slapping the dogshit out of him—couldn't keep his hands off the girls. Gilberto had eaten pussy, garbage from dumpsters, several dicks while locked up at Huntsville, a ration of shit from most of society, but damned if that Ripside bouncer sumbitch was on the list of eligible shit-givers.

He'd fix that mu'fucker. He lifted a five-pound box of black powder and a roll of firecracker fuse from Joe's Surplus and made a half-assed bomb. It detonated all right, at 3:00 a.m.—blew in a back wall and broke some windows. Cops never really did much looking for the perp, but Gilberto changed territory. There were topless bars and dope to be had on Harry Hines, miles from that fucked up neighborhood.

* * *

They called her C.J., which didn't make a hell of a lot of sense because her name was Gretchen. With a snake tattooed around her left leg, winding around North to disappear at the vital junction, she was a stripper at The Green Dog Topless Club on Harry Hines. Strippin' beat whorin' her mama had told her. At 22, with ten years ingestion of every substance known in the penal code, C.J. was pretty much down the chute to the stripper junk yard.

Then, *HE* walked in. A skinny, swarthy little rat, he patted C.J. on her rapidly- expanding-beyond-stripper-approved ass and it was lust at first sight. A tattoo of a bird on his right forearm, C.J. was too dumb to recognize it was an eagle. Stoned himself, he had no way of seeing just how damned hard she really looked in the dim, smoky light. But Gilberto was too fucked up to have seen her much more clearly in bright sunlight.

"Yer tits ain't big enough to dance on no stage," he said.

Any stud that articulate was irresistible in C.J.'s world. She was sleeping on the sofa of another stripper who lived nearby. For the next few nights, they nearly wore the old, overstuffed relic out.

His family was deposed Middle Eastern royalty, he said. He was still the legitimate ambassador to the United States from the far off land of Pushmata. Hey, for all the hell she knew, Dallas was in Canada and she couldn't have picked east from west on a marked map, let alone find or even know the Middle East existed. Gilberto had come up with the idea from a wino he'd heard preaching on a corner down the street.

The inevitable squabble exploded into a full lover's quarrel, then a fist fight, then a 9-1-1 domestic disturbance. Ambassador Gilberto split before the cops got there. C.J. showed up at the Dog that night with a make-up covered black eye. No problem — the joint was dark anyway and customers weren't looking at her eyes.

He'd take care of her ass, all right. He still had a part box of black powder and a couple feet of firecracker fuse from the Ripside bombing. He wadded the powder in a discarded sack, stuck in the fuse, slipped past the bouncer, and lit that sucker on the floor beneath the urinal — then beat it. Maybe nobody told him it was against the law to set off a bomb when the joint was open for business.

As he cleared the door, two drunk bikers walked in the john and were in the "ready" position when the bomb went. One guy went backward into a wall. When they bagged him he was indistinct like a sack of water. The other guy saved his honor to the end. The blast blew his right hand out through the roof. Unfortunately, his small American dick was in it. Dead of blood loss and traumatic shock the morgue would rule.

Homicide sent out Red Harper and Maria Martinez. Harper, in Homicide since before color TV was big, tough with a rim of red hair surrounding a bald pate. He was never without a nasty cigar stub in a corner of his mouth.

Hernandez, in Homicide eight months was beautiful, smart, tough, and at all times preceded by boobs as big as a fat boy's head. She put out to no cops, male or female.

In ten minutes, they'd found C.J. who immediately took a shit on his Excellency. The deported ambassador to Pushmata, or some shit like that she said. She had no idea where he might be, of course. "But I got his cell phone number," she beamed, eyes not fully focused. She then solemnly pledged never, not ever, not never to have any contact with him again. "Them knockers real, honey," she eyed Martinez's assets. "You could make a bundle on the stage around here."

Half of Dallas's finest spent the next week kicking asses and taking names. No ambassador was located. Gilberto, hiding in several rat holes was safe, sort of. Nobody knew who the hell he was. But, dumber than a cardboard box, he could fix that easy enough.

In a sink hole inside a crime-ridden neighborhood, nobody was particularly surprised when another bomb went off at the Green Dog Topless Club. Dispatch reported a victim had been ambulanced to Parkland. "Blown all to hell" they said in cop-speak radio code.

Harper and Martinez had no idea who or what the

ambassador might be, but they sure as hell recognized C.J. wringing her hands in the ER hallway.

"What the fuck about not never, not no time, seeing this turd," Harper asked.

"Mu'fucker come back," she stammered. "I'm fucking innocent."

"Of what?" Martinez asked.

"Puttin' that bomb...tryin' to...on the Green Dog manager's car. He had a premature ejaculation...the bomb did, I mean."

They stepped into the victim's curtained cubicle. A skinny little man lay on the gurney, attended by several staff. "Believe the ambassador to Pushmata is found," Martinez said.

"Kiss my ass, you pig mu'fuckers," the semi-conscious patient spat groggily.

"Pigs," Harper rolled the cigar. "Damn mister ambassador, you're way behind the curve. While you're settin' down there at Huntsville waitin' for the needle cocktail, you can learn ugly cops insult shit from some of the three hundred other fuckups on death row."

The young surgeon turned angrily to Harper. A skinny kid from suburbia with no conception of Gilberto's world, he exploded into self-righteousness. "Jesus Christ officer, no need to get all redneck here." He pointed at Gilberto's bandaged arms, both stubbed off above the elbow. "Don't you see this man has maimed himself for life."

"Helluva point, Doc," Martinez said above her forty pounds of tits. "His Excellency here is gonna have to figure out a whole new way to jerk off."

"Oh fuck me," C.J. wailed from outside the cubicle. And several hours later, the previously angry but now in love young surgeon did just exactly that.

© 2013, Gary Clifton

THE THREE SISTERS
Jack Bates

At night you can't see where the waves break off the horizon. All you get is the crash as the water hits the sand and the chilly tingle as the foam sweeps over your foot. At night you have no idea how endless the ocean is.

As children, our father took us to the ocean whenever he could. We spent those vacation days frolicking in the surf, no tension, no rivalry. He would take us out no farther than our knees, and he would point at the waves giving them names and showing us how to catch the curl and ride one in. Sometimes we would just kneel there and let the waves hit us. We created a vocabulary of our experiences.

A large, rogue wave that towered on the horizon and crashed with a thunderous roar was a King Kamehameha. Father said these were the ideal for body surfing. Slappers were smaller waves that snuck up and broke directly on you, slapping your belly or your backside. A Bubbler was a wave that looked intimidating but died out in a festival of boiling foam. Then there were the Pointers, so named because all they did was roll over your toes, which is what a ballerina used when she went up on point. We had asked why not Toesies and father had said that would be silly. His laughter was contagious.

Occasionally, my father told us we needed to keep our eyes out for the Three Sisters. The waves were part of Great Lakes lore. He was so alive telling his three daughters how the waves came at you one at time but in quick succession. His arms swept out over the water; his eyes got as big as the noon day sun. I don't know about the other two, but I was captivated.

The first wave was said to be thirty feet high and it

crashed down over the bow of a boat pushing it down into the water. Before the boat had a chance to right its course, a second wave smashed down even harder and pushed the bow back under the water. The last of the three sisters, as high as our fourth-floor balcony at the tiki resort we stayed at, drove it completely under to the bottom of the lake.

"They're real bitches," Dad said. Even Mother laughed.

The Three Sisters we faced along the ocean shore were never this deadly. Father called out the waves to us while we stared them down, laughing as they broke around us. In reverse order of our birth he would name them, ending with Elena, the wave that forever loomed over me. Elena and Jenny could stand their ground, the rush of the undertow sucking their toes into salty mud. Father would reach out and catch my hand to hold me up from the pounding of those three quick waves.

This was the wave mythology as taught to us by our father, a man who had hoped to impart this knowledge unto a son but was blessed with three daughters in the absence of this heir. Father knew very little about raising girls, having grown up in a house of all boys. He never knew how we fought on so many levels of mean. I was the last born. By then he and Mother were well into their forties. They called me a miracle baby, but my two older sisters called me Oops.

Elena, the oldest, and Jenny, the middle, were never kind to me. It had already been a struggle for our father's attention before I was born but now that I was there, the baby, what little attention they got from him was now divided by a third. Consequently, we argued and fought. The constant bickering and posturing pushed my father to his breaking point. He thought we were arguing over boys and clothes and bathroom time but he never caught on that all we wanted was time with him.

Our mother knew. When he wasn't around she'd sneer at us over her Manhattan, blow cigarette across the linoleum table we ate our lunches at. "The way you ladies go on and on," she'd say, her smile coiling like that of a snake poised to strike. "You forget that there's only one woman in this house deserving of your father's attention and that woman is me."

To hear her talk, it made our actions perverse. All I wanted was for him to be my dad. I think even Mother felt she had to compete with us. I know she felt that way about Elena. It was hard not to.

Elena with her hair spun as fine as corn silk, so golden the sun bowed its head to her. A constant reminder of the young woman with perfect skin and killer body that first caught my younger father's eye. Jenny and I never came out the victor in an altercation when pitted against Elena. All she had to do was flash her smile and our father unequally divided our punishments.

When the time came for Elena to go off to college, I thought my father was going to have a nervous breakdown. Maybe this Michigan farm boy created by the gods of lightning and ore was depressed about approaching fifty. As we aged, so did he. My mother was always there to remind him of this inevitability.

Having Elena around reminded him of his youth. Now he had to grapple with the fact that his Elena, his centrifuge to his past, was going to become some other young man's companion. Oh, there had been boyfriends all through high school but none of them could ever compete with Father. Elena chewed them up and made chum of those boys who would have gladly supplicated at her feet.

Maybe that was why she never stayed with anyone for more than a few weeks. Compared to the god our father was, they were mere mortals.

Elena went missing the fall of her second year away at a state university. I think my father knew as soon as it became apparent Elena had disappeared that when she was found, she would be found dead. Mother maintained her demeanor through the entire ordeal. The police visited just about every other day. The three local news channels all but used our bathroom. And, of course, there were the crackpots.

We got calls from psychics who said they knew exactly where Elena would be found. When my father asked one how she knew his daughter was dead, the woman told him she'd had a vision of a reporter saying it on TV.

Then there was the guy who pounded on our door at three a.m. He insisted he'd been tracking a demon for decades that had been targeting young women on college campuses. The demon was harvesting these young women to be succubae that would eventually be used to open the doors to the last days. He could prove it if my dad would just go out to his van with him and look at what he had on his laptop. The cops hauled the man away and towed his van.

It was no secret that I was the last to see Elena alive. I was a junior in high school the year it happened. Father said it was time for to visit college campuses to prepare for my post high school education. I didn't want to. Jenny was still living at home and going to a junior college; I wanted to do the same. Elena agreed to let me come up for Little Brother/Little Sister weekend. My father offered to drive me but mother insisted it would be better if I went alone in her car. She said I needed to understand when I left for college, I was on my own. They would not be driving back and forth every weekend like they had Elena's first year.

I told the police the weekend had been fun. Elena had taken me around to some bars and parties. We had tailgated before a big football game and partied after. Yes, I told them, I had been drinking. They assured me that wasn't as important right then as knowing what happened to Elena.

"Do you remember anyone acting strange around your sister?" Detective Ryan asked me during the first interview.

"It was a college town," I told him. "There was all sorts of strange going on."

"Can you be more specific?"

"Well, there was the one guy who cornered her at a

house party and went on and on about America's shadow wars. That was a lot of fun."

"Did they argue?"

"No. He was high and she was too and they just seemed to fall into this weird conversation."

I watched my father as I told the detective this tidbit. I saw the pain in my father's eyes. I wanted to smile and tell him that I would never betray his trust like Elena had. I would always be his princess he could lock away and visit whenever he wanted to.

But I could tell from his despair it wouldn't matter. Elena was his only princess and he had let her out the castle gates and now she would never come back.

"What about boyfriends?" Detective Ryan asked.

"What about them?" I asked. I really wanted a cigarette but I couldn't light up in front of my father. I looked at my mother. For the first time all day she didn't bother to have one of her own. It was like she knew I needed the smoke around me.

"Did she have any?"

"There was a guy named Michael," my father said. We were all surprised by his voice. When he looked up, his eyes were wet.

"That was last year, daddy," Jenny said.

"So they broke up?" Detective Ryan asked.

"They were never really together," Jenny said. God, I wished she'd shut up. This was my moment. Father was counting on me.

"What happened with this Michael?" Detective Ryan asked.

Jenny was about to tell him how Michael had found Elena cheating on him with one of his roommates. It would have sewn up a suspect for the cops, maybe two. Father knew nothing about it. If he learned of it then, in front of a stranger, it would have blown apart his heart.

"He was a college boyfriend," I said. "Things happen in

132

college."

"Do you go to college?"

"I'm still in high school. But I saw enough that weekend to know what goes on at college. People hook up and break up hourly. No, if you're looking for anyone suspicious, I'd look into the guy that was talking about covert armies and handing out X to anyone who asked."

"Did you ask?" Detective Ryan asked.

"No," I said.

My dad made a coughing sound. My mother finally lit a cigarette. Detective Ryan left.

Lake Solitude is a large, inland lake not far from Elena's school. Men who rose before the sun too get a jump on ice fishing pulled her arm up through the hole they cut in the ice.

They used dental records to identify Elena. There was no water in her lungs. She had died before being dumped into the water, weighed down with a backpack filled concrete blocks. The bag hung backwards over her chest, the belt fastened across her back. A student ID card clipped to a zipper gave up Dave Bannerman, he of the late night anti-government lectures. Detective Ryan phoned to say Bannerman had dropped out of school the semester after Elena went missing. His whereabouts were unknown.

My father sank even deeper into his depression. It permeated the house. Only mother carried on, somehow more buoyant in her mood and actions than she should have been for losing a daughter. Maybe she was trying to lead by example. Jenny spent less and less time at home. One night a few weeks later, with the specter of Elena wandering around the house, I went out back to have a smoke behind our garage. Jenny was there already having a cigarette.

"What are you doing here?" I asked. "You don't smoke."

"I do. I just don't want Daddy to know."

"Does he even notice what we do? Does he even notice us?" I asked. I took a drag from her cigarette.

"Of course he notices us," Jenny said. She snatched the cigarette back from me. "Sometimes you're such an idiot."

"Elena was his whole life."

"She was the first born. It only seemed like he paid more attention to her because he knew her longer."

"So you felt it too."

"Felt what?"

"Father loved her more than he loved us."

Jenny jetted a long stream of smoke. "He loved us equally. He always told us so."

"It was never equal."

"Now is not the time to be jealous of Elena."

"Now is the perfect time to be jealous of Elena. Even when she's not here she's still here. She's all over that house. Dad can't walk down the hall without crying."

"Cut daddy some slack, Delia. God, what do you expect? He lost his daughter."

"I'm his daughter. And I'm here."

"Funny," Jenny said. She finished the cigarette, pinched off the end, and put the butt into a zipper locking plastic bag. "I hadn't thought of how far you stood in Elena's shadow."

"What do you mean?" I asked.

"I've been thinking of how convenient her murder was."

"Murder?"

"No one kills themselves by strapping a backpack of concrete to themselves."

"It was probably that anarchist," I said. The cigarette wasn't having its usual effect on me. My throat burned. My words felt laden with toxins.

"You mean the anarchist no one can find? How is it the only two people who saw them at the party would be our dead sister and you?"

"There was a lot of booze and drugs, Jenny. If you had gone away to school you would know these things about college life."

"If I had gone away to school, you'd have Daddy all to yourself, which is what I think you've always wanted."

Jenny got the last word in that night. I watched her go back into the house, pulling her running jacket close. I finished my cigarette with tears in my eyes.

Weeks went by. Father eventually came out of his funk. At least when he wasn't at home. I cut class one day and went into town to surprise father with lunch. He wasn't there. Nancy, his secretary, said he'd already gone to lunch. She told me that for the last week or so he'd been leaving every day at approximately the same time. Sometimes he came back smelling of smoke and stale beer. He'd lock himself in his office. She could hear him crying.

Nancy asked if I wanted to leave the food I'd brought with me. She could put it in the break room fridge. I thanked her but carried it out with me. When I got to the lobby, I dropped it into a garbage can.

I was mad at my father. On the street, with tears burning my eyes, I looked up and down the block until I saw a small, grungy looking place called Frankee's. It had no windows but a triple-stacked stripe of glass brick running across the front and bending along the side let a little muted light into the dank hole.

I opened the door. It was like watching vampires scatter. The afternoon light flowing in momentarily blinded the handful of afternoon drinkers lining the bar. The shaft illuminated a rectangle of shame at the corner. Father sat facing the door. He held an empty shot glass in the air. The giggling, blond, bimbo he drank with finished hers and took a drag on a smoldering cigarette. She turned and squinted at the open door.

It was Jenny.

"Hey, in or out," the bartender yelled.

I was out.

Neither of them said anything to me that night. I don't know if they realized it as me. They were too far gone by the time I got there. The sun was in their eyes. Why would they suspect me? I was supposed to be at school and I wasn't Elena.

Mother and I ate dinner alone.

"Where's Father?" I asked.

"He's passed out." Mother smiled. Her eyes slid at me more than rolled. She lit a cigarette over her mac and cheese. "Drunk."

"I got it. And Jenny?"

Mother took up a forkful of the faux yellow pasta with her cigarette hand. "Be happy with your mother's company, Delia."

I poked at my own meal, dragged the fork tines through the watery sauce. Upstairs I heard Jenny retching. The toilet flushed. Mother hummed some empty tune she channeled from the spheres.

Father was already at work when mother found Jenny dead. The EMTs said it looked like Jenny asphyxiated on her vomit in the middle of the night. There was trace regurgitation on her pillow. It looked as if she had passed out face down in bed.

There was no police investigation. The coroner said the findings were consistent with accidental death. Another tragedy, nonetheless, for the already tragic Regan family.

Father couldn't function any longer. The spiral he tumbled down had no end. He slept in the basement. Mother carried on with her life but there was no interaction between them. The food I took down to him went uneaten. If I turned a light on for him, he moaned and whimpered until I turned it off. He preferred the dark. Mother said he was trying to return to the womb.

When the EMTs returned less than a week after their last visit, the police did investigate. It was all a formality. Mainly for insurance purposes, mother said. They wanted to make sure there was no suspicious activity. One accidental death in the house appeared to be standard. But two in less than a week?

Father lay sprawled at the bottom of the stairs. Detective Ryan said it looked like in father's emaciated condition he had been too weak to make it up the stairs. He might have had a spat of vertigo and had toppled backwards down the stairs, his head striking the concrete, the trauma being too much for his system. The coroner would have the final say, of course.

"Of course," mother said. She slipped on her reptilian smile. Detective Ryan couldn't see it but I knew all too well this was how my sisters and I had been raised by her: Not to be polite but to be detestable.

I almost said, "What else could it be?" But I knew what mother would say. "Why don't you tell us, Delia?"

"I didn't have anything to do with it." I said it under my breath as Detective Ryan stepped out the door and Mother started to close it. They both stopped and stared at me.

"Did you say something?" Detective Ryan asked. Mother's smile twisted over his shoulder.

I shook my head. Tears stung the corners of my eyes. What did it matter now that Father was dead? Mother suspected. Jenny had suspected. Father was too deep in his grief to ever know.

"Nothing," I said. It came out like a croak. I broke down into tears. Mother closed the door. She dropped a fresh pack of cigarettes next to me on the couch.

"Here, Delia. You don't have to sneak them anymore." Mother slinked her way up the stairs.

I knew that night I could no longer live in that house. There were too many shadows. And her. My mother. I couldn't live with her. I dug the keys to my father's car out of his junk drawer, grabbed my purse, and hit the road. There was two hundred dollars in his wallet and a credit card. I drove all night.

The road is long and lonely in the dark. Light plays tricks on your eyes. What looks like someone or something standing along the shoulder is nothing more than the void of space and time. The void opens sometimes and drags people away. I was going through the Jellico Mountain pass out of Kentucky when I began to wonder if Daddy's car could fly.

I pulled off the road into the Tennessee Welcome Center where I slept until a groundskeeper tapped on my window and told me my lights were on. The sun was up. I was hungry. I checked my phone. My mother had not tried to call. I thought about calling her but what would I say? "Hi, mother. It's Delia. I've taken father's car and I am leaving. I can't stand the thought of being in that house without him."

It was the truth.

Partially, at least.

And she would know it.

She would know that Jenny had been right that night I found her smoking behind the garage. There had been no party the last time I saw Elena. It was just her, me, and this guy who gave her free X. It probably wasn't totally free. After they had both passed out, I took my hand and pinched Elena's nose closed. When her mouth popped open, I used my other hand to hold her jaw shut. It was that easy.

Bannerman freaked in the morning when he couldn't revive her. I watched from the bedroom as he shook her. When Elena didn't budge, he looked around for me. I stayed hidden in the closet watching from the slats in the door. He found the note I left.

Hey, sleepy head, I had to head for home. Thanks for the fun. This is our little secret from dad, okay?

I signed it with Jenny's name. What did he know about me?

I waited until night and carried Elena to mom's car. Bannerman's backpack was in the back seat. Perfect. It was like a million scattered puzzles pieces all locking together on their own. Even Jenny's death worked in my favor. Drowning in her own puke. All I had to do was hold the back of her head and keep her face in the pillow.

And father? I took in a deep breath. The car was rife with the tang of my father. I had nothing to do with that. Not directly. He had lost his two daughters and forgot he had me. Once, for my twelfth birthday, he had asked me what I wanted. He said I could have anything in the world. I told him all I wanted was his love. He laughed and asked "What's the price tag on that?"

I guess now there was an answer.

I went to the ocean alone. At midnight I stood on the beach of the tiki resort where father had first taught us of the waves. The Pointers greeted my toes and pulled my feet deeper into the coffee colored sand. Off shore the King Kamehamehas roared majestically. A few Slappers flitted against my belly. The spray was cool, the rumbles soothing. I stepped into the waves and waited to join my sisters where we could endlessly roll and clash together.

I wished my father could be there to play with us once more.

Forever.

FORMULA AND METH
Ryan Sayles

"No, that's not how you snort it. *This* is how you blow a rail."

Along the webbing between her thumb and index finger, Angelina lined out enough meth to kill a horse. It was how she would snort it in the back of class her junior year of high school. Easier to hide from the judgmental, prying eyes of Ms. Merser, the crazy cat lady teacher. Now, eighteen months and one baby later, she's backstage at the Nitty Gritty Titty, a hip and happenin' strip club, showing all the new blood how to prep for a hard night of courtesy tugs and the judicious application of baby powder.

"Just remember to exhale before your nostril gets too close to the line. Don't wanna puff that shit into a snowfall. Waste." Angelina exhales far away from her hand, puts her cute little button nose to the rail, and in one quick swipe across her hand's webbing that line of powder disappears into her brain cavity.

Eyes twitter, burn and water like they're putting out their own fires. A cough, smile. Drainage down her throat. Tastes like salt and chalk and bitter pinpricks. "No waste. It's a party foul. That was one lap dance right there. The next lap dance will pay for formula for my sweet little Bella."

Yes, Angelina, like so many other American teens, named her baby after *Twilight's* lead twit.

The new blood just stare. One of them, with the very unoriginal name of Candi, is choking back her gorge from having to blow Detrick, the manager. He sat in his ragged office chair, still smelling like last week's chili dinner farts, and lifted his gut rolls for her. The stench, a complicated mélange of musty crevice and dank, unwashed human skin, crawled up her nose like a bold insect. Salty and vile, it was. The price of admission onto his golden stage of fast cash and self-esteem.

From somewhere on the other side of the wall, the DJ announces: "And now for your pleasure, the hottest, wettest pussy this side of eternity, the gash Brad Pitt wishes he was slaying, the *real* Angelina!" Like a pro boxing match.

"Well, they're playing my song." Angelina jumps up, snaps her T-back undies and goes out there. Cheers and a rainstorm of singles meet her.

* * *

It's going to be a good night.

High rollers seated front and center, wagging George Washingtons as she passes by, working her feminine whiles for all they are worth. *C'mon, rent,* she thinks as she slides down the pole, upside down, fully nude and raging from the meth. Her head reaches the stage just as the song ends. *Perfect timing.* She hangs there, spread eagle, and enjoys the applause. Gets up. Collects her bills. Off on the prowl through the poorly lit tables where men are waiting.

She knows better and stays away from the fat creeps wearing the same clothes they wore yesterday. Those dudes, rolling pennies and stealing from their elderly mothers' bank accounts to come here and get some hot chick to tickle their junk, they were the ones who would follow her home some morning and eat her. Maybe burn the place down with Bella inside it. Those are the predators.

She sticks to the guys who are clean, shaved, done-up. Guys who drink something sophisticated that says *here for the experience* as opposed to *I'm not even going to try and hide the fact I want to rape you.* Knowing the nuances of exotic dancing is what separates the famous gals from the ones that slip off into full-blown prostitution and die from botched back-alley abortions.

Finds her mark. Lone dude sitting at a three-top table, sipping from a mixed drink. Sidles over, letting her nipples brush his exposed skin as she leans in and whispers all hot and moist, "Take me to the back room."

"Price?" He says, husky. Playing along.

"Twenty-five a song. But, if you have the cash, I have all night."

"Don't take this the wrong way, this is nice and all—" he loosely gestures to her titties brushing along his skin in an obviously intentional manner, " —but I've been holding out for your friend over there." He nods to Madonna, some ginger tramp who moved here from Idaho last year. "I was waving her over here when you showed up, so..."

Angelina smiles. "I understand. She needs the money anyway. Gotta kill that itch, ya know?"

The dude's smile stops abruptly. "Are you bullshitting me?" He sits up straighter, locking eyes with Angelina. Got his attention. "Because if you are just so I'll drop some cash into your thong—"

"Calm down. I'm just trying to give the best service I can provide. Madonna is a sweet gal, and I promise, she'll fuck you. Easy. She fucks everybody. Just wear a rubber. Because no, I'm not bullshitting."

Angelina takes his chin into the cup of her hand and leans close. "But I can tell you have a wife at home even though you switched your ring to another finger. You get what Madonna has, and you'll give it to the missus. Just wear a rubber. Bye bye."

No wasted time. "One song, then we'll see where it goes from there."

Angelina smiles. Can taste the payday. She takes his hand, leads him back. Near the private rooms she sees Simpson, winks. Simpson, the biggest man this side of eternity and a bouncer for the hip and happenin' Nitty Gritty Titty, nods imperceptibly. Knows the game is on.

Angelina pulls back the curtain with a sly gesture that

jiggles her boob. The mark's eye follows. "Wait," Simpson says, one step forward. "Get your drink, bro."

The mark looks back to the table. Sees his glass. He looks back to Simpson, raises an eyebrow.

Simpson smiles. "The waitress will bus the table. Other dudes will sit down. Don't want you to lose your seat, bro."

The mark still stares. "Well, *bro*, I'm doing this one song at a time. We won't be but a few —"

Simpson blows him off. Stays cool. "Just don't want to see you lose twelve-fifty when you haven't drunk half of it. I'm lookin' out for you. Plus, trust me, *bro*. You're gonna buy more than one song. *Trust me*."

The mark shrugs. Says, "whatever." Gets his drink. Goes inside with Angelina. Pulls the curtain closed.

* * *

His drink is on the table next to them.

Angelina reaches under the table and pulls out an airplane bottle of Jim Beam. Sits it next to the glass. Pushes the mark down to the chair, jumps into his lap. The room is small and dark, but low lights allow him to see all her curves and the small skim of glitter across her smooth flesh.

The music outside is deafening. Inside here it is a roar, but the effect of intimacy is not lost. The song pulses and she begins a private dance.

Gyrates as she allows him to press his face into her cleavage. Work her breasts with his lips and tongue. She stares off into the distance, placid face and rolling eyes display how boring the job has gotten. But she makes little breathy noises, lets her breath hitch. Makes him think she's into it. Runs her small fingers through his hair, grabbing handfuls. Dude starts to purr. Distracted now.

She moans, reaches around behind herself and, with practiced effort, removes a small over-the-counter eye dropper bottle from her vaginal cavity. *Glad this didn't pop*

143

out on stage she thinks as she lays a few drops in his drink.

Re-inserts it. Finishes the dance. She fake-collapses into him, as if a lap dance could give her an earth-shattering orgasm. Her lips on the sweaty flesh of his neck. She rubs herself up his chest until her eyes meet his. She licks his mouth, says, "Let me serve you."

He smirks. "I'll buy some pussy, if that's what you're taking about."

She smiles, takes his drink and holds it to his lips. "I like my dick to taste like bourbon."

"This isn't bourbon," he says, finger tapping on his glass.

"Your tongue isn't a dick either, silly." She giggles, grabs the Jim Beam and jiggles it like a dinner bell.

"Oh...I get it." The mark looks down to his tenting pants, asks, "Won't that burn though?"

"I don't let it sit long enough to burn." She nibbles at her lip, plays coy.

He takes the hint and swigs from the glass. Sets it down with a single gulp left.

"Uh-uh," she says. Picks the glass back up. "In here, you get your money's worth *on everything*. House rules."

"Fine." Bottoms up.

She rubs herself on him for the next thirty seconds before the drops take effect. Just as she is slowly pulling his zipper down, he slumps back, eyes roll to whites, muscles relax like he's dead, pisses himself. Angelina helps herself to his wallet.

* * *

Angelina leans out of the curtain, sees Simpson waiting like a good boy. "Four hundred, all in twenties except three tens and ten singles. Hurry."

Simpson nods, goes to the shitter for some privacy. He keeps a small stable of dancers who are willing to pull these stunts. His older brother cooks meth, which he slips to the girls here and there. His younger brother launders fake bills. Poorly made fake bills, but they pass a cursory inspection. Simpson keeps a stash of them in his locker, and what amounts to a cash register in his pocket.

He counts out ten fake singles, three fake tens and the rest in fake twenties. Goes back. Hands Angelina the money. She hands him the real dough, palms the bunk shit. Adjusts the time on the mark's watch and his cell phone, repacks his wallet, leaves.

* * *

The mark wakes to Simpson's rather large, rather black hands picking him up rather roughly.

"If you're gonna shit on my dancers, pass out in the back room and just in general be a motherfucker, you can go somewhere else. Got me?"

The mark is groggy; the reality of what is happening hits him like wrecking ball. "Wa-what?"

"I said if you come here, you act like a client, not a douche. I don't like what Angelina says about you. Anyway, you've slept enough. We ain't no fucking hotel for shitbirds."

"But I didn't—" the mark looks at his expensive watch. "Oh my God! It's almost five in the morning! My wife! What is she—"

The wristwatch on the tree trunk arm dragging the mark by the collar says it's barely past eleven p.m. But oh well. These things get missed easily in tense situations.

Carrying him out to the back alley, Simpson says, "Pawing at her, calling her a bitch, get rough and then drink until you pass out right fucking there? I should fucking kill you."

"No dude! That's not what happened at all—"

"Yeah right. Get the fuck outta here!" Simpson throws

the dude out the back door. Hits the frigid pavement. Bounces his head. Simpson's bark the only thing besides shame that follows him out.

"Come back and I'll have some prison buddies rape and shank you."

The door slams. The mark starts to cry just a little and is out of the story and into the cold, hard world.

* * *

"Your brother isn't cooking tonight, is he?" Angelina asks, taking her cut from Simpson.

"Nah. He cooks on Mondays. Tonight is when he parties. Hell, he's probably fucked up right now."

"Good. I hate Bella sleeping above the apartment where he does that." Although she enjoys the meth Simpson slips her, lately time has been getting away. She shakes her head, says, "Dunno why I asked that."

"No worries. Didn't I get Detrick to give you off on Mondays?"

"Yeah." Angelina takes Bella to a friend's on Mondays just for that reason.

"Right, right. And you still got that Russian grandma comin' across the hall to check on her?"

"Yeah. It works out. The old bitty thinks twenty bucks a week to check on Bella — mind you, this is after a spoonful of Robitussin DM so she's tuned out until ten in the morning — is a steal. Says she can't sleep anyways so I bet she's over there like six times a night."

"Watch that broad. She might snatch the kid one night and sell her to the Bratva."

"What the shit is a *bratva*?"

"Russian mob. Sell her back to Commiestan or whatever."

"You think she'd do that?"

"Sure." Simpson laughs. "You never thought your baby

146

daddy would commit suicide and then he did it. These hard-up johns come walkin' on in here, they never think you're gonna drug and rob them and you do it."

"Yeah, but I do that for my baby." She smiles. "There's a difference."

"Sure. Sure. Of course there is. My bad."

"And by the way," Angelina says, getting ready to go back out on stage. "Don't bring up Ethan. I know he wasn't the best or anything, but he loved me."

"Baby daddy loved you? This the same guy in that picture over there on your dresser?"

"Yeah."

"Ol' dressed in black, hatin' Jesus, cuttin' himself baby daddy?"

"Yeah."

"What would possess you to fuck him anyway?"

In a moment of terrifying honesty for Angelina, she says, "He told me I was pretty."

Eyebrows raised, Simpson smiles like the devil. "*I* think you're pretty."

"Ha. Learned my lesson already." Angelina hears her name. "Ready for round two?"

* * *

By five a.m. they've pulled their con on six other dudes.

"This was a good night after all," Angelina says as she stuffs her earnings from everything inside her purse. Simpson walks her out to her car, absently looks at his phone.

A text from his alchemist brother, time stamped three hours prior: *juan orderd big score no more party 2nite. cook. stall A- vapers wil go a way.*

"Damn it," Simpson mutters. He hates it when his brother gets down and then fucks with cooking. Juan always orders late into the production cycle. Fucking Mexican is too

147

lazy to get his order in on time. "Angelina," Simpson says, takes her arm. "How about breakfast on me?"

Angelina checks her phone. Her stomach growls at the thought. All she had to eat that night so far had been meth, a couple of Jell-O shots and the perversions of men. "Well, I guess I have until ten a.m., right? Thanks Robitussin DM!"

She giggles loudly. Simpson smiles like the devil again.

* * *

By nine Angelina has eaten three pancakes and let Simpson do what he wanted.

He drops her off at her car and leaves, saying, "See you tonight." For all the time he'd known her, he's never asked her real name. As he leaves, he checks his phone again, sees another missed text, this one time stamped at half-past eight.

"Huh, musta been while I was trying to figure out her bra..."

The text, again from his brother: *o shit.*

* * *

Angelina swerves and honks through a throng of emergency vehicles and rubbernecking neighbors.

They stare at her like she's on exhibit. Like she's helicoptering tittie tassles while painting with oils and singing an aria. Her stomach figures out the gravity of the situation before her head does, and starts twisting in knots without being told.

Police tape. People in reflective yellow directing her where to park. Angelina lives on the fourth floor, east side. The Russian is on the west side. Simpson's brother cooks on the third floor. East side.

On foot, chilled from the fire hose spray's mist, Angelina approaches in awe and tries to make sense of the building's condition. Rancid smoke still flits about through the air, grabbing at her like the greasy fingers of johns at the club. Groping for a free feel. Snowflakes of ash rest nearer the building, debris peppers the sidewalk.

The first two floors are the same dull brown they always were. The third floor is gray-black with soot fanning out, climbing the windows. Somewhere, a pane of glass falls and shatters like a dream. The fourth floor is black as death, brittle and ruined.

The fifth floor looks like it collapsed inwards. The smashed-in skull of the building, caved into its smoldering, empty head.

EMTs skulk about, shaking their heads. Empty gurneys. People crying. Cops demanding answers from people who are too stunned to speak.

"Oh shit..." Angelina stands numb. New formula and a teddy bear in one hand, the other hand clutching a purse filled with dirty money and methamphetamines. Even she knew Simpson's brother cooks on Mondays, which is her day off and she'd take Bella and go spend the night at a friend's house. That's how it was. How it is. How it will always be.

She stares at a cop, asks, "Did Simpson's brother cook *last night?*"

The cop furrows his brow. "What? Whaddya mean?"

Angelina, the desperation and horror clutching at her stomach, all in knots and wanting to vomit, it climbs her throat. Claws her tongue. Stings the back of her eyes as tears well up and spill over.

"Do you think he would do that?"

THE BIGGEST MYTH
Tom Pitts

"The biggest myth about the money business is that people get hurt when they don't pay." Christophe was standing in Jerome's kitchen, looking comfortable, at home. "You mind making me a cup of coffee? You got any of the good stuff. I only want a cup. It's still early for me."

Jerome nodded, but didn't get up.

"Anyway, as I was saying," Christophe went on, "The biggest myth about the loan business is that people get hurt. You take a guy, good job, working hard to pay his bills, meet his obligations; what good is it going to do if he can't make it to that job?" Here Christophe paused and waited for Jerome to answer. When he got no response he said, "None, that's what."

"Mr. Lysikov, I've made payments."

Christophe held up his hand. "I know. Trust me, I'm completely aware of your account and where it stands." Christophe reached out and turned the faucet on, then turned it back off. His back was to Jerome. "You knew when you came to me that I deal mostly with gamblers. Guys who need a little flow to keep their roll going. I get that. I understand that kind of animal." He turned to look at Jerome. "You know what we do when a gambler doesn't pay? I give Billy Mac a call down at the bookie office and tell 'em to cut the guy off. That's it. Simple. Usually does the trick, 'cause a guy wants to have a line down there. He's already underwater so he can't use his credit cards for those websites on the islands, he's gotta keep things local. And, believe me, he wants to keep playing." Christophe pulled out one of the chairs from the kitchen table and sat down across from Jerome. "Thing usually rights itself."

Jerome crossed his hands in front of him and kept his gaze locked on Christophe. He wanted to give him all his attention, his utmost respect. He was already nervous having the man in his kitchen. No way he thought that the man himself would show up at his house. Not with his deep purple suit with a paisley handkerchief sticking out of the pocket looking like some kind of flower. Not smiling and being polite and acting cultured the way he was.

"Jerome?"

"Yes," said Jerome. He caught himself holding back saying, *sir*. That would be too much, laying it on too thick.

"I said can I get a cup of coffee."

"Oh, yes. Of course. Sorry." Jerome got up quick to brew the pot. When he stood, his chair scraped the linoleum. It was loud, scared him. Reminded him how on edge he was.

Christophe didn't seem to notice or care. He went on talking. "When you came to me with this cockamamie idea of yours, I knew it was a risk. This isn't a couple of G's to a guy I know can repay, guy that's a doctor or lawyer that loves his sports. I thought to myself, what's this Jerome think I am, Wells Fargo?"

Jerome was making himself busy at the counter, spooning the coffee into the filter, pouring the water into the top of the Mr. Coffee.

"Then I said to myself, oh yeah, Wells Fargo doesn't do start-up loans for drug dealers."

Jerome suddenly felt cold.

"I mean, that's what this was, wasn't it? A start-up? You acted like you knew what you were doing, but, really, if you did, I wouldn't be sitting here, would I?"

Jerome hit the on switch and turned to face Christophe, not knowing whether he should nod or shake his head. The water began to gurgle and bubble through the coffeemaker.

"Where was I? Oh yeah, the biggest myth about the money business is that people get hurt. I mean, if a guy has a job, he's got to be able to get outta bed and make it to work.

That's if you want him to keep paying. How's a guy gonna pay you back from a hospital bed?"

There was silence. It was a long moment before Jerome realized he was supposed to answer. "He can't?"

"That's right. He can't," said Christophe. "But that's a guy with a job." Christophe looked at the coffee pot to see how it was brewing. He inhaled deeply through his nostrils and let his lips curve into a soft smile. "Smells wonderful. Can't beat that smell. Nothing better." He cleared his throat and went on. "You take a guy like yourself, a guy with no job. A drug dealer—a want-to-be drug dealer at that. I think that's the kind of guy who doesn't want a job. That's the kind of guy who wants to cut corners. He doesn't want to get out of bed and earn his money every day. That kind of guy is a risk. Do you have real cream?"

Jerome didn't know what that meant, so he said, "Sorry?"

"Real cream. For the coffee. You have real cream? I don't take it with sugar, just cream."

Jerome opened the fridge and pulled a small carton of half-and-half, making sure the expiration date was still a week off. He set it on the table, but kept standing, waiting for the coffee to finish.

"A guy like that is a risk. You understand what I'm telling you?"

Jerome nodded.

"So when you came to me with this business idea, I said to myself, no, this is not a good idea. That was how long ago, Jerome?"

Jerome shrugged.

"Maybe that's your problem. I didn't recognize it at the time, but you got no head for figures. You want to make it in business, you got to have a head for figures. It was four months and three weeks ago, Jerome."

Jerome didn't like the way his name sounded when Christophe said it.

"Ten thousand is a lot of money. It may not sound like it to you, but it is to me. Let's see now, ten thousand at five points. The first week you give me the five hundred; that buys you another week. But then you decide you have to leave town for a while. Where to? I don't know; I don't care. We're still in good shape, you and me. But that's another four weeks. Five hundred a week you're piling on. We're then at twelve thousand. You got to come up with six hundred a week."

Jerome was starting to feel dizzy. He sat down in the same chair as he had before.

Christophe said, "Looks like the coffee's done." While Jerome got back up and took a ceramic cup from the cupboard, the math lesson continued. "Again you give me the points. You tell us some story about the deal gettin' fucked up, and apologize to my man and give him the six. But we're still carrying the twelve. Next week, we don't hear from you. Another week goes by, nothing. You're now at thirteen-two. You call my friend down at the office and tell him you've got something, but you never show. Three more weeks until we hear from you. You show up at the store with five, but now you're still above fourteen. We take the five, and as a gift we take off a week, but that means seven hundred a week. Are you following this, Jerome?"

Jerome turned and set the coffee down in front of Christophe. He wasn't following it. He was dizzy again. He didn't like where this was going. He knew what he owed now. Eleven hundred a week. Twenty-two thousand in principal.

Christophe said, "This is good coffee. Really good. Not too strong, just right. I love a good coffee early in the day. If I drink it too late, it gives me headaches."

"Look, I'm doing what I can. I'm seeing about selling my car."

Christophe cut him off. "How did we get here, Jerome?" He leaned in a bit, trying to make his voice sound soft and comforting. "What happened?"

"I told your boy. The fucking guy took a walk on me. Skipped with the ten thou and I've been trying to dig my way out ever since."

"Twenty-two is not digging yourself out, if you don't mind me saying. It's digging yourself in."

"My car is a 2008. It's got be worth at least fifteen thousand."

Christophe held up his hand. "I'm not in the used car business. I think I already made it clear that I'm in the money business." He took another sip off of the coffee. "Delicious. What ever happened to the guy you were in business with? The guy who skipped."

"I dunno. He took the cash. I thought it was a go. Then, boom, I never heard from him again."

"You look for him?"

"Of course I did."

"What's his name?"

"Sonny. Sonny Richards."

"That his real name?"

"How do I know? Sonny Richards is all I know. He lives at 1437 McAllister. Upper flat. I've been there many a time, but there's no one there now. *For Rent* sign up in the window."

"Sonny Richards, huh? 1437 Mac? Tell you what, I'll have my friend look into it. See what we can find out."

"Thank you, Mr. Lysikov. I appreciate everything you've done for me. I appreciate your patience. If we can find this Sonny, I know we can get this straightened out. I can — *you can* — take what he owes me and turn it over yourself."

"I told you, I'm in the money business, I'm not a drug dealer. I'm a loan shark for Christ's sake, why would you think I want to get my hands dirty with drugs?"

Jerome said, "The Apaches had a name for a guy like this Sonny. Something like Indian-giver, but I can't remember it now."

Christophe wasn't listening, he was saying, "This coffee isn't too hot anymore. You mind if I use your microwave and heat this up a little bit?" He stood up without waiting for an answer and hit the button on the microwave and the door swung open. Christophe set the cup inside, shut the door, and hit the timer.

"Yeah, the Apaches had a word for what this guy did to me," said Jerome again. "Tomako or timi-something."

Christophe said, "The Apaches, huh?" He was watching the cup turn inside the microwave.

Jerome noticed the cup had been spinning too long. The coffee was beginning to bubble and burp. "The Apaches had a name for everything. They were a great people, the Apaches."

Christophe opened the microwave door and carefully took out the cup.

"Careful," said Jerome. "That shit is gonna be way too hot."

"No," said Christophe. "It's perfect." He turned toward Jerome and threw the boiling coffee into his face.

Jerome raised his hands just in time to get the scalding liquid on both his hands and his face. Jerome screamed, "*Apache. Apache.*"

"Apache, huh?" Christophe stepped closer to Jerome and smacked him in the forehead with the ceramic cup. "What's Apache? The secret word of the day? Who's listening, you piece of shit? You think the calvary is coming because you're yelling Apache?" He smacked him with the cup again and this time the handle broke. The cup tumbled to the tile floor.

Jerome kept saying it, screaming it, "*Apache, Apache.*"

"No one is coming, Jerome. No one is going to save you. That cop you think is listening? He's on lunch. Yeah, he's having a nice *long* lunch, on me. You know how much it cost to get him to do that? Six-hundred bucks. That's about half a week's vig from you. You stupid fuck, did you really think you could just set me up and this would go away?"

Jerome was crying now, from both pain and desperation. He held his head in his hands and kept his face down. He was waiting for a bullet.

"No, fuck-hole, I don't want your car. I don't want your money anymore either, 'cause you don't have any. You own this place though. Free and clear. Inheritance can be a beautiful thing, huh? That's what I want. That's the only thing that will clear you. You sign over the deed and this will all go away. I've got it drawn up; all you need to do is sign it."

"But this house is worth..."

"I know what it's worth, I checked. Ask yourself this: Is it worth more than your life? Because you're in deeper than the money now. You called the cops. You're a snitch."

* * *

Christophe came out of the door of Jerome's house and walked straight to his car. He wore a big smile on his face. The sun was shining, and in the natural light, his suit looked even better.

He opened the car door from the sidewalk and got in on the passenger side.

The driver asked, "Did he go for it?"

"Of course he did, Sonny. He gave up the house just like he was going to give up you and me. I explained it to him. Some of these guys are real slow; you got to separate myth and reality for them. He's now a firm believer."

BAD MOVIE
Pete Risley

It was Saturday night and there was this new zombie movie that was supposed to be a hoot. I didn't want to see it too bad, but Yo did. I just wanted to go out, and he had the car, so we hit the multiplex. The movie started at like 9:15. We did split a 40 on the drive over, and Yo might have had a couple before, but it's not true that we were all drunk and shit.

It was raining and thundering a little when we got out of the car; had to run for it. Inside there was a long line for the movie—all people in high school, pretty much. All the other movies had short lines because there wasn't anything else worth seeing. There were some kids from our school there but nobody who really mattered. It was noisy like usual, people talking in little groups, bullshitting around waiting for the screening room doors to open, and right in front of us happened to be these three stupid kids, like sixth graders. They were all excited, babbling, squealing when they laughed, mimicking voices from TV, jumping around and shit. Real irritating little homos.

Then these babes got in line behind us. There were three; two of them okay but a little skanky, but the other was this bad little blonde. She was like maybe fifteen, big eyes with that raccoon eye makeup, bare midriff with her jacket open even though it was a little cold out, low riders; made her look like a little slut. Which I like, of course. Who doesn't?

I caught her eye, I could tell. A lot of girls stare at me right off because I look good. Hey, I'm handsome, I admit it. Sounds like I'm bragging, but it's just true. People say it all the time. You know that old dead actor named James Dean? His movies suck, but he looks kind of like me, people say.

He even makes expressions like me, facial expressions. My sister has a couple of his movies on DVD, and I can look in the mirror after seeing them and make the same faces. Yo, who's a homely-ass mutt, he tried to call me a "pretty-boy" once. I mean, just once; he didn't say it again when I whacked him upside the head.

See, Yo—his real name was Josh, Josh Yoder—he was a big strong kid, he could kick anybody's ass, and he liked to, since that was about all he was good at, but I could always handle his shit. He wanted to be popular at school, but for that he needed me more than I really needed him, never mind his dad's fucking Grand Am. I don't even like Grand Am's, but my folks didn't have a car at all.

Anyway, this little blonde, she was one to pretend she wasn't impressed, an act I was used to. It means they're real interested. She turned her head after our eyes met for a second, put her long blonde hair behind her ear, pouted and started talking and giggling in a cute squeaky voice to this one girl she was with. Cute and knew it; sure, they always know it. Knew I was watching her, too, primping and skipping around to show herself off, practically shaking her little butt at me.

Meanwhile, one of the dweeb kids in front of us, kid with these little rectangular glasses that are supposed to make you hip, was trying to impress his butt buddies by talking like that old vampire dude from the real old Dracula movies. He said like, "the soon-to-be-dead are among us here and now—there, and there and there, and there!" He turned around when he said that and pointed his finger at Yo. Bad mistake.

One of the other kids, the tallest one, almost as tall as me but scrawny, was grinning and laughing like it was a Chuck E. Cheese's birthday party, but when he turned and glanced at Yo and me, the looks on our faces, he clammed up and looked jittery. And he was the tall one, you know?

I mean, he didn't act that scared, but a little was enough,

because it didn't take much for Yo to catch that scent of fear and go for it. Plus I wasn't inclined to discourage him right then, because these girls behind us were watching, you know. I'm not sure these little wussy boys had even noticed the girls; they didn't have dicks yet, if they ever would.

The third kid, the littlest guy, he had a black pixie haircut like the Beatles or some shit that his mom probably thought was cute on him. He looked like the wussiest one, but he was just smiling, watching his buddy with the glasses put on his show. The stupid kid who'd pointed, with the glasses, was still rattling on about vampires or some shit with this big grin on his face like he was Jay Leno.

"Kid's pretty funny, huh?" I said to Yo, but loud enough for the girls to hear. The girls snorted with amusement, or one of them did — the blonde, I hoped — and the wusses heard that and all three of them, even Jay Leno, got real still, like hamsters when a cat's in the room.

"Fuckin' smartass," said Yo in this deep voice he always put on when he was fucking with somebody. He put his second finger to his thumb and flicked Jay Leno on the back of the head, hard. Yo had these big fucking hands.

"Ow! Hey!" Jay Leno said, too loud, like a six-year-old would, rubbing his head where he'd been flicked. A girl behind us shrieked with glee, and somehow I knew that time it was the blonde, and a bunch of other people in the line heard it too, turned around to look and were cracking up. "Dat wuz smart," somebody said in a retard voice, and others were mimicking "Ow!" in a high-pitched homo voice just like the wussy kid.

The tall kid looked like he was going to start crying right there — fuckin' chickenshit — and the little pixie guy looked pretty worried too. All of them stayed quiet, like they were sad all of the sudden. There was a lot of chatter going otherwise, not because of Yo and this kid anymore, just the usual shooting the shit.

The doors opened finally, a relief to the wusses I'm sure,

but this wasn't going to be the end of it.

We all filed in, past the slow-ass ticket-takers in their white shirts and black trou. A loud preview was showing as we walked into the showing room. Yo was headed for seats down front, but I put a hand on his shoulder and pointed to a spot where the wusses had just sat down. Yo nodded and grinned. He always looked like Goofy from Disney cartoons when he smiled like that, even in the weird light from the movie screen.

We sat, and before long I heard the same squeaky giggling as before from the seats in the row behind us. It was my little blonde and her buddies. I turned my head and rolled my eyes, letting my mouth hang open just a little. It was a look I'd practiced at home with this one James Dean movie. Me and the blonde exchanged glances again. She looked real excited now, but again, she tried to hide it, looked away and put on the fake pout. I kept watching, and after a couple seconds she looked right back at me, smiled real wide like she couldn't help it, but then went back to the pout and looked away.

Yo started to bring up his foot, to put it in the face of the scaredy-cat tall kid who was sitting in front of him, but I said, "Be cool, wait for the movie to start." He grinned and nodded.

The previews went on forever, and the movie finally started up. It was the usual thing, a little boring at first but pretty soon had some good zombie attacks with a lot of spurting blood and shit. The zombies in this movie were fast and did these evil cackling laughs. I let it run on for a good while before I elbowed Yo to remind him of the wusses waiting to be fucked with. Had to elbow him a couple times, I guess he'd gotten wrapped up in the movie.

He nodded, raised his foot and put it over the back of the tall kid's seat into the side of his face, but fixed on the screen again as a real rotted zombie chomped into a bonneted baby's skull, while everybody laughed and shrieked and shit. Yo was laughing too. He had a real deep, retarded-sounding laugh.

"Hey, quit it!" said the tall kid, with a whine in his voice, pushing Yo's foot away. He put it right back, and the kid got up and moved to another seat, way at the far end of the aisle. Yo looked at me and grinned open-mouthed, bobbing his head in a silent laugh.

A bunch of people chortled, but Yo seemed to lose his amusement all the sudden. Zombies on the screen were now running down the aisles of a nursing home, carrying chainsaws and decapitating old folks in wheel chairs, while more zombies came up behind them, catching the old wrinkled up white-haired heads and stringing them together by the hair as they ran, with the heads still screaming as the zombies strung them together. It was pretty cool.

Yo bent over to ask me right up in my ear, "You think heads could still scream like that?"

"Naw," I said, "only in movies."

"Not even for, like, a second?" I just shook my head no, 'cause I wanted to watch the movie myself at that point.

Yo laughed heartily again as a zombie attacked a fat black custodian carrying a vacuum cleaner, backing him into a corner, taking the cleaner away from him and beating his wide-eyed terrified face all bloody with the base of it. Then the zombie used the vacuum to suck the guy's face completely off, his eyeballs too, which came out of the sockets with a pop. Everybody in the theater went nuts over that. The zombie himself did this real insane laugh all through it. It was real funny how Yo's laugh sounded just like the zombie's laugh, only deeper, which got me and other people nearby chuckling along.

After a while though, the carnage onscreen all seemed about the same, and I wondered if the blonde girl was still thinking about me. I heard some murmuring, and turned around in my seat to see, to my dismay, that she and her girlfriends were talking to some guy sitting behind them. I

161

turned back around, annoyed.

But then somebody tapped me on the shoulder. It was her. First time I got to look right in her face. She was really cute, close up even, and acted a little nervous. "'Scuse me, would you like this popcorn?" She held up a large, half-empty tub of dry, unbuttered corn.

"Don-naaa," said one of her friends, as if surprised at her.

"You don't want it?" I said.

"No we don't want it," said the blonde. Donna.

I didn't want it either, but took it, of course, exchanging smiles with Donna. When I turned back around, I had an idea. "Want some?" I said to Yo.

"Yeah, great," he said, putting the container between his knees and digging a big handful out.

I leaned toward him. "Hey, Yo, we're neglecting the sideshow, man," I said.

"Wha' sho'?" he said, with his mouth full, munching.

"The wusses. Why are we letting them live?"

"Th' whosis?"

"Them." I pointed.

"I don't fuckin' care," he said.

"We could decorate them a little." I mimicked taking a piece of popcorn and tossing it unto the head of the Jay Leno kid, who was sitting in front of me. I noticed even as I did this that the pixie kid had gotten out of his seat, excused himself past a couple people and walked back up the aisle. Might have heard me talking and was going to tell on us, but might also just be going to the bathroom.

"Yeah, I guess. Popcorn's greasy anyway." At that, he started tossing the popcorn onto the kid's head. He frantically brushed it off, whimpering a little. A girl behind us squealed out a laugh, but another said, "It's not funny."

"Cool it for now, we might have a little snitch on our hands," I told Yo, but, amused by the wusses' reaction, he kept tossing.

162

A light went on at the side of my face, a flashlight. One of the ushers was pointing it, a big older guy. He spoke sternly, though in a low voice. "Excuse me, sir. You and your friend will have to leave. Right now."

"Why, we're not—"

"Right now, or we'll have the police here in two minutes. You've disrupted the show enough already. Out." The pixie was standing beside him, with a big snotty scowl on his face. Fuckin' snitch.

"I didn't do anything," said Yo.

"Ahhhh," I heard a girl say, "that's not fair." It was my little babe Donna.

"Good riddance," said another. That was that one friend of hers. Cunt.

"C'mon, let's split. Movie sucks anyway." I got up, and Yo groaned and got up after me, and we trudged up the aisle with the usher walking behind, none too fast so that it didn't look like we were intimidated. We chuckled a little, too, I did anyway. People we passed glanced at us warily, though the movie got loud just then, sounded like machine-gun fire. Yo stopped for a second and looked back at the screen. I could tell he was bummed. I think somebody in the audience said "asshole," up near the exit, but they probably meant the usher rather than us.

Once we got to the lobby, the guy with the flashlight stopped and stood with his arms folded watching us leave, like he was the sheriff running us out of town. A couple of the other ticket takers, girls, came up and joined him, glaring at us. I wondered which girl the fucking jerk was trying to impress. I was going to flip him off, didn't bother, just turned around and smirked at him as we reached the doors.

We went outside. There was a brisk wind, felt good after the rain. The puddles bobbed with light from the tall parking lot lamps. Made me want to do something, get some fucking kicks before the night was over. To see that Donna, talk to her, maybe get her in the car even. Hell, the night was young. I checked my watch, it was after eleven. We were in there longer than it seemed, the movie would be almost over.

"Fuck, man, I wanted to see how the movie ended," said Yo.

"Yeah, me too," though I didn't really. "You wanna wait and see if those fuckin' wusses come out? It's about over."

"Yeah, let's do that. I'm pretty pissed off. Fuckin' seventeen dollars to see the movie." Actually, it was eight-fifty a ticket, but he'd paid my way 'cause I was broke. "You know what, man? This fuckin' pisses me off the more I think about it," he said.

"Little fuckin' wusses, man," I said. "Did you see that one who went and got the usher to throw us out? Looked like the mean guy from the Three Stooges. Ever see the Three Stooges?"

"I feel like kickin' somebody's butt, man," Yo said, lighting up a cigarette. "I'm serious. Watch the whole movie to almost the end and don't get to see it. People fuck with me they get fucked up, man. You know?"

"I know it," I said. This was just vintage Yo-man.

"After they come out an' shit, we'll go back to my place and get some more beer," he added. "My dad's got a bunch in the garage."

"That'd be cool. Hey look, here comes some people, must be over." I didn't see the wusses, or Donna, among all the kids coming out the entrance. I looked around the parking lot. "Let's get behind that pickup over there, if they see us they'll just run back inside."

We did so, and pretty soon the wusses came out among the crowd, the pixie, the tall one and the one with glasses, not looking very happy and walking fast. Maybe they figured we could be waiting. And there not far behind them was my little fox Donna and her two skanky friends.

The wusses were probably headed into the mall to get picked up by their moms, but as it happened, they walked

164

right by us. "Hey, buddy," said Yo in his menacing voice, stepping out. He was talking to the pixie, glaring at him.

"You guys better leave us alone," said the Jay Leno one, his voice getting high like with helium. They all looked scared, especially the tall one; he was shaking like a Chihuahua.

"You didn't have to run and snitch like a little fuckin' girl," said Yo, as if he was seriously scolding the kid. "You could of just said 'quit throwin' popcorn on me,' and I would have."

"We don't want anything to do with you," said the pixie. His voice wasn't shaking, but you could see from his eyes he was about pissing his pants.

"It's not cool to be a fuckin' snitch, man." Yo grabbed the kid by the collar, put his foot behind his ankle, tripped him, and sat on him. "I don't like fuckin' snitches, man." He backhanded the kid across the face. I could see this was going to be bad. Yo was real pissed about the movie, I guess. These kids' parents might be there screaming any minute.

The kid, to my surprise, tried to punch him back. Yo grabbed the kid's wrists, turned his head and said, "Didja see that? Tried to suckerpunch me!" People were gathering around the two of them and me, some glaring at us, some smiling because they liked to see a fight, like I usually did, but not now. Yo was getting all carried away.

"Let him up, Yo, we gotta go," I said. "Let's go."

To my surprise, Yo punched the kid in the middle of his face, pretty hard. You could hear a crunch, and the kid started to shriek. His nose looked squashed, there was blood coming out of it. He hit him again.

"Stop it! Stop it!" a girl standing by kept saying, like a tape loop. I started worrying somebody in the crowd might jump in to be a hero. I saw Donna then, in the back of the crowd, craning her neck to see.

"Jesus fuck, man, c'mon!" I grabbed at Yo's arm, and at that moment, the kid tried to punch him back again, a

165

straight-up punch, missing his face and hitting him square in the throat. I guess he was strong for a little guy, or else hit Yo just right. I heard this loud snap.

Yo made a long weird bellow, rolled off the kid and curled up sideways on the asphalt. He put his hands around his throat and pumped his legs real hard, shuddering more and more, and the bellow turned into this awful snorting sound. He snorted faster and faster, couldn't seem to stop.

He looked up at me, his eyes begging, but there was nothing I could do. The snorting got more and more hoarse, 'til it was just a hiss. His face was getting dark, like bluish grey, you could see it changing real fast, just darker and darker. Girls in the crowd watching, maybe guys too, started to scream and cry.

The usher who'd thrown us out was there, talking on his cellphone, putting it flat on his shoulder as he yelled at the crowd to stay back. Then Yo, his face shiny and almost black even under the bright light of the lamps, made another sound, like he was gargling some mouthwash, only harsher. After a few more seconds, it ended.

He still seemed to stare back at me, and his tongue was sticking out of his mouth, bunched up real thick. I hate to say, but he looked even more like Goofy that way. I couldn't look at him anymore. I heard a faraway siren.

I don't know what was happening right after that; it's kind of a blur. There was some old fat guy with a chin beard and glasses yelling at me and crying. I don't know how I know this, but I'm pretty sure he was one of the wusses' dads, probably there to pick them up. I decided not to talk to him.

Somebody yanked me by the arm and led me to sit down in a car. I thought it was Yo's car, but once inside I heard this staticky talk from the dashboard, and thought, when did Yo get a shortwave radio? But it was a squad car. A cop was asking me some questions in a loud, slow voice like he was talking to an idiot, but the questions didn't make too much sense. It was like a dream where slow, stupid stuff keeps happening and you get all frustrated.

The one thing I recall clearly was looking out the window and seeing Donna, a little distance away, talking to another cop. "We were there, he didn't do it, it was the other guy," I heard her say a couple times, while her girlfriend who didn't like me was pulling at her, saying, "Donna, Donna, my God."

Maybe it was because my heart was going fast, but it was like what I was seeing before me was galloping, like a movie that's out-of-kilter, so that light from the lamps reflected in rain puddles kept jumping around real frantically in a pattern. It felt like I was getting hypnotized.

They left me alone for a minute, and as I sat quietly in the squad car, there was Donna again. Her friend was gone, and she was all blonde and pretty, standing a few feet away right under a light pole so the light shone down on her and brightened up her hair to almost white, just like an angel or something.

She cocked her head to one side, smiled real sweet and waved at me. Damned if I didn't wave back like everything was cool, automatically doing one of my James Dean faces. It's crazy, but I remember thinking that it was just fate, destiny, that this was supposed to happen, my days hanging with Yo were over, and now there'd be Donna. But what would I do for a car?

I was out of my head. It turned out it didn't matter, anyway, because I never did see Donna again.

© 2012, Pete Risley

THE PEEPER
C.J. Edwards

Jimmy Wade had been watching her for a month. She had smiled at him when she walked her small poodle around her front yard as the movers hauled her things into the renovated double. He hadn't been sure what to do about that. Pretty girls never smiled at him. His pudgy frame and pimple-scarred features didn't inspire smiles, even from the homeliest of girls. Living with his mother after the age of thirty didn't help much either. So when those bright, even teeth framed by plump lips flashed in his direction, he had turned away to hide the crimson sheet that flashed across his face, and the erection that sprung up against his sweat pants. He almost didn't make it to the mini-barn behind the house to spill his junk into the oily rags piled behind the John Deere riding lawn mower.

From then on he had taken every opportunity to catch a glimpse of her. From her mail he had discovered her name, Carley Jacobs, and from the White Pages online, her phone number. Her Facebook account had provided him with a wealth of knowledge, even some shots of her in a bathing suit from a spring break spent in Cabo. They now hung on the wall in the back corner of the mini-barn. He didn't dare keep them in his room for fear that his mother might find them. She had discovered him in the bathroom once when he was thirteen with a Victoria's Secret catalog swiped from a neighbor's mailbox.

"You filthy little animal," she'd screamed at him. "I'll not be having such dirty sin in this house." Then she snatched away the catalog and proceeded to beat him with it as he fled outside. All the while she screeched her condemnation of the foul nature inside the souls of all men.

Banished to the barn, he could still hear her calling on the Lord to save her from having to witness such abomination.

After that first month of watching Carley from afar, glimpses of her from his bedroom window as she walked her dog, or as she mowed her lawn, Jimmy finally worked up enough courage to take a peek in one of her windows. They were quick and furtive sorties at first. Her half of the double had a single stretch of a privacy fence separating it from Mrs. Jeffries's house next door. Mrs. Jeffries was Carley's landlord, and Jimmy did odd jobs for her from time to time. The fence didn't fully enclose the yard, and there wasn't a security light.

Darts across the street turned into strolls, which then became lingering skulks in the shadows beneath her windows. As spring grew warm, Carley would often leave her windows cracked open to let in the evening breeze. Sometimes Jimmy was treated to phone conversations between Carley and her girlfriends. He became intimate with the sound of her voice, especially her laugh. Boldness, nurtured by continued success, led to his first extended peek into the living room.

It was a Wednesday night. He had crouched just below the open window listening. The TV was on, and he could hear Ryan Seacrest hosting *American Idol*. During commercial breaks, Carley would call her friend Amanda, to discuss the performance of their favorite contestant.

"Did you see their faces when he hit that high note?...Oh my god I know...He is so hot. Too bad he's gay...He is too...Okay, yeah whatever..."

After another commercial, Jimmy finally worked himself up enough to raise his eyes level with the window sill. Another male crooner was belting out a remixed Michael Jackson eighties hit when his eyes collided with the sight of Carley's bare legs as she sat on her faded couch painting her toe nails. He could smell the tang of the polish that she spread across each nail with a red-stained brush. His body began to shiver as blood rushed to his groin. She had just finished with her right foot, and was preparing the left, when Carley's poodle perked up his ears and growled. Jimmy ducked as the curly-haired dog bounded to the window.

"What is it Max?" Carley said.

Jimmy ran. This time he didn't make it to the mini-barn. He was forced to climb up to his room to change his briefs. As he stripped off the sticky underwear, heart still pounding from almost getting caught, Jimmy realized that he had to do something about the dog.

The next couple of days Jimmy kept to his room, plotting. By the weekend he had a plan. When Carley went to work the following Monday, Jimmy walked over to the window where Max had almost exposed him. It was cracked as usual, security pegs preventing it from being opened all the way. A crack was all he needed, for now. Sliding up the screen just enough, Jimmy set two moist doggy treats on the sill and waited. He was rewarded by Max's snuffling nose followed by his pink tongue licking up the tiny treats.

Jimmy returned two more times that day with offerings for the little pooch. On Tuesday he followed the same schedule. Wednesday he began feeding the treats directly from his fingers to the poodle's mouth. Before the week was out Jimmy and Max were good friends. Jimmy almost felt bad about what he was going to do next.

On Friday nights, Carley would usually go out. She would sleep in the following morning. On these occasions she would let Max out into the small fenced in area behind her half of the double, and then go back to bed. After a week of making friends with her dog, Jimmy watched from his bedroom that Friday evening. He had seen Carley come home from work, and three hours later, watched her red Honda back from its parking space into the alley and pull away. Before going to bed, Jimmy set his alarm to wake himself at six a.m.

170

* * *

Strangling Max turned out to be easier than expected. After luring him from the yard with more treats, he took the dog to the min-barn. Inside, while Max gobbled up a pile of the meaty bits, Jimmy looped a thin cord around the dog's neck.

"That's a good boy, Max."

He tied one end to the bottom of the mower, then took a firm grip on the other, and jerked. Afterward, Jimmy pushed the lawn tractor to one end of the barn's interior, pried up three of the floor boards, and dug a shallow grave.

When Carley had knocked on his door later that afternoon, for a split second, Jimmy thought he had been found out. He stood, face frozen and mute, staring at her. Sweat beaded on his forehead, and a lonely trickle snaked its way down his spine.

"Hi," she said. Her smile was thin. "I live across the street. I was wondering if you might have seen my dog Max today." Her hand reached out. In it was a lost dog poster with a picture of Max's curly haired face set in the middle of the paper. His little head cocked to the side, his open mouth made him look like he was smiling.

Relieved, Jimmy took the poster. "Um, no. I haven't seen him."

"Okay. Thanks anyway. Please, let me know if you do." She turned to go.

"I could take a few more of those," Jimmy said, and pointed at the stack of posters in her hand. "Maybe post a few for you?"

"That would be so sweet. Thank you," she said.

With Max out of the picture, Jimmy resumed his visitations. He overheard the tearful conversations Carley had with her mom, then her sister, about poor old Max. Different emotions flitted across his mind. He sampled each one as he watched and listened to her distress. Guilt was never a good flavor. Guilt was what he felt when his mother chastised him for some new offense, or filthy male habit he had acquired. Sadness worked all right. When he saw those tears trickle down her soft cheeks he could almost taste what it would be like to sit down beside Carley, put his arm around her, and squeeze away her pain with his urgent fingers.

After savoring each, Jimmy settled on satisfaction. He could still feel the rough cord tight against his hands, vibrating between his fingers while Max had flopped, then twitched, eyes bulging, his little teeth snapping at the still air inside the barn. The thrilling satisfaction reminded him of the feeling he got while jacking off into the dirt outside Carley's window, while he watched her folding laundry in a t-shirt and shorts.

The weekend following Max's disappearance, Jimmy began to realize that the relationship between him and his beautiful neighbor must progress to the next level. She needed him closer, so she could finally get over her lost pet.

Lifting the spare key to Carley's house was as easy as switching it with the same brand of key he had purchased from Ace Hardware when he stopped over to see if Mrs. Jeffries needed anything. Now, all he had to do was wait. The following week seemed to drag as he anticipated Carley's Friday girls' night ritual.

In his darkened room the following Friday, Jimmy watched until Carley's car made its backward turn into the alley and drove away. Not able to contain his anticipation a moment longer, he pulled on a black windbreaker and skipped down the stairs. Before he made it to the door his mother called to him from the front room where she was hunched over her Bible.

"James Lester Wade, where are you going?" Her steal eyes probed his face. "Out to do the devil's work?"

"No, mother."

"Look at me when I'm speaking to you."

Jimmy turned and raised his head from his chest where it had fallen when his mother had called to him.

"You're up to no good. I can smell the sin on you boy." She pointed her Bible at him. "Just like your father, always thinking your dirty thoughts. Don't think I don't know what you're always doing out in that shed."

His face boiled red. His mother cackled. She made him think of sour milk.

"God will send you to the roasting pit for it. You, and your filthy little hands!"

Jimmy bolted from the door. His mother's laugh chased him from the porch. It wasn't until he reached the shadows beside Carley's house that he unclenched his fists. He felt a stab of pain in his right palm where the spare key had jabbed deep into his skin. He felt the blood recede from his face. His heart rate and breathing returned to normal.

When his fist inserted the key into the lock on the back door it stuck. It was a copy, and hadn't been used much. He pulled it out, put it back in, and jiggled. The lock turned. Jimmy stepped into the kitchen. After the door was closed and locked behind him, he turned to face the short hallway that lead to the front of the double. The smell of roasted chicken hung in the air, fading into the underlying scent of candles, and the slightest hint of perfume. He stood there for a long time in the light of a single florescent bulb left on over the sink. Jimmy closed his eyes and breathed deeply. He listened to the silence, wallowing in anticipation.

The digital clock on the stove had read 9:45 when he had let himself in. A loud hum shook itself from the refrigerator. He flinched, and opened his eyes. Jimmy looked at the clock. It was 10:10. He moved towards the living room, glancing around at the familiar furnishings as he went. Not able to wait any longer, he climbed the stairs, passed the bathroom door, and approached Carley's bedroom. Jimmy's fingers brushed a towel draped over the dresser as he entered. It

173

was still damp. The smell of perfume was stronger here, coiled around the aroma of moist fabric.

Jimmy's knees shook. He crossed to the unmade bed and sat down on its edge. The soft sheets and comforter invited him to stretch out on them. He pressed his face into Carley's pillow. The rest of his body shook. He reached a hand down into the front of his sweat pants.

There was a click. Jimmy froze. He felt his blood crash to his chest as it fled from his extremities, leaving the prick of needles on his skin. His ears strained. Someone had opened the back door. Footsteps tapped on the white linoleum, then disappeared when they reached the carpet of the living room.

Rolling from the bed, Jimmy peeked through the window that looked out over the back yard. Carley's Honda sat in her parking space idling. The parking lights spread an amber glow over the gravel.

"Fuck," he whispered. If he hadn't been so turned on, he might have heard the car pull up.

A creak announced Carley's arrival at the stairs. Jimmy's head snapped back and forth as he looked for a place to hide. There was no time to get out a window, or hide in a different room. The closet was an open cutout in the bedroom wall across from the bed. It didn't have a door, and it sunk about two feet deep, with two foot wings stretching to either side of the opening. He crossed the room in two strides. The left cavity was filled with extra blankets, pillows, and shoe boxes. The right had only an umbrella and an extra curtain rod next to it. Brushing past the clothes, he squeezed himself as best as he could into the tight space.

Carley reached the bathroom. Jimmy could hear the sink faucet come on, water making gulping noises as it found the drain. The water shut off. Maybe she'd just needed to use the sink and whatever she had forgotten was downstairs. Maybe she wouldn't come into the bedroom, or at least not to the closet.

Light flooded the bedroom. Jimmy shut his eyes. He had read somewhere that if you didn't look directly at someone they might not realize you were so close by. There was a sound of clothes rustling. A shadow fell across Jimmy's face as Carley's body blocked the light from the room from where he crouched in the closet. He could feel her next to him as she began picking through the clothes on their hangers. The light taste, almost memory of her fragrance, was replaced by a heady sledgehammer of her perfume and bare skin. It was too much. Jimmy's eyes wrenched themselves open.

Carley stood mere inches from the tip of Jimmy's nose. The bedroom light fell in a halo onto her blond hair. She was shirtless. When he saw her breasts loosely bound in her black lace bra, he gurgled deep in his throat. His hand rose to cover his mouth. For a moment, Jimmy held onto the hope that she wouldn't notice him, that she would select a new top, and leave him undiscovered.

Carley scrunched her lips into a delicate pout as she picked through the hangers. Jimmy didn't know whether it was the sound in his throat, or the movement of his hand that alerted her to his presence. It probably had been a combination of the two. In the end, it didn't matter. What mattered was the look on her face, and the sound of his mother's voice in his head.

"Now you've done it, you filthy boy!" he heard his mother trumpet. "I always knew you'd get into trouble. Just like your father."

For the smallest of moments, Carley's face didn't register anything at all as her eyes met Jimmy's. Then the gravity of what she was seeing washed across her face. It started in her eyes. Those thick eyelashes rose, pulling the lids high. Wide pupils dilated even more until they banished all of the blue from her eyes. The carefully prepared blond hair tossed. Her nostrils flared.

The head toss trickled down through her chest. Her

arms came up. Her hips squared toward him, and then her knees sagged, almost collapsing with shock. Carley's feet writhed while they fought with the decision of whether to fight, or make a run for it.

As Jimmy took all this in, something occurred to him. For the first time in his life he felt...powerful. The terror taking shape on Carley's face and spreading across her body was because of him. Someone actually feared him. His chest filled, blood exploded through his muscles. Adrenalin stabbed at his heart, flooding his veins with a lustful inferno. He saw everything clearer and brighter. Under Carley's perfume he could smell new sweat spring to life along her skin, her hair spray, soap, the leather of her belt, and the musk between her legs.

Carley's lips peeled back as a scream built in her chest. Jimmy burst from the closet. His heavy frame slammed into Carley's tiny one, his hands clamped over her mouth with stunning force. He heard the hiss of air forced from her lungs as one of her high heels gave way and her back struck the floor with Jimmy's weight pressing down upon her.

Jimmy felt Carley's teeth sink into his palm. To avoid being bitten again, his hands slid beneath her chin onto her throat. At first he just wanted to keep her from screaming, but then his grasping fingers severed Carley's lungs from her air supply. Jimmy found that he liked the way her eyes bulged, and the pretty purplish color that spread from his hands up to her hair line as he choked her. He clamped down harder and her body began to writhe beneath him. The sound of her heels stomping up and down was muffled on the carpeted floor. Manicured nails clawed at his fingers as Carley tried to buck him off with her hips. Jimmy got hard again.

White splotches were now splattered across the purple skin of her face. Her mouth gaped and her teeth bit at the air that couldn't reach her lungs. She looked like a goldfish, Jimmy thought. The one he had as a child. He would pull it from the water to watch it twitch and squirm. Heat stained Jimmy's sweats as Carley urinated. It washed across the skin of one of his thighs. He came as Carley's body stilled. Her pupils opened wide, and the sea blue color of her eyes disappeared.

Jimmy was panting like a dog when he rolled off of Carley's limp, lifeless body. He lay staring up at the blank ceiling for a while, and attempted to process what he had done. When his breathing steadied, he rolled over onto his side, propping his head up on one hand. A silky smile grew on his lips. He stared at Carley's face, now blooming with tiny red dots from neck to eyebrows. Her features gazed at him and he could see the whites of her eyes turning crimson. Now she was even more beautiful, he thought.

* * *

The next morning, Jimmy stepped out of the mini-barn and wiped sweat from his face. His hand left muddy smears across his nose and cheeks. A couple houses down he heard a car horn blare. He walked around to the front of the house and glanced across the street. Standing next to a moving truck was a large-breasted girl in a tight t-shirt and shorts with the word PINK stenciled across the ass. She turned. Her long red hair flicked over her shoulder. When she saw Jimmy looking at her, she waved.

© 2011, C.J. Edwards

SEVERANCE
Jim Wilsky

Friday afternoons at Speery Lance Investments' corporate headquarters were typically very slow and this one was no different. By four-thirty that afternoon, the parking lot had only a few scattered cars left and the building was almost empty. The last few diligent workers were finally heading out.

Peeking from the restroom door opposite the elevators, Abbott watched the uniformed guard get up from his desk in the middle of the lobby and walk slowly to the back wall of windows. The view was gorgeous from there, overlooking a large terraced patio and two acres of manicured grounds. He could see that the old man was lost in thought. The guard just stood there staring out at nothing, hands on his hips.

Henry Duggart was one of the few employees at Speery that Abbott had ever really respected. The old man was a loyal worker who had worked for the company for almost thirty years and he was a solid family man who never complained. He was probably thinking about having dodged the inevitable for another week. Abbott knew the man had to be aware that the cutbacks and downsizing were going to get him sooner or later.

"Henry?"

Startled, the old guard turned to Abbott's voice which was right behind him now.

"Henry, look, I don't want to do this but I don't have any choice. Believe me, this isn't about you. Not about you at all." As Chris Abbott was talking, he shrugged off his overcoat and let it drop to the floor. The guard looked at the coat and frowned, his gaze drifting slowly back up to

Abbott's eyes.

"Mr. Abbott? What, but, what're you doing here? Whatcha got there?" Henry asked him and pointed at the long skinny Fed Ex box Abbott was holding.

Abbott smiled at him.

"Mr. Abbott?"

The former Speery exec still said nothing but took the box and set in on the floor, standing it straight up. He took tape off the end, reached in and pulled out a long sword. It reflected the lobby lights off its gleaming blade. It was slightly curved, with a gold and white handle. There were ornate designs at the hilt and on the hand guard, with a braided blue and crimson tassel.

"It's fuckin' beautiful isn't it? It's called a Mameluke. Marine Officers saber, passed down to me from my grandfather." Abbott gazed along its shining length and then smiled over at Henry. Abbott's eyes were burning way too bright, like two little suns.

Henry tore his look away from those terrible eyes and stared at the sword.

"Mr. Abbott, you don't want to be doin' this. Whatever it is you're up to. Y'all put that away and just go on now. Ain't no need for this, jist head to the house." The old man's voice was a whisper and Abbott felt sorry for him. He was just trying to do his job and keep this from getting any more out of hand than it already was.

With his free hand, Abbott pulled out the Beretta from a shoulder holster under his left arm. The barrel of the gun was extended by an expensive suppressor, an added accessory that he had bought only a week ago.

"Not much time for chit chat Henry. I'm sorry, I really am, but I gotta go."

Henry's eyes opened wide and he stepped back slowly. Still smiling pleasantly, Abbott raised the pistol to the security guards waist.

"I saw his Jag in the lot but just to be sure, he's still up

179

there right? The hard-working CEO, waiting until everybody else is gone to make it look good." Abbott's voice had a quivery sound to it. Excited and terrified at the same time. Even he noticed it. It was almost like he was teetering on the edge of a very deep drop. That couldn't be though, his mind's voice told him. Hell, he had already fell off that ledge.

Abbott giggled at the thought and then he laughed out loud. It came out as a short bark.

He'd been told two months ago that the company had decided to go in another direction. "The next level," "a new focus," "changing course" and all the other empty corporate fucking phrases had spewed so naturally out of Bettencourt's chubby little pink mouth. Well today was game, set and match.

"HENRY! Goddammit man, pay attention, I asked you a question!" Abbott was grinning even more now, showing perfect teeth.

The bank of elevators dinged twice and two different doors opened.

The five people walking out of the elevators filed out, not looking back to where Henry and Abbott were. They were only looking ahead, out the front doors, and two days of freedom.

Both men watched this small group of employees head out the front lobby doors.

"Now look here Mr. Abbott, Missus Bettencourt came and picked up her husband. They was headed out to do somethin'. Spur of the moment. 'Bout an hour ago. That's why his car is still out there." The guard's eyes stayed on the sword.

"Henry, I appreciate what you're trying to do. I really do. Now I need you to walk into the men's room over there. Quickly. Do it right now. Just gonna tape you up, I promise, that's all. Gotta keep you quiet for a bit."

"I can't do that. Put the gun down Mr. Abbott. You ain't

no killer." As he had been speaking, the man was reaching slowly for the safety snap on the .45 automatic on his hip. A gun that had never been drawn, let alone fired.

"Well, Henry...as it turns out I think I am."

Just as the guard managed to unsnap the holster, Abbott squeezed off two quick shots, which sounded like loud coughs. The old man fell sideways, hitting a chair and then glancing off a low coffee table on his way down to the floor. He was holding his stomach tightly but he'd also been hit farther up the chest, near the heart. There was a lot of blood on the marble floor already.

Abbott looked down at him for a moment longer. The guard's eyes were staring up at the ceiling and he saw him blink once, then once again more slowly. His bloody hands were now sliding away from his stomach wound.

The sudden buzzing of the lobby desk phone jerked Abbott's attention away from watching the dying man.

He trotted quickly over to the elevators and pushed the up button.

The phone at the guard's desk stopped, and then started again.

Abbott watched intently as the digital numbers above the mirrored doors of the middle elevator kept coming down.

He was sweating heavily now and it was stinging his eyes. He swiped at his face with a sleeve and held the sword pointing down, snug against his right leg.

The elevator dinged.

Swishing doors opened and there stood Hugh Davidson, a senior accounting manager. A mid-level fucker and always would be, but he was also a terrific brownnoser if there ever was one. Davidson was laughing about something with Marcy Gotts, the little queen bitch from human relations.

They both looked at him for only a moment with frozen smiles, then jaws dropped and mouths slowly opened as they recognized him. Davidson saw the long-barreled gun first and he actually pointed at it like the idiot he was.

Abbott put a foot forward and blocked the elevator door.

Davidson blubbered something unintelligible and frantically pushed the button to shut the door anyway. It bumped Abbott's foot and opened again.

"Hey gang, TGIF!" His voice was loud and unhinged. He smiled at them and they both stepped back to the far wall of the elevator.

"Mr. Abbott, I don't know what you think you're doing but you need to leave the premises immediately." Marcy Gotts stuck her chin out and up, evidently deciding this had to be handled firmly. It was HR 101: take control of the situation, simple as that.

"Is that right MARCY?" His voice was just under a shout. The gun swung her way.

"Abbott, please, look, just..." Davidson held a hand up as he finally found his voice. The accounting manager gave Gotts a quick look that said please shut the fuck up Marcy and then glanced back to Abbott.

There was a long silence as they both stared at Abbott. She was just starting to say something again when Abbott decided he had heard enough out of Marcy fucking Gotts. The Beretta reported with that same loud popping sound. The bullet went almost perfectly through her left eye, blew straight out the back of her head and made a clean hole in the elevator wall.

Amazingly, her body stayed upright for a second, as if she'd been somehow nailed to the wall. Abbott thought she looked like some sort of one-eyed zombie right out of a movie, complete with blood streaming down her cheek and a gaping mouth. Finally though, the purse she'd been holding plopped down at her feet. Slowly the body sagged and slid downward, ending up in an almost perfect squatting position, with her head lowered between her knees.

A dark, wet stain had spread quickly down Davidson's pant leg. Apparently the accountant couldn't bear to look at Abbott, so he stared at the floor and squatted down too. His hands were held out in front of him.

The elevator to Abbott's left dinged and he quickly stepped in with Davidson, pushing the seven button once and then again. Just before the doors slid shut, he caught a confused sideways glance and double take from Kevin Portman as he walked by.

Portman, from sales and marketing, wasn't quite sure what he'd just glimpsed in the elevator, but whatever it was, it hadn't looked good. He kept walking toward the front doors, although his walk was a little quicker. He fumbled for his phone and then dropped it twice while trying to dial.

On the way up, Abbott stepped around the crouched body of Gotts, put the long barrel directly on top of Davidson's shaking head and shot straight down. As he passed the fourth floor, Davidson's body was still jerking as he put another round in the accountant's right ear.

He slapped a fresh clip in so he'd be good to go if he needed it. Holstering the Beretta, he looked at his watch. It was 4:51 and he still had plenty of time. Bettencourt never left until at least five thirty on a Friday.

Holding the sword at the ready now, he didn't even notice that the entire floor of the elevator was a shallow pond of blood.

* * *

Richard Bettencourt loosened his tie and stared at the ceiling of the boardroom.

"Is that it then boys and girls? Are we done here?" He was having a conference call with the West Coast division managers on speaker phone.

The phone on the table beeped and Bettencourt looked at Meghan's light blinking.

183

He put her into the conference call purposely, just to make her a little more uncomfortable.

"I said no interruptions, but I suppose we're about done here Meghan, what is it?" His tone was pissy and curt.

"I need you in your office immediately Mr. Bettencourt. It's a personal matter, can you switch to line three please?" Her voice had a little quiver to it.

After making it clear that no, he would not fucking switch to line three, he told her to meet him in his office. Bettencourt signed off with everyone on the conference call. He stood up stiffly and straightened his pants, brushing them off and fussing with the creases. He wondered just what the hell this could be about.

Meghan never spoke in that manner, so he had known immediately that it was probably something serious. Could be business, but it could be his bitch of a wife, his wild ass daughter or the new little slut he'd been seeing lately. It might be any of those, or all of them combined.

He stalked over to the door that connected the boardroom to his private office and opened it up with a rush. Jeannie stood there waiting, nervously clicking her pen.

Her eyes were like saucers and he noticed she was almost looking over his shoulder, not directly at him.

"What the hell is so important Meghan?"

"I'm very sorry about this Mr. Bettencourt. I just, well..." she looked sideways and down. Her hand went to her forehead.

"WHAT, what is it goddammit?"

"Someone needs to talk to you right now."

"So, are we playing twenty fucking questions here or are you going to tell me who?

"A woman named Taylor called for you, Ms. Taylor Breen. She said you had her number and to call her right away, right now, or she was going to do it. No more threats she said, this time she's promising she'll do it."

He looked at his watch.

"It's almost five Meghan, why don't you go on home. I'll make the call and see what this all about." His voice and tone had suddenly changed and he was almost pleasant about it.

He ushered her out of his office, shut the door and sat down slowly in his chair. He really needed time to think this thing out. That stupid little slut, just who the fuck did she think she was?

A moment later, he heard Meghan scream. It was a shrill and awful warble that seemed to go on and on. Then there was nothing. Bettencourt stood shakily and spread both hands on the desk for support. He had no intention of going out there of course, Meghan or no Meghan. Something fell and shattered out in the foyer and he stared at the closed door. There was another scream but this one had no force to it and it ended abruptly.

Ten seconds of stone silence ticked by, then there was three quiet knocks on Bettencourt's door.

"Taylor?" his legs failed him just then and he sat back down hard.

"TAYLOR?"

The door opened and Abbott stuck his head in.

"Ohhh no, it's much worse than that, it's me! Is this a bad time RICKY?"

Bettencourt noticed a thin spray of blood that was misted across Abbott's forehead, nose and cheek. There was a red glob on his chin too, almost ready to drop off.

Frozen in body and mind, Bettencourt had no words.

"Good, won't take a second." Abbott stepped in grinning, almost cordial. He held the dripping sword casually and walked to the big desk. There was a good amount of blood on his shirt as well.

"I only have one quick item on the agenda today — severance packages." He cocked his head then and rolled his eyes upward. "Sirens, Ricky. Hear 'em? Still a long ways off

185

though. Never make it in time."

Bettencourt cleared his throat but couldn't manage to say anything.

"Anyway, I'll be brief. This not my cheap-ass severance package, or even severance packages in general we're talking about. No, I want to specifically detail your severance."

"Now then. Chris. I—now, hold...just a moment here." Bettencourt choked out this meaningless bluster, raising his left hand as a traffic cop might.

"Just a moment here," Abbott giggled. "Oh man, Ricky, that's so perfect, so you."

The horizontal swing was textbook, swift and perfectly delivered. At first, Bettencourt just stared at his left hand without any real comprehension. It had flopped awkwardly over to the very corner of his desk. It fascinated him for a second and he didn't really comprehend what had just happened until he looked at the resulting stump at his wrist. It was pumping blood like a garden hose. His high scream easily eclipsed Meghan's.

After that it got very sloppy. Abbott missed several times. He had to chase, stab and slash quite a bit more than he wanted to. All the while, Bettencourt was crying, pleading and slip sliding around on his own blood. Finally though, the job was done. It was a good thing, too, because Abbott could hear them getting closer and closer.

The first SWAT guys that came in ready to rock and roll, found Abbott with his hands up in the air, sitting at one end of the large conference table. The sword, slathered in red, and the gun lay on the other end. In the middle of the table was a centerpiece that was somehow balanced upright but leaning precariously to the right.

Its mouth was forever puckered in an o shape and the eyes were almost comically frozen wide in shock. It was a little nicked up a bit to be sure. The right ear was missing as was most of the nose, but Abbott was so pleased that it

186

hadn't flopped over yet. That would've ruined the entire effect. Hopefully the forensic guys would get a good shot of it.

THE HONEYMOONERS
Chris Leek

"I know you're in there Earl, open the door you no good bastard!"

Good things might come to those who wait, but trouble always seems to show up right away. I thought I'd ditched Amberly at a truck stop outside of Parker Junction, but here she is pounding on my motel room and shouting up and down the lot. I crawled out of bed and peeked through the drapes. It was barely light, but I could see that she looked pretty pissed. The color of her face was just about a match for that strawberry hair of hers. I must have put 250 miles down since I ran out on the check at that Tasty Freeze and left her preening in the rest room. God knows how she found me way across Arizona, but I'll be dammed if I do.

The old timer who runs this place looked kind of pissed too. He was hitching up his pants and hurrying across the parking lot as fast as his dumpy legs could carry him, which truth be told, wasn't so quick.

"Earl, open up or I'll bust this sucker down."

"Now, now missy what's all this about, I can't have you hollering out here and disturbing all my guests."

The old fella was out of breath, his face all red and puffy from sleep, or whiskey, or maybe both. I wasn't sure who he meant by *all*, as I was the only fool staying in his over-priced flea circus. But I could guess what was coming and couldn't help feeling a little sorry for him.

I've known some hard women in my time, not one of them could stand toe to toe with Amberly.

"Just what in hell does it have to do with your sorry ass what my business is?" she said, her hands firmly planted on her hips. "A big fat nothin' that's what."

The old boy's face was having trouble deciding between shocked, surprised and scared.

"Now, easy there miss, there's no need to be rude, I was just..."

"Miss? Do I look like some damn miss? My name is MRS. Johnson and my cockroach of a husband is holed up in there," she said pointing right at me.

I had the lights off so she couldn't have seen in, but I ducked just the same, call it instinct.

"Well, I'm sorry mi...Mrs. Johnson, but you're mistaken, that there room is taken by Mr. Doggett."

"I don't care if he's calling himself Roy fuckin' Rogers, this here is my Earl's truck," she said thumping the hood of the Silverado I'd left parked outside.

If I'd thought Nancy Drew here was gonna show up again, I would have traded the damn pickup. I should have done it long before now anyway, but I liked the ride, which is the sort of dumb shit that will hang me in the end.

"Alright, alright just take it easy ma'am," he said taking an involuntary step backwards. "I think I'd best go call Gonzo, down at the sheriff's office, he can sort all this out."

"Fine by me," Amberly said, folding her arms and aiming a hard stare at my door.

If some hick deputy runs the plates on that truck he ain't gonna find no Tom Doggett or any Earl Johnson for that matter. If I'm real unlucky he might turn up an Arlo Baker from Amarillo. Arlo had recently passed away, kind of sudden like on account of the bullet hole he had in him. I was only looking for odds on the Rangers over the Padres, but things got a little out of hand and instead I wound up with a rock and a hard place. Neither one is doing me much good.

I took Arlo's old double barrel Ruger from off the dresser and stuffed it under the mattress, kicked his veterinarian's bag in the closet and went to unlock the door.

"What in god's name is all this rumpus?" I said making

out I'd just woke up, which I had, if you thought about it.

"Ah, Mr Doggett, this here woman..."

Amberly shot him a look that would freeze a forest fire.

"I mean to say, this lady, says she's your wife?"

"Hey honey, when did you get in? I didn't hear you knocking guess I was sleeping right deep."

"Having no conscience will let you do that I suspect," she said and pushed past me into the room.

"Sorry if we disturbed you sir," I said giving the old boy my best smile.

"No harm done I suppose," he said running a hand over his balding pate. "But there was just one thing Mr Doggett, that lady there said your name was Johnson?"

"Of course, you'll be needing a little something extra for the double occupancy and all," I said and slipped him a twenty.

"Right, well, much obliged," he said, making the note disappear.

"Goodnight then," I said and shut the door on him, before he thought up any more fool questions.

* * *

Amberly was sat on the bed smoking a cigarette and looking like she had something on her mind.

"You're a piece of crap Earl Johnson, you know that. I ought to bust you in the chops just for half of what you put me through."

"Tough day at the office," I said pouring a shot of Wild Turkey into a chipped jelly glass and handing it to her.

"Don't you be messin' with me right now," she said and snatched the glass.

She emptied it in one swallow then held it out for refill. I cut out the middle man and gave her the bottle. She snatched that too and drained close on a fifth. I should have known that any women who could drink me under the table

190

was going to end up being a righteous pain in the backside. When she finally came up for air, she let me have both barrels.

"I had to hitch all the way down here you son of a bitch. I been sworn at, spat on and felt up. Not to mention propositioned by a one-eyed Mexican truck driver and his skanky girlfriend."

"Now that's a show I'd pay money to watch," I said and immediately wished I hadn't.

"Well fuck you too, is that any way to speak about your own god damn wife, hell we ain't been married but a week."

"Shit Amberly, I keep telling you a Vegas wedding don't count. How many bona fide preachers do you know that dress up like Elvis and make you to promise to love each other tender and don't be cruel?"

"The state of Nevada says it's legal and I got a piece of paper right here that proves it."

She had been beating me over the head with that damn license ever since she got it.

It wasn't like I had any of this planned. It just sort of turned up on my doorstep, like a truck load of poor relations on Thanksgiving.

I'd just got out after a six-month stretch in the Neal County lock up and was wanting nothing more than a long weekend drunk, thought maybe I'd get myself laid too. You know, just to knock the rust off things. Somehow I wound up running for the State line in a stolen pickup with a dead horse-dentist-cum-mob-bookie riding shotgun, and bag full of dirty cash stashed under the seat.

It was while I was trying to put some distance between myself and that gigantic gopher fuck in Amarillo that I run across Amberly, waiting on tables at a gulp 'n' blow diner. The following day had me hung over, tattooed and hitched. I'd figured of the three, the tattoo would be the only one I couldn't shake off.

"Amberly, look I ain't the marrying sort, what with the

191

job keeping me travelling an' all."

"You ain't no equine dentist either; you're a lying no good."

"Sure I am, you want for me to give your eaters a quick polish up?"

"You callin' me a horse now on top of it all?" she said and started blubbing.

"Aw Christ, don't start that; look I'm sorry alright."

"You never even got me no ring," she said, puffing smoke and sniffing.

"I'll go fix that, first thing."

"You mean it?"

"Sure I do, now why don't you go freshen up and I'll get us some ice to rattle in that Turkey."

Amberly looked up at me with those big ole blue eyes and wiped her nose on the cuff of her jacket. She might be tougher than a two-dollar steak and part fuckin' blood hound to boot, but she ain't so bad once you get past the rough edge of her, and besides the TV set in my room was broke.

I waited until I could hear the shower running before picking up the ice bucket and taking a look outside. It was real quiet. I scanned the highway both ways, but nothing was moving on it. I slipped out and walked over to the ice machine. The sky was glowing pink with the sun getting ready to break. It was already pushing seventy and you didn't need to hear the weatherman on KPLX to know it would be another damn hot one. I leaned up against a rusted out vending machine by the motel office and lit up a smoke.

"That's right, Texas plates...Well if it's on your way; I'd sure appreciate it..."

I caught one half of the old boy's phone call through the open window and I could guess the rest. Seemed twenty bucks didn't buy you jack in this dust hole.

I hustled back to the room and found Amberly wrapped in the only towel, drying her hair with my best shirt.

"Get dressed, we gotta go."

"Are you crazy? I just got here," she said around the cigarette clamped in her lips.

"Amberly I ain't foolin' that old coot has sent the law coming down here."

"So?"

"So, if you don't want your new husband doin' five to ten, then quit dragging your ass."

"Just what the hell are you tryin' to say Earl?"

"Look, I'll make it real simple for you, either we leave now or I'm likely sunk. The why ain't important."

"That dog won't hunt Earl, you best tell me what this is all about or I'm fixing to stay right here," she said flicking her ash on the floor and staring at me, all expectant like.

"Fuck, okay, I give. Go fetch me that veterinary's satchel from out the closet."

"What you plan on fixing up the Sheriff's teeth for him?"

I could have happily gone to work on that smart mouth of hers right then. The look on my face must have told her as much, 'cause she stopped running it and went to get the bag.

"Here," she said holding it out.

"Go on then, open it."

She sat down with it on her lap, fiddled at the clasp and peered inside.

"Well fuck me with a hat on."

"Kind of a game changer ain't it?"

"Is them all hundreds?"

I nodded. "That work for you?"

"Sugar, I reckon it'll do," she said and started hunting for her panties.

Amberly was hopping around the room pulling on her shoes and cussing. I was sat out front waiting in the truck when I remembered the shotgun. That Ruger had a barrel crooked as the number seven and was neither use nor ornament. Hell, it was older than I was and should have been with Arlo at the bottom of Santa Rosa Lake, either that or in a damn museum. Like I said, it's the dumb shit that does for me.

"Okay, I'm ready," Amberly said, climbing in the truck.

I jumped out and went to fetch the gun.

"What, we stayin' now?" she called after me.

I got back behind the wheel and seeing as I had stolen the only pick up in Texas without a gun rack, I slid the Ruger down the back of the seat.

"I ain't even gonna ask about that," Amberly said, folding her arms.

"That'll work just fine," I said.

We swung past the office and the old boy came to the door to stare after us. I flipped him off and was enjoying watching his jaw drop as I rolled out on the highway

"Shit Earl!"

I snapped my head around and saw a northbound semi bearing down on us. I mashed the gas pedal and stripped some rubber. The truck driver laid on the horn and locked up his brakes. His box trailer started to fold like jack knife and tried to overtake him. I ain't exactly sure what happened after that.

* * *

I came around sometime later chewing on the steering wheel and breathing in gasoline fumes. Blood was running down my forehead and messing up my last clean shirt. I looked around for Amberly, but the passenger seat was empty and somehow downhill. It took me a moment to realize the Silverado was sitting ass first in a drainage ditch.

"Hey you, you alive in there?"

"I can't swear to it," I said peering through the crazed windshield.

I could just make out a metal name tag called Gonzalez and another badge that read Maricopa County Sheriff's Department. There was a pretty good chance they had a lawman pinned to the back of them.

"Get your hands up where I can see 'em and your ass out of the truck," Gonzalez said, pointing his fancy plastic pistol at me.

"Well, which is it to be, officer?"

"What?"

"I can either get my hands up or I can open the door. I can't do both."

"You best get one up then, and don't go trying nothing funny with the other."

"I wasn't figuring on playing with myself, if that's what you mean," I said

"Just get out the damn truck," he said.

I tried the handle, but the door seemed wedged. I leaned back and gave it my shoulder. The damn thing popped real easy and I tumbled out head first into the ditch.

The long arm of the law grabbed hold of my collar and dragged me up the side of the wash.

Gonzalez shoved me over on the hood of his cruiser and cuffed my hands behind me, just like you see them do in the movies.

"You carrying anything you don't want to be arrested with?" he asked patting me down.

"You mind me askin' exactly what I'm being arrested for."

"I ain't figured that out yet, let's just say I don't much care for the look of you."

"Ok so I ain't nobody's bargain, but if ugly is a crime we're both in trouble."

"Listen you smart mouth bastard, I've got a dead truck driver, a dead motel clerk and then," he paused and spat a gob of tobacco juice. "I got you."

I looked across the highway and saw what was left of the rig. It was sat on flats amongst a pile of cinder block and roof tile which until recently had been the motel office. Well that meant my lousy driving would pass unnoticed, but when Gonzo here got to running the truck tags he'd have more than tobacco to chew on.

Just then there was a squeal of anguished metal followed by a volley of cursing. I had been wondering where Amberly had got to.

"Who else is in that truck with you?"

"I don't rightly recall."

He put his hand around my neck and bounced my head off the hood.

"Stay put and don't do nothing dumb," he said and vanished into the culvert with his hand hovering over his holster like a nervous gunfighter.

I leaned over on the cruiser, bleeding again and trying to think up something that might explain a stolen truck and a fuck load of dubious greenbacks.

Gonzalez wasn't gone long. He appeared from behind the pickup with his hands in the air and a surprised look on his face. Amberly came up behind him holding the Ruger out in front of her like a kid with a stick hunting for a Piñata.

"Jesus Amberly, what in hell are you doin'?"

"Damn it Earl, don't you go givin' my name to no lawman, you wanna write down my address for him too while you're about it?"

"You don't got an address."

"That ain't the point," she said, keeping a bead drawn on Gonzalez. "Now mister, I don't want to shoot you and you don't want to be dead," she told him, cocking the hammer.

"Easy there lady, that old burner has a kink in it big enough to shoot round corners. If you get to yanking that trigger you're gonna blow us all to hell an' gone."

I couldn't recall if that thing was even loaded, but he was likely right about the result if it was.

"Well don't just stand there Earl, go an' get a hold of his pistola," Amberly said, ignoring Gonzo.

By now I was getting the hang of married life, so I did

196

what I was told and started fumbling behind my back for his Glock.

Gonzalez wasn't about to let himself get bushwhacked by an auto wreck in handcuffs and a brick-top crazy with a bent up side-by-side. I don't suppose that kind of thing would make for good reading in his report. He snatched at the pistol and bought it around to aim at Amberly.

Self-preservation being one of my stronger suits, I dived for cover under the car.

But it turns out Amberly is no slouch in that department either, without missing a beat she swung the Ruger around and cold cocked him on the side of the head. Gonzalez stood dribbling tobacco juice and swaying uncertainly for a moment before folding like fresh laundry.

"I guess that's done it now," I said, struggling to sit up.

"Would you rather I let him arrest your no good ass?"

"No, no, I suppose I wouldn't."

"Well shut your pie hole then," she said and heaved the shotgun into the ditch.

"How's about you come get these cuffs off me."

"Hold your damn horses."

Stuffing the Glock in her jacket, she started rifling through old Gonzo's pockets. I'd lay odds this wasn't the first unconscious body she'd checked for loose change.

Amberly pulled out his key chain out and jingled it at me. I shuffled over on my backside and held my arms out behind me. I could feel her trying a few keys before she found the right one and my hand came free. I started to get up and she yanked on the cuffs, sitting me back down again.

"Park it Earl." She ratcheted the empty bracket around the limp wrist of Gonzalez.

"God dammit Amberly," I started, but she had already disappeared down into the wash swinging the keys around on her finger.

"Amberly quit foolin' and get me loose."

She came back with Arlo's money bag and a big smile on

197

her face that I didn't much care for.

"You know Earl, I've been thinking, how about if I keep this," she said patting the bag, "you can forget about getting me that ring."

"Just what the hell are you talking about woman?"

"I guess I ain't the marryin' kind either sugar," she said and popped me a kiss.

Without another word she tossed Arlo's bag into the police cruiser and jumped in beside it.

"Amberly, you lousy..."

The rest of my words were swallowed up by the roar of a V8 as my nearest and dearest fishtailed down the shoulder with the parking brake still set and the rear tires smoking.

I sat in the dirt, watching the Crown Vic's taillights until they shimmered out in the haze. I tugged on the cuffs and Gonzalez groaned beside me. Pretending like we were married, I leaned over and punched him hard on the jaw.

DONALD DUCK AND THE AVIAN SNITCH
Richard Godwin

"I'm telling you she's got a parrot stuck up her arse," Micky said.

Jo-Jo stirred his coffee.

"What the fuck are you talking about?"

"I'm saying Nancy has always liked birds, right? I managed to get her to shave it down to two fucking birds, two parrots to be exact, and one of them has gone missing."

"So you assume, as we all would, that it's living up your wife's arse."

Egg dripped from Micky's fork as he waved it at Jo-Jo.

"Every time she bends over she makes a sound."

"Must be all them beans. Are you going to eat that?"

Jo-Jo made a move for Micky's sausage, which sat in a pool of grease on his plate.

"Get out of it, you fucker."

He stabbed at Jo-Jo's hand with his knife.

"I tell you Micky, ever since you did those drugs you've been talking shit, absolute fucking shit. You sit there letting your food get cold, you spray me with egg, you need to sort yourself out mate."

"Nancy's the only one I need to sort out. I ain't joking, we went shopping the other day. She was getting some tins off the shelf in the supermarket and as she bent over I heard this noise."

"Sound like a fart?"

"No, it sounded like a groan, an erotic one."

"An erotic groan?"

"Aw, ooooh."

"You winding me up?"

"And why would I do that me old son? Partner in fucking crime, right?"

Micky shook his head, and squirted tomato ketchup all over the remainder of his food, chewing ravenously.

"There was a case of a woman in Alabama," he said, "who liked a bit of anal. Her husband said she had capacity."

"Capacity?"

"He lost a tool box up there. She used to sing gospel you know. Well, she got excommunicated from the church because her parrot kept singing 'fuck all y'all' in the middle of the chorus."

"She probably had Tourettes."

"No she fucking didn't. She farted feathers. They found a spanner up her when she died. And you know what she died of?"

"Bullshit?"

"Myxo-ma-fucking-tosis me old son."

"That's what rabbits get."

"Who fucking cares? You might think I'm talking bollocks, but I know there's something up Nancy's arse."

Jo-Jo leant forward.

"Stop taking drugs, Micky."

"Don't you lecture me, sitting there with a fucking ton of metal in your gob. All those piercings, you could get infected."

"Some women like them, I got one on my knob."

"So I heard."

"What about you?"

"What about me?"

"You go around with you head shaved wearing a week's stubble, you think that looks sharp?"

"You could be damaged by your own jewelry."

"Are we gonna do this fucking job or what?"

"Yeah."

200

There was mischief dancing in Micky's eyes as they paid for their lunch. Then they left the cafe, stepping out into the debris strewn street.

* * *

"Now, he's on his own, so we're in and out quicker than a whore's snatch," Micky said, when they got to the small post office a few streets away.

"I know the score."

They put on their masks.

The man behind the counter didn't look up as they walked in. He didn't hear Micky lock the door. He only let out a small gasp when he put his paper down and saw two men with guns dressed as Donald Duck standing in front of him.

"Give us the money and you won't get hurt," Micky said.

They waited until he opened the back door and then Jo-Jo went into the office where he stacked the bundles of cash into the holdall.

"Easy," he said.

As he was leaving he saw the old man's finger hesitate on the panic button and he smashed him across the head with the butt of his gun.

They ran from the shop. They removed their masks in a back alley, dumping them in a dustbin.

"You know what I'm going to spend this on?" Micky said. "I'm going to drug Nancy and stick an endoscope up her arse."

Jo-Jo tapped his temple.

"You're sick in the fucking head, mate."

* * *

Nancy was sleeping when Micky got home. He stood in

201

the living room as evening fell outside the window, and opened a tin of Boddingtons.

A parrot stood on one leg in a cage staring at him.

"We did the job and I'm loaded, me old son," Micky said.

"Up yer arse," the parrot said.

"Jo-Jo is..."

"A fucking cunt."

The squawks and obscenities roused Nancy, and she came downstairs.

"Micky, are you teaching Freddy to swear?"

Her negligee was open at the front, and Micky ran his eyes down her body.

"Fancy a quickie, Nance?"

"I've got to do my night shift."

"Come on, let me give your arse a slap."

"Charming."

"You're not hiding something up there are you?"

"Like what?"

"What happened to Sammy?"

"I told you, he flew out the window the other day. Have you seen him?"

"I've heard him."

"Where?"

"Every time you bend over."

She went upstairs to dress while Micky opened another beer and made faces at Freddy.

"Oooh I like a cock ring," Freddy said.

* * *

As Micky got drunk, Nancy was straddling Jo-Jo in her stilettos. He was lying on his kitchen floor as she lowered herself onto his cock and licked her lips.

"I love your metal. This one rubs my clit just right, you naughty man," she said, chuckling.

202

"You ain't half got the best arse, Nancy."

She pounded his cock until she collapsed on top of him and dripped two drops of sweat onto his eyebrow piercing.

Afterwards, as she dressed, Jo-Jo said, "Micky said anything weird?"

"Like what?"

"I'm worried about him."

"Have you two been up to mischief again? I don't want him going back inside."

"No, we've been as good as gold."

"So why are you worried? He don't suspect nothing."

"He was saying some weird things about parrots."

"My Sammy's disappeared."

"He says he thinks it's up your, you know."

"My what?"

"Your backside."

"He's mucking around."

"No. I think he might hurt you Nancy, I'm serious, he had this look in his eyes, wanted to stick something up there."

"He'd never."

"Watch him," Jo-Jo said.

* * *

That night Nancy woke to find Micky peering up her nightdress with a Maglite.

She kicked out and knocked him onto the floor. He lay there with the beam of light pointing at the ceiling as she stood up.

"What the bleeding hell do you think you're doing?"

"I want to look at your arse."

"Go back to sleep, Micky."

"Show me your arse," he said, getting to his feet.

"What do you want to put up there?"

"Who said anything about that?"

She looked away, and Micky grabbed her arm. Nancy slammed her first into the side of his head and kicked him in the groin.

"You're sleeping on the sofa tonight."

"I knew I was right," Micky said, as he stumbled down the darkened staircase.

* * *

He was woken early by the sound of Freddy saying, "This one rubs my clit just right."

He was standing outside Jo-Jo's flat when Nancy got into the shower.

Micky kept his finger on the bell until Jo-Jo opened it, then he smashed him in the face, knocking him backwards into the hall.

"You fucking slag, you've been shagging Nancy."

"I said you were fucking mental."

"You told her about the endoscope."

"Bollocks."

As Jo-Jo got up, Micky grabbed his nose piercing, ripping through his septum.

"The parrot's grassed you up."

He slammed Jo-Jo's head repeatedly into the wall until he wasn't moving.

He went to his lock up on the way home. He fed Sammy and cleaned his cage, then took two pictures of him on his mobile.

Nancy was in the kitchen when he got in.

"I got something to show you, Nance," he said.

Her eyes were brimming with tears as she stared at Sammy.

"Where is he, Micky?"

"He's safe, but if you want to see him again I want you to do two things."

"Are you blackmailing me?"

"Yes. Stop shagging Jo-Jo and tell the cops I was with you yesterday afternoon, all afternoon, we were having sex."

"Are you mad? Me and Jo-Jo."

"He's admitted it. Jo-Jo's not the sharpest tool in the box, I tell him I think there's a parrot up your arse and he tells you."

Nancy hung her head.

"It was only a fling, Micky. I was angry because you went inside."

"You're my alibi, Nancy."

"You won't hurt Sammy will you?"

"Not if you do as I ask."

* * *

Micky had already made the call, given the local police the tip off. It wasn't the first robbery Jo-Jo had committed, he'd carried out a spate of them in the previous weeks. When Nancy was fucking Jo-Jo, Micky went back to the alley and got Jo-Jo's Donald Duck mask. He stuffed it under his sofa when he left him lying in the hallway.

Jo-Jo found himself arrested later that day and immediately grassed Micky up. But when the cops visited him, Nancy stood firm by her alibi.

Micky returned Sammy to Nancy who cosseted him as Micky got drunk.

"I swear those birds are the only things you care about," he said.

It wasn't long before she realised that Sammy wasn't well. She took him to the vet and returned teary eyed.

"He's got psittacosis, Micky," she said. "They've given him shots."

"That'll sort him, Nancy."

Micky had himself vaccinated a few days before.

That night as Nancy slept, he put on some gloves and rubbed dried parrot droppings from Sammy's cage into

Nancy's mouth.

SLAY RIDE
Mark Joseph Kiewlak

She was tied up on the seat next to me. Her legs were handcuffed. The car was moving fast. I think her name was Lily.

"Don't be afraid, Lily," I said. "I won't let them hurt you."

One of them smirked. The one on the passenger side. Outside, scenery flew past. Trees. Rocks. We were in the mountains.

"Don't go getting all heroic," the driver said to me. He was short and had all the cuddly warmth of a fireplug. He was smoking an unfiltered cigarette.

I struggled against the cuffs. Another layer of skin got peeled off my wrists.

"Ho ho ho," the passenger said. He was big all around. His head nearly touched the roof. He was wearing a pea green jacket that he couldn't have zipped up if he wanted to.

"What are you," I said, "the fucking potbellied giant?"

"Watch your language," the driver said. "There's a kid present."

I looked over at her. She must have been all of eight. Her wrists were so small they'd tied her up with phone cord. Me, they used handcuffs. Rope on my ankles. Smaller cuffs on hers. No sense to it. No rhyme or reason. About what I'd expect from a pair like this.

"Where we're heading," I said, "my language is the least of her problems."

Potbelly half-turned in his seat. "You think you know where we're heading, smartass?"

"Can't be anywhere good," I said.

More scenery rolled past. My ears popped. We were

207

heading downhill now. It was starting to snow.

"You guys got the money," I said. "Why not let the girl go?"

"What do you think, we're fucking stupid?" Potbelly said. "We let the girl go she'll tell on us."

"Look at her," I said. "She's terrorized. She's in shock. She's not going to remember any of this."

"They got sketch artists. They got hypnotists," Potbelly said. "She'll tell."

"You're not worth a hypnotist," I said.

The girl still hadn't moved. She didn't struggle. She didn't even look scared. I leaned over and narrowed my focus to just the two of us. "I got hired to find you," I said. "To protect you. And to bring you home. I'm going to do all of those things. You just don't be scared, okay?"

Her expression was blank. She had no coat but she wasn't shivering. Her Mickey Mouse sweatshirt was a little ragged around the edges.

"If you kill her," I said, "they'll never stop looking for you. If you let her go, all they lose is money. They won't be as interested in finding you."

"They'll be interested," Fireplug said.

"They've got all the money in the world," I said. "But only one daughter."

"We can't let her go," Potbelly said. "Not now."

I looked at Lily. There was a tear running down her cheek. She didn't seem to notice. I looked again. Her sweatshirt was way too big for her. Her pants were too short. Her socks didn't match. They weren't her clothes.

"You fucking scum," I said. "What did you do?"

Nobody in the front said anything. The air got thick.

"You fucking scum, answer me."

Potbelly was turned away. Fireplug held the wheel with both hands. "We can't let her go," he said quietly.

"Fuck you," I said. "Fuck the both of you bastards. I'm going to fucking kill the both of you."

No one else said anything. The snowfall was increasing. The car was picking up speed. All I could see was red. It's not that I never ran into this before. But you never get used to it. If you get used to it you're a monster.

I slammed myself against the door. It wouldn't open. I fumbled behind my back to grab the latch. There wasn't any.

"This used to be a cop car," Potbelly said. "Those doors only open from the outside."

"Shut your fucking mouth, you fucking pervert," I said.

The girl hadn't moved during any of this. The road was all hairpins and narrow. We skidded more with each turn.

"You don't care, do you?" I said. I addressed myself to the driver, Fireplug. "You don't care what happens to us. To any of us. You don't care if we crash."

"What are you talking about?" Potbelly said.

"He feels guilty," I said. "That's why we're out here in the worst possible weather on the worst possible road. You could've shot us and dumped us anywhere. Even that warehouse where I found you. This is something different. Your buddy wants us all to die."

Potbelly looked unsure of himself. He gazed at his partner. Fireplug kept his eyes on the road.

"That true?" Potbelly said. "You trying to kill us?"

No answer.

"You trying to kill us 'cause we messed with that girl?"

No answer.

"Just 'cause we messed with one lousy little piece of rich white ass? You trying to kill us for that?"

The car skidded heavily into a turn. My stomach dropped out. We sideswiped the guardrail a bit before he got it back under control.

"Stop the fuckin' car," Potbelly said. "Slow us the fuck down and stop the fucking car."

I moved as close to Lily as I could. I reached behind and got hold of her wrists. I started working to tear loose the phone cord.

"We shouldn't have done it," Fireplug said.

"Stop the fucking car," Potbelly said.

"We shouldn't have done that to her."

Potbelly had a gun out. It was pointed at his partner.

"Don't make me shoot you, Lonnie. I don't wanna fucking shoot you."

The car slowed down a bit. I had Lily's arms free. She didn't try to move them. I needed her attention but she was blank. Just blank.

"What's wrong with you, man," Potbelly said to his partner. "It was just fun. It was just a little fucking entertainment to pass the time. Christ."

The car was almost at a stop. Outside was nothing but swirling white. A few bare tree trunks told me we were still on the mountain.

Lonnie the Fireplug put it in park and turned to his partner. "Put the gun away, Francis."

"I can't," Potbelly said. "I can't trust you no more."

"Put the gun away right fucking now."

The larger man, Francis, did as he was told. I tried to get Lily's attention on my ankles. On the rope that was keeping them tied. She wasn't looking. At anything.

"Now get out of the car," Fireplug said.

"Here?" Potbelly said. "We're gonna do them here? Right on the side of the road?"

"Get out of the car," Fireplug said.

Potbelly opened his door. Both men got out. An arctic blast of air swept through the car. Lily didn't react to it at all.

"Now get them out," Fireplug said.

Potbelly opened the door on Lily's side. When he took her by the arm he noticed her hands were loose. He didn't seem to care. And she had no reaction to his touch.

"You fucking twisted scumbag," I said. "You fucked her up good, didn't you?"

"Get him out too," Fireplug said.

Francis the Potbellied Giant took out his gun and

pointed it at me. "Slide out of there," he said.

I climbed out of the car and stood in front of Lily, shielding her between myself and the car. We were all on the same side with the car between us and the road. Over Fireplug's shoulder, I could see the shiny gray guardrail and how the land dropped away from that point.

"Give me your gun," Fireplug said to his partner.

"My gun? What the fuck's the matter with your gun?"

I felt something at my ankles and looked down. It was Lily. She was trying to untie the rope.

"Just give me your gun, Francis."

"I don't trust you, Lonnie."

"Give me the gun."

"I don't trust you no more."

The wind was whipping flakes into my face. I could barely keep my eyes open. My cheeks were numb.

"Francis."

"What, Lonnie? Fucking what?"

"The gun."

Francis the Potbellied Giant reached over and handed his gun to his partner. Fireplug took the gun and shot Potbelly six times in the chest. The sound of the shots seemed to echo forever on the deserted mountaintop. Potbelly landed on his back near the guardrail. He wasn't moving. Fireplug still had his back turned to us. Lily had loosened the rope enough so that I could kick one leg free. I charged at Fireplug through the snow with my head down and my hands still cuffed behind me. I hit him at full stride with my shoulder just as he was turning. The force of the impact drove him backward toward the guardrail. I kept pushing with my shoulder and he stumbled backward over the railing taking me with him. I hit the snow and slid on my back, picking up speed until I slammed headfirst into a tree and caught myself on one of its broken branches.

I tried to catch my breath. I looked for Lonnie the Fireplug. There was nothing but a deep groove and a trail of broken branches disappearing out of sight down the mountainside.

I turned over on my back. My hands were still cuffed. I began very slowly to push myself upwards, digging my sneakers into the snow as best I could, steering toward tree trunks and upturned roots whenever I could. My hands were useless and numb. My wrists were scraped raw.

It took a long time. When I reached the guardrail I saw that Lily was still standing by the car right where I had left her. Francis the Potbellied Giant was dead. The snow had turned red all around him. I crawled over to his body and ordered my hands to search his pockets for the key to the handcuffs. I couldn't feel the key but I saw that I was holding it. I dropped it once. Then again. It disappeared in the snow and I started to lose consciousness. Then Lily was there beside me. She took the key and unlocked the cuffs. I looked down at her ankles. They were bleeding from where the cuffs had scraped her. I searched Potbelly's pockets again but I couldn't find the key to her ankle cuffs. I got to my knees. Then to a wobbly stance. I lifted her in my arms without feeling it and carried her toward the car. It was still running and warm inside. I got the door open and tried to place her down on the front seat. She wouldn't let go of me.

"Home," she said.

I got in the passenger side and pulled the door shut behind us. I turned the heat on full blast and held her to me until feeling returned to my body.

"That's right, Lily," I said. "I'm taking you home."

2011, Mark Joseph Kiewlak

CRIMINAL LOVE
Mike Monson

"And what kind of work do you do?" I asked this asshole, knowing full well he was a worthless piece of shit who lived off of his wife's full-time wages.

Dude scowled at me and looked over at his sweet hot Connie, rolling his eyes. We were all together at a table at the White Hawk Bar in the Super Wal-Mart Shopping Center in North Modesto.

"Hey," he said, "I ain't no career man like you with your suit and shit."

Suit? I had on Ross Dress for Less cheap-ass off-brand khaki pants, a raggedly button down navy shirt and a decrepit blue blazer I'd gotten from an oxygen-tank-hugging dying man at a garage sale. How the fuck is that a suit?

This guy with his Harley t-shirt, black jeans, motorcycle boots and huge gut was dumber than I thought. Jesus, what did he think I was, some kind of an executive or something because I wore a blazer with gold-colored buttons?

The truth was that I was making just over minimum wage and was completely broke — but tonight all that was going to change.

"So what do you do then," I asked, "for money? How do you make a living, support your household?"

"Dwayne builds custom bikes," Connie told me. "Like on American Chopper."

She looked at Dwayne with raised eyebrows, almost like she was trying to put him on the spot, challenging him to answer my questions. Dwayne looked away. I could tell that I was getting freezed-out. Assholes like this, if they feel disrespected or challenged, they pretend you don't exist, even if it is you buying the beer and whiskey. It's a talent.

"Oh really," I said. "Can I see one? Do you have pics on a website, or in your phone?"

Dwayne ignored me. He had no idea I'd been fucking his wife for months and that I already knew all about him.

American Chopper? What bullshit. *His* reality show would be called American Jailbird. Dwayne liked to put on a front of being some kind of chopper-building biker-criminal, like a cross between Jesse James and Sonny Barger. But he never made any money of his own and spent all of Connie's salary on drugs and liquor for himself and his friends. He didn't own any tools as far as I knew and had never even owned a bike; their only vehicle was Connie's ten-year-old Toyota Tercel.

"So, Cal, are you going to be able to help us out?" Connie asked.

"I dunno," I said, "that depends. Do you have the cash?"

Connie brought her purse from her lap to the table top.

God she was good-looking: deep brown skin, long wavy black hair, stunning bright blue eyes.

"You really got it?" I asked Connie, "All twenty grand?"

She nodded and gave me that sweet smile that melted me.

"Okay," I said, "I'll make the call."

Connie had taken her feet out of her sexy high heel shoes and was running her toes up and down my leg. I loved this but hoped Dwayne couldn't see what was going on under the table—I didn't want us to do anything to tip him off too soon.

Dwayne knew that Connie and I had met while I was a temp at the insurance company where she worked as a secretary. They put her in charge of me when I was called in to help with one of her bosses' tedious filing projects. For me, it was love at first sight. For Connie it took a while, but I eventually wore her down.

Soon we were at each other constantly — in our cars, in my apartment at lunch, in the freaking supply closet. In between, she gradually told me all about Dwayne: the beatings, the frequent jail time for offenses like possession, public intoxication, making criminal threats, the occasional assault — all the low life petty shit.

I dialed the number. "Amos, it's on."

...

Connie had recently gotten a nice little inheritance from her aunt. She somehow managed to convince Dwayne to not blow it all right away, telling him that her friend at work had some huge drug connection that could turn their twenty grand into one hundred (right, like *that* was going to happen). At first he'd threatened to beat Connie for even having a male friend at work but the hope of large amounts of ill-gotten dollars calmed him down.

"Okay," I said. "You guys follow me."

I got in my old Honda Civic. Connie drove the Tercel. I took them out of town about ten miles into the thick of the vineyards and almond orchards, where old farm and ranch houses lie far from the eyes and ears of neighbors or random passersby.

We pulled into Amos's long dirt driveway. I reached under my seat for the Smith & Wesson 38 and put it into the right pocket of my blazer. Amos had given it to me recently and had taught me how to use it.

It was dark by now — pitch black the way it gets out in the country away from the lights of town. There were no stars.

Amos's huge ranch house was lit up. I could see his brand-new Mercedes S65 AMG sedan and his fully restored 1958 Corvette parked by the side. Amos, all in black and looking badass, was standing on his porch, with his arms crossed, a Glock 31 in his waistband.

I think Dwayne was impressed. This was certainly looking like a big-time drug deal — especially when he saw the suitcase on the dining room table. It was open and stuffed with dozens of little clear plastic bags, each full of white powder. The powder was actually baking soda—but Dwayne would never know that.

"Wow," Dwayne blubbered, staring at the suitcase. He looked at Amos. "Are you Amos Frane?"

Amos just stared at him like he was inspecting an insect he was about to crush with his boot.

"Fuck, I've heard a lot about you, man," Dwayne said, "I sure appreciate this opportunity."

"Shut up," Amos said. "Both of you sit down and show me the money."

They sat and Connie pulled a paper bag from her purse and emptied it out onto the table. It looked like twenty grand to me. I grabbed my gun, cocked it and put the barrel on the back of Dwayne's head.

"Sorry, Dwayne," I said. "I'm afraid you were misled. This ain't no drug deal. It's a hit. And you're the target."

Amos pulled his piece and aimed it at Dwayne's face.

"What the fuck!" he screamed and looked over at Connie. His wife stared back at him with cold eyes. Man, I was so in love.

"She can't help you, you piece of shit," I said. "It was all her idea."

I pulled the trigger. Dwayne fell forward onto the table. Connie moved fast to pull the money away from the stream of blood that was quickly oozing out of her husband's head.

This was all good. Amos was my uncle and he was an extremely successful criminal: contract killings, home invasions, various acts of extortion. I'd idolized him all my life and I'd been begging him to let me to join up with him and his crew for years. He'd always put me off, saying he didn't think I had the "proper commitment."

I was pretty sure that bringing him twenty grand and proving I had the guts to pull a trigger was ample proof of my commitment.

"Now the bitch," Amos said.

I hadn't expected this. I looked at Amos. He nodded toward Connie. "Do it."

"Cal?" Connie said. She was shaking, crying.

I didn't move.

"You didn't think we could let her live, did you?" Amos asked me. "She is a loose end to this deal and you know that I do not allow loose ends. You kill her now and we keep this thing within the family the way I like it."

I couldn't think straight. This was not what I had had in mind.

"You do it or I will," Amos said, pointing his Glock at Connie. "And if I have to do it it'll make me rethink the power of your commitment, if you know what I mean."

I looked at Connie. She was terrified — and so lovely.

I started to raise the .38; my hand wavering, unsteady.

"You said you wanted to be a badass criminal, nephew," Amos said. "Prove it. Now."

"Please, no!" Connie was getting hysterical.

I guess I'd waited too long. Amos squinted his eyes at Connie and took aim.

Connie screamed, and that's when I shot him. Amos had taught me well, the bullet struck his heart. Once he was down, I shot him again, in the head.

I was confident no one had heard anything. I went to Connie and hugged her tight. We made love right there on the floor next to the bodies and the money and the blood. There was no stopping us.

The child we conceived that night is now ten years old. He is a boy and Connie and I spoil him rotten. The three of us live in Amos' house — you could say we are prospering.

Cal Frane has become a respected name among certain people not just in Modesto, but all over the Central Valley and much of the rest of California. I'm especially well known for being a vicious, cold killer and for the fact that I never allow loose ends.

I like to keep things in the family.

PERFECT CHAOS
Tyler M. Mathis

I'm sitting in my car, staring at the bank, a weathered stone fortress that conveys an aura of impregnable security. The granite is merely a façade, however, and the security entirely passive: a battery of cameras jutting from the walls, a silent alarm, and six employees—four tellers and two loan officers—instructed never to play the hero.

I should really get back to work. I'm already five minutes late and the gym is over the bridge, out toward the suburbs, but I'm rooted to the spot. There has to be a way...you hear about guys pulling off clean bank jobs all the time...

"Hey hey, pardner!" the bum shouts at me through my open window. I call him Wolfman Jack, because that's who he sounds like. "Lemme spritz up dat winshield fo' ya!"

I motion him away, but he spritzes up my windshield anyway, just like he did the last two times I was down here, leaving behind a filmy residue that can only be removed in a car wash. Wolfman Jack is down on his luck, and I tipped him for his services before, but not today. Hell no. Enough is enough.

"Man, fuck you, big man!" the Wolfman says to me. I twiddle my fingers at him, his cue to go find another windshield in need of spritzing.

The perfect bank job, I'm thinking, sitting here. I'll need a disguise, as I'm bound to be caught on camera. Witnesses are inevitable; I need a plan to control them. But the main consideration is *time*—the more I have, the more cash I can heist from the vault. And the only way I can buy time is to keep the cops away from the scene. But how?

And it hits me, like a piano plummeting out of a cartoon

sky...

* * *

"It starts with one of the oldest tricks in the book," I say to them. "You cause a diversion, something so big that every cop in the city has to respond."

Anvil takes a long drag off his butt, and abruptly crushes it out in the plastic ashtray. He hasn't changed much since jail, except for a couple of new tattoos, his ham-like arms now completely covered with various incarnations of swastikas, confederate flags, and images of death to all non-whites. Personally, I never bought the master race bullshit espoused by Anvil and his white supremacist brothers in the slammer. Ours was a relationship built on service, and survival. You might think a guy as big as I am — six-four, two-forty — would be left alone in jail, but the opposite is true. To take down someone my size was to earn respect. Aligning with the Aryan Brotherhood kept the wannabe tough guys from fucking with me. In return for their protection, I was occasionally called on to beat someone into complying with the Brotherhood's directives. I'm not proud of what I did for them. That's just the way it was.

"Whaddaya got in mind?" Anvil asks, his blue eyes unblinking.

I pause while a waitress in Daisy Dukes and a halter top lays down another round of beers at our table, carting the empty bottles away. "An explosion," I say. "But not just anywhere. The Federal Building is a few blocks from the bank."

"Shi-it!" Anvil says, laughing.

"Hear me out, Anvil. Look, I'm not sayin' it has to be in the building. I was thinkin' in the dumpster out back."

"The fuck good does that do?"

"Media hysteria," says Russel, the third guy at the table, who will serve as my partner should the heist go down.

With a look part annoyance and part humor, Anvil listens as Russel elaborates. "Think about it: a bomb goes off at the Federal Building. The media will run with it before they get all the facts, maybe even spin it as a terrorist attack. Every cop in the city will respond. Personally, I think Johnny's idea is brilliant."

"Really, boy? Well who the fuck asked you?" Anvil glares at Russel, who looks duly terrified. He should be. "Anyway," Anvil continues, addressing me, "so you want me to plant a bomb on federal property. Last time I blew somethin' up cost me fourteen years; somethin' like this could put me away for life. Why the hell should I help you?"

"Because this bank's loaded, Anvil. Me 'n Russ can pull half a million clean, I'm sure of it. Piece of it's yours if you help us out."

Anvil laughs. "Think you're gonna pull off this caper with a dexter like *him*?" He points at Russel and laughs some more.

"He's what I got," I say.

"And I have nothing to lose," Russel says sternly. It's the truth. We were cellmates and fast friends, two educated men cast into a barbaric system of *correction,* where we were reprogrammed for our new lives as career criminals. Russel was an accountant by trade, sent up for embezzling his clients; he now works in a meth lab for the most powerful drug lord in the city. I did six years for assaulting a fellow fraternity brother, nearly beating him to death for fondling my girlfriend's ass. My parole officer wrangled me the job at the gym, stacking weights and mopping sweat off the machines. I make my actual living in the locker room, peddling steroids to my fellow muscleheads.

"All right, so the explosion draws the cops away," Anvil says. "What happens then?"

I smile. "Chaos. And it works completely in our favor."

"How so?" Russel asks.

I've got Russel and Anvil nodding by the time I'm done

explaining. In addition to the bomb, we'll also need the Brotherhood to supply us guns and some essential props.

"Hundred grand'll cover it all," Anvil says. "I'd want fifty G's up front from anyone else, but I'll take twenty since you always done right by the Brotherhood."

Steep, yet generous. I don't have twenty G's to put up front, but I'll get the money someplace. Maybe the Russians I push steroids for can advance me the cash, yet another dangerous proposition, with exorbitant interest, but it'll be worth it.

"Fair enough," I say, confident that my plan is going to work. It *has* to work. I'm in debt to the Aryan Brotherhood the instant that bomb goes off, amount due in full no matter how the job turns out...

* * *

Russel and I sit in the car outside the bank. I check my watch: 9:58 a.m. The bomb is set to explode at ten sharp; we'll make our move the moment it hits the radio news.

I check my new look in the rearview mirror. "Man, these fake glasses are stylin'," I say to Russel as I admire the rectangular tortoiseshell frames.

"Ja, fer sure," Russel says. "And don't forget to give Billy Idol his hair back."

"Fuck you, dude." I tilt my head and inspect my spiky blond dye job, applied just this morning. "I'm a brush-cut government golden boy. You're just jealous, Mr. Peabody."

Russel snorts, reaches up to turn the mirror on himself. He shaved his head this morning, is wearing a fake brown mustache, and looks nothing like the Russel I've known for the past four years.

I discreetly remove the .45 from my shoulder holster, point it toward the floorboard and chamber a round. Russel takes the cue and does the same. He heaves a heavy breath. "Think we'll have to shoot anybody?" he asks.

"You better damn well be ready to."

"That's not what I asked." Russel locks a stare on me, awaiting an answer.

"What do you care? You have nothin' to lose, remember? You're all in, Russ. You gotta shoot, I suggest you do it."

Russel looks at the dashboard, the heaviness of the situation hitting him hard in the eleventh hour. It hits me as well — the pressure of having to steal enough to pay off the Russians and the Brotherhood *and* make out fine for ourselves, or it will all be for naught.

Neither of us choose to continue the conversation. On the radio news, last night's baseball scores are interrupted by a breaking news report: a bombing at the Federal Building on Elkins Street—

"Let's go," I say. We stride up the stone steps, through the glass doors and past the ATM into the bank lobby. All four tellers are present, though only two lines are open. I count five customers altogether. Only one of the loan officers is in today, a blond man with a world-weary look about him. We march toward his desk, the soles of our dress shoes clacking in time on the marble floor.

The loan officer asks, "May I—"

"Treasury Department," I say. Russel and I flip open our wallets to expose fake Treasury Department badges. "I'm agent Sharp; this is agent Peabody. Are you the manager on duty?"

Our bad haircuts and cheap suits must certainly mark us as treasury agents, because the man pops up from his chair like a soldier being ordered to attention. "Yes, sir. Grady Maddox." He pauses, begins to offer his hand to shake but stops, sensing we don't have time for such pleasantries. "What can I do for you gentlemen?"

"Mr. Maddox, a bomb has exploded at the Federal Building four blocks away," I say. "We fear this may be a terror attack, and that chaos might ensue in the streets. I hereby order you to close immediately, as your bank may become a target for robbery."

Maddox looks perplexed. "Terror attack? I haven't heard any such thing."

"Check the local news," Russel says, pointing toward the computer on his desk.

Maddox's jaw drops as he confirms the breaking story streaming live on a news radio station. "Possible terror attack..." he mutters; then: "Yes, sir. Immediately." He jogs to the counter, heading off the customers, who now number seven. He tells them of the terror attack — omitting the word *possible* — and announces that the bank is closing. Five customers dash for the door, but two stay behind and demand that their business be attended to before closing. Russel and I step in, shooing them away with our phony badges. One of the tellers follows them at my order, locks the outer door behind them and returns to the counter.

"Grab your things and head home," Maddox says to his tellers. "I'll lock the vault."

I pull my gun and point it at him. "You'll get in it first." Maddox gasps and raises his hands; one of the tellers shrieks. Russel draws his pistol. "All of you, move it!" I say as we herd them toward the open vault. "Touch an alarm and you're fucking dead!"

* * *

Russel and I exit the bank, each of us shouldering a burlap sack stuffed with cash. I'm guessing we've got well over a million dollars between us. We locked the bank staff in the vault; the timer lock will open in two hours.

As I predicted, the streets are getting a bit chaotic due to the media's speculation of a possible terror attack. I bowl through the stream of people rushing past on the sidewalk, clearing a path for Russel, and we reach the car. I go around to the driver's side, open the rear door and deposit my sack in the backseat. Russel opens the passenger front door, clutching his sack to his body.

"Hold it right there, jack!" says Wolfman Jack, the windshield-spritzing bum, who is pointing at Russel's forehead a crude revolver that looks like it was fabricated by a stoner in a high-school metal shop. I draw my gun and sight in on the Wolfman. People continue to hustle by on the sidewalk, ignoring the scene or altogether oblivious to it. "Uh-uh, big man!" the Wolfman says to me. "I'll pop this muthafucka square in his bald fo-head." He laughs. "I knowed you was casin' this joint, big man. You best believe you gonna pay me today!"

But the Wolfman is having a hard time covering Russel and watching me at the same time. "Get lost, Wolfman," I say. "I'll blow your fuckin' head off the moment you grab that sack."

"I'll git him first, big man."

"Oh no!" Russel gasps, looking skyward.

"Oh bullshit!" the Wolfman says. "You 'spect me to fall for that old gag?"

From down the street comes a woman's scream. The Wolfman falls for this unexpected diversion, turning his head for an instant, and Russel — not the violent type at all — surprises me by swinging into action. He drops the sack and smacks the gun from the Wolfman's hand. It goes clattering onto the sidewalk, lost in the shuffle of feet.

"Aw, hell no!" the Wolfman says, looking helplessly toward the sidewalk. Russel picks up his sack and jumps in the car. I wedge my gun between the front seat cushion and the center console, within easy reach, and we haul ass, leaving Wolfman Jack to cry over his lost fortune.

"Way to go, Agent Peabody!" I say as we pull into the crawling flow of traffic. Russel whoops with joy, something I've never seen him do, as he looks into the sack of money between his legs. He pulls out three stacks of hundreds and whoops again. "Yeah baby!" he shouts.

"Take it easy, bro," I say. "We ain't outta this yet."

"Set for life, Johnny!" Another whoop as we creep toward the bridge that will take us over the river and out of the business district, toward the suburbs. Russel continues to play with the stacks of money.

The business district gets a little seedy on its outskirts, the financial institutions and law offices giving way to pawn shops and check cashing joints. I see a couple of hood rats looting an electronics store. One is boosting a stack of DVD players; the other cradles a small plasma TV under one arm while brandishing a gun with his free hand.

Traffic is moving a little faster now. We traverse one intersection and then another, almost hitting a crossing car because its driver decided to run a red light. Only one more intersection to go before we reach the bridge onramp and make a clean getaway...and wouldn't you know it, the light is turning yellow. "Come on!" I growl, flooring the accelerator and nearly striking the rear bumper of the jackass in front of me, who's driving far too slowly. Finally he wakes up and speeds through the intersection as the light turns red. I follow, laying on the horn as I run the light.

Crunch! My head hits the roof stanchion between the front and rear doors as the car spins out of control. Russel flops into my lap and then flops back over to the passenger side. We hit something—I don't know what—and stop with a spine-whipping jolt. Dazed, blood leaking into my blond-dyed hair, I look around. We're up on the curb, the front end of our sedan split in twain by a light pole. "Shit," I say, looking around. Russel is knocked out cold, his head lolling to the side, blood oozing from his nose.

Stacks of money are scattered everywhere, and people are descending on the car—shouting, pushing, fists and fingernails flying. A woman and a young man are playing tug of war with a stack of hundreds, spittle flying as they argue. The paper band on the stack rips; Franklin's go fluttering everywhere. Angry shouts mix with cries of joy as more bystanders join the greed-whipped frenzy. Russel's door is pulled open; his limp body flops onto the pavement. A guy in a Muslim prayer cap hauls Russel's sack of money from the car, only to be jumped by several looters for his efforts. He goes down beneath an onslaught of feet and fists.

I've seen enough. I reach for my gun but it isn't there; it must have gone flying in the accident. But no matter. Adrenaline has built within me, and I fly into a rage more fierce than any I experienced during my heyday of shooting steroids. I push the door open, slamming it into several people and knocking them flat. Four people are trying to wrest my sack of money from the backseat. I grab a boy by his pencil neck, launch him up and over the crowd. A woman rakes my face with jagged nails already bloody from another victim. I punch her in the face, feel her eye socket shatter beneath my knuckles. Snatching my sack of money, I turn about and plow through the maelstrom like a fullback smelling the goal line on Super Bowl Sunday. But there are too many of them, all clutching and clawing for the sack. I don't let go and I don't go down, but it doesn't matter. Somehow the sack rips open; stacks of hundreds and fifties cascade in a torrent onto the sidewalk. I punch people's faces in, stomp their bodies into the concrete as I fight to recover some modicum of my fortune.

Gun shots, close enough to smell the powder. People scatter. I reach down to scoop up more money, but only loose bills remain — filthy, bloody, the bedding beneath trampled bodies. A scream, and two more gunshots. Two gangbangers are approaching, each holding a pistol horizontally and shooting anyone in their path, pausing now and then to pocket the money dropped by their victims. One of them locks eyes with me. I run, hearing the snap of a bullet as it whizzes over my shoulder. Another bullet grazes my arm, ripping my suit jacket. I keep running and they keep shooting, though no longer at me. I've made my getaway.

I jog to the bridge, slowing to a walk as I head over the span. Traffic is frozen in a total state of gridlock. Many of the motorists are out of their cars, some standing on their hoods to get a look at the road ahead. A fistfight is in progress a few cars away.

I don't dare count the money I recovered, not in front of all these people. I can only guess at what's in my pockets. Forty grand? Maybe sixty at the most. Barely enough to pay back the Russians.

Not nearly enough to pay off the Brotherhood.

HIS GIRL
Matthew C. Funk

It wasn't until Carson aimed the gun at the girl's face that Ron began to panic.

"If I need to tell you one more time, gas man," Carson's white-rimmed lips sped, "I'll send her brains into your fucking Beer Cave."

Ron quit inching toward the alarm under the counter. He quit breathing. His mind choked on the idea of a world where such a thing could happen to the girl.

Not just any girl. Jenny. His Jenny.

"Alright, son." Ron tried shuffling toward the lockbox. His legs were ice. Just like Jenny's blue stare, lost in the gun barrel.

"Don't 'son' me, old man! Put your safe's cash in my hand!" Carson thumbed the Colt's hammer.

"Alright."

None of this was alright.

Hold-ups did not happen in the universe of Ron's Cotham Mercantile. Boys like Carson went on to jobs as tobacco field foremen, not meth-starved felons. And girls like Jenny were heaven on Earth.

Nobody should be able to hurt heaven.

A glance at Jenny's face showed Ron she was more than hurting. She was shaking like she'd been stitched out of insects.

That got Ron moving. He had to make it better, soon as he could.

"There's a good boy." Carson sneered. He stepped closer to Jenny. Ron shook his head.

"Just don't."

"I will."

Ron couldn't imagine how anyone could.

"Just please don't." Insistence ran out of gas in Ron's tone. He'd thought he knew Carson.

Ron had sold Carson his first *Sports Illustrated* — the NFL preview, 2004 — and had seen the excitement leaping in the boy's features. Carson had always dropped spare pennies from his change in the counter dish. Carson had bought packs of energy drinks and never snuck smokes and always paid for what he opened and ate in the store.

"I so fucking will." Carson brushed a chestnut strand of Jenny's hair from her temple with the gun barrel.

Ron had known Carson. But not nearly as well as he knew Jenny.

He studied her face, as if he'd not already memorized it: The cherubic softness of her cheeks. The eye makeup, swept sloppy by her inexpert hand. That pink ribbon mouth.

That mouth could make a smile that would crack a Devil's heart: Full and immaculate, but for one crimped end, like a bow on a present that'd been handled too roughly.

That mouth was a pale line now.

Those lively blue eyes were empty lamps.

Ron's hands were wrestling with the lockbox before he knew what they were doing.

"Hurry it up," Carson hissed. His hand slid over Jenny's neck.

That neck wasn't meant for fingers like that, nails bitten to a moist saw. It was meant for kisses.

"I am." And Ron was, for Jenny's sake he was, but his fingers wouldn't work the lock.

"No, Ron." Carson set the barrel in a direct line against Jenny's brain. "Is that your name? Ron?"

"Yes."

And Jenny flinched. Ron wondered if it was because she knew his name: She used it every time she came in — every time since she was still in a training bra. Always his name and always that little crinkled smile.

"Ron, what you're doing now is called fucking around." Carson sneered at his joke. "I'll give you five to quit it, then I let the air out of her head."

Ron's face set serious. His fingers firmed. They turned the combination on the lock.

Jenny's head wasn't full of air, Ron wanted to yell. It was full of talk of angels in the clouds and faeries in the trees. It wondered aloud about rock concerts and big cities. It was a font of wonder.

Ron would have given all he had to know what else was in that head — to hold her one evening and just listen.

"There's a good man." Carson nodded. His Colt only dented deeper in Jenny.

She wasn't making a sound now.

Ron coughed out a frustrated breath.

"Just ease off her."

"Just fuck yourself."

Jenny was quiet as a work of glass.

There was a lot she hid, Ron knew. Jenny needed listening.

She needed holding. Tending.

Her jeans were always tattered. Ron had given her patches for them, but still they found places to split. Her jewelry's random scheme spoke of discount binges at the flea market. Jenny always paid with change. And Jenny sometimes had bruises — peeking through her jeans' gaps, glowing just below the long sleeves she always wore.

Jenny wanted for much and needed more.

Right now, she needed saving. Ron popped the safe, waved the wad of cash.

"Right here, son."

"What did I say about the 'son' shit?" Carson jabbed Jenny's head to a sharp angle.

She still made no sound. Ron looked for pain on her face. It was blank.

He saw her hand skirting for a beer bottle set in the

cooler door.

Ron waved the cash again. "Here! Here it is. Take it."

"You come and give it."

"Here!"

"Quit playing!"

"Here, Carson!"

Matches struck behind Carson's glare. His jaw shoved as if to take the blow of his name on the chin. The Colt's aim took Ron.

Ron smiled. Jenny was safe.

Not safe from her bruises' source. Not safe from having to forage for good things. Not safe from whatever made those blue eyes shine so bright, but safe for now.

"You know me?" Carson shook his head. "Not fucking smart, Ron."

Jenny snatched the bottle and whipped it into Carson's head in a single motion.

Carson fell. Jenny went down atop him. Her lithe little form hunkered, chest heaving.

Ron dashed around the counter. Jenny was pulling a knife from Carson's belt.

"Quick, Ron!" Jenny's voice was wind chimes in a summer storm. "Quick!"

"It's alright now, Jenny," Ron ran down the aisle, desperate to see relief welling in the eyes Jenny's mane of brown hair screened.

"It will be." Jenny flipped open the knife.

She lanced its point into Carson's neck. Metal separated muscle, jerky with Jenny's fevered sawing. A ragged gap opened. Blood fled, sputtered, shot wild on the aisle stacks.

"Jenny." Ron called her. Even at four feet distant, she seemed a world away.

"Got to finish him off! He'll come back, like in the movies! They always come back."

Carson bucked, fought, settled. Jenny's slicing clacked the linoleum.

The eyes Jenny locked on Ron had never seemed so full of brightness. Her face was calm again. Her voice was just crystal and breeze.

"Okay," Jenny said as Ron squatted beside her. "Help me pull his head off. Then we can be sure."

"Jenny," Ron's arms reached to do what they'd always hungered for — to hold her. They couldn't. They could no more embrace her than they could molten metal.

"What?"

"Jenny, you're out of control."

Jenny stared. Ron searched it. They were the same eyes as ever.

"Me?" Jenny beamed with crimped lips. "I've never felt more in control."

The smile fled.

"You're the one who seems out of control, Ron!" Jenny's eyes leapt over Ron like fleas. "I see you — I see the way you look at me. I know what that look means!"

"Jenny, no." Ron trembled out the words.

Jenny snorted. The knife point tented the skin under Ron's jaw.

"At least my uncle doesn't lie about what that look means." Jenny's tone took on an animal arch. "I don't like lies."

"I'm not..."

"Not?"

"I'm..."

"You're totally out of control; you can't even form a sentence!" Jenny leaned her brow to nearly touch Ron's. Her breath raked his quaking face. Out came that smile, same as ever, ready to crack any heart. "I know how control works, though."

Ron didn't know how anything worked anymore. He could only stare as Jenny whisked his thin hair, gathered, seized with a rude lover's passion.

"It's like uncle says: There are rules," Jenny said. "Some

rules you can break. Some rules break you."

Jenny tugged. Ron nearly spilled back. The blade opened his skin; a blaze of pain to him, not even worth a flinch from Jenny.

"Jenny, I need..." Ron began, almost toppling.

"No." Her chimes were caked in something rough now: Another voice of motor oil and pig blood and soiled bedsheets. "I'll tell you what you need, Ron."

The knife sailed through the skin of his face and blue eyes sunk straight through to the rear bone of his skull.

"You need to give me that cash, Ron," Jenny grinned. "Then you need to lie face down like a good little girl."

Ron's wounds and Jenny's smile split wider.

"Do it for me," she said.

NEVER TOO OLD FOR FUN
McDroll

Beeny found a mangy dog, dead for days. It was lying on the council rubbish dump and he knew it would make perfect target practice, a gift from the gods. He wondered what damage a handgun could do to real flesh. Would there be a *thwump* as the bullet hit the carcass?

He poked at its scrawny arse. Would the bullets go right through the dog's body? Gingerly he toed it again. Gave him a funny sensation the dog could still jump up at him, suddenly spring back to life.

"Agh! Fuck, shit!" Beeny swung round to see that Jango had pounced ninja-like at him, pulling his parka hood over his head. Bloody hilarious.

"Oh man, that was dead brilliant. Look there's keech running down your leg!"

"Fuck off Jango, there is not; you're just a fuckwit. The gun could've gone off, I could have just pulled the trigger..."

"Aye, and shot yourself up the arse!"

Jango laughed at the funniest stunt he'd pulled for a long time but Beeny seethed with indignant rage.

"It's no' a real gun anyways," pointed out Jango, "do you think I'm daft. Where would you get a real gun, you know, one that fires actual bullets?"

"Is so real!"

"Don't be stupid, give it here. Let me see, it's one of them imitation jobs."

"No, it's mine and it's the real fuckin' deal. It's a semi-automatic Makarov pistol. So stick that up yours!"

"Bollocks! You been having a wiki-leak again? Let me see it."

Jango held out his hand for the gun.

"Naw, you're not having it. I got it last night in the pub from a Polish guy, took me out the back. He had it wrapped up in a black bin bag."

"And what? He just 'gave' it to you?"

"Stop being a wanker, 'course he didn't." Beeny kicked at a stone, hitting the dead dog. "He said I could have it on a five-day trial and if I like it I can buy it off him for a hundred spondulicks."

"And this Polish guy just let you walk away with it? What did you do? Stick it up yer jumper?"

"No...aye...well, what else was I supposed to do with it?"

"What was the Polish guy's name? Did he give you his mobile number?"

"Don't know and nope."

"And you don't think that there's anything unusual about all that? No wee bells ringing or wee lights coming on in that huge brain of yours?"

"I've just got it for five days. If I don't like it he'll take it back..."

Jango closed his eyes and rubbed his close-cropped head. Never in his life, knowing already how stupid and naive Beeny could be, did he ever, ever think that he was this stupid.

"Give me the gun." Jango stretched out his hand.

"No. Fuck off. It's mine." Beeny stuck the gun into his parka pocket.

"Is it loaded?"

"Aye. 'Course it is, it's a bloody gun!" Beeny grinned at Jango and stuck his chest out, proud of his new found power.

"Christ!"

"What? You're just jealous 'cause I've got a piece and you haven't. With this I'm going to hit the high times. I don't need you anymore and your poxy wee robberies. Now I can do anything I want and get some real dineros." Beeny turned, and just to make the point to Jango about what a big man he now was, he fired off a couple of rounds into the dog's rear end. "You wee shitting beauty!"

"Stop it! That's enough. Fine, if you're sure that's how you want it." Jango looked Beeny straight in the eye. "So come on, share your master plan because this I have to hear, and put the bloody gun away."

"K Jango, Here's my offer. Let's do a job on Friday night but this time I'm in charge. I'll call the shots and you'll go along with me. Let's see if you can take it Mr. I Know Fuckin' Everything. I'll select the target and then I can have first dabs at the good stuff for once. Got it? Do we have a deal?"

Jango nodded. Give Beeny enough rope and all that...
"Is that an affirmative?"

"Aye, it is. You're on. You're the big man. Let's see what you're made of."

* * *

One a.m. and Jango cut the lights in the battered white transit and crept into the crescent. There's not many posh areas in Irvine but Beeny had managed to find one in a secluded, green-hedged and wrought-iron gated oasis, far away from the damp high-rises and pigeon-splattered pavements of their more regular stomping grounds.

"You sure about this Beeny? Is this not a wee bit out of our league?"

"Fuck's sake man, I tell you, I know what I'm doing. This is an old house, the windows and locks are going to be dead easy to do. A wee breenge from your shoulder and we'll be in."

"And your auntie told you this? Is she sure? Sounds a bit too good to be true to me!"

"I tell you, it's true. She's cleaned for them for years and she says they're so fuckin' rich, go abroad on holidays all the time but too fuckin' stupid to put in proper double glazing or new locks on the doors! Anyway, folk like them, they'll just claim back on the insurance if anything is missing. It's win win."

"Right, okay, what do you want us to do?"

"She says they're all out tonight, away to some big do in Glasgow so all we do is get in and back out without the neighbors seeing us. C'mon."

Leaving the van at the end of the drive, Beeny and Jango slid out, stayed off the crunching gravel, and stepped out into the pitch-blackness. They could just make out the house in the distance with its white painted gable looming. Silence hung in the velvet air. Beeny gripped the gun.

An owl hooted and Beeny's heart froze before doing a triple flip.

"Get a fuckin' move on man," wheezed Jango.

Heading off again, at a brisker pace, Beeny repeated their mantra, "Quick in, quick out."

A few minutes later they reached the side of the building, quickly slipped around the corner and looked for the back door. Reaching out his hand, Beeny felt the cold iron of the doorknob, gave a quick breenge to the door with his shoulder, the lock gave way and they were in. Standing in the dark of the room, they both gasped for air.

* * *

Upstairs, old Mrs. Reynolds stirred in her bed. She had changed her mind about going out but woke when she heard the slightest creak coming from the ancient oak floorboards. Beside her, Hugo sniffed the air, hair on the scruff of his neck already standing on end.

"What is it boy? Do you hear something?"

Stepping into her slippers, she got out of bed; Mrs. Reynolds patted the dog on the head as they both listened for any more movement.

Bang!

The dog moved first, heading straight for the door with Mrs. Reynolds only a few steps behind. Pretty sure somebody was moving around downstairs in the old laundry, and they'd just walked into the old tin bath that sat in front of the sink where the family put their outdoor shoes before tramping mud through the house.

"Shoosh boy, let's take this quietly, we don't want to give ourselves away," the old woman whispered to the dog, keeping a hold on his collar to stop him from bolting down the stairs as he so obviously wanted to do.

"Right Hugo, let's go see who we've got visiting tonight, shall we? Let's have a bit of fun with them!"

* * *

"Could you not see that great big tin bath right in front of your nose, you stupid eejit?"

Beeny glowered back at Jango, "It's fine, chill, there's naebody at home, it doesn't matter. Come on. Quick in, quick out."

Jango shook his head and sighed at Beeny, hoping for once that their luck might be in.

Beeny knew he needed to open the door from the laundry just far enough, squeeze through, head into the hallway, look for the room on the left where he'd been told to go by his auntie; look for paintings and small knick-knacks. Better money than Xboxes and Argos jewelry.

"This way Jango, come on, get the bags ready," Beeny whispered over his shoulder as he pushed open the sitting room door.

Once inside, he shone the torch around and gawped at the opulence; over-stuffed sofas, open fire with a high mantelpiece, grand piano covered in family photos and glass display cabinets clinging to every wall.

"I think we're in fuckin' Buckingham Palace, Jango!"

The boy stood in awe and it was only when Jango threw the bags down on the floor beside him that he awoke from his stupor and remembered why he was there.

"Right, come on, grab stuff and fill the bags up, but watch out just in case the corgis bite your ankles," Jango laughed as he pushed past Beeny.

* * *

Behind the sitting-room door, Evelyn stood with Hugo, listening to her two unannounced visitors. Chuckling, she waited for her moment, knowing that it wouldn't be long before they attempted their escape. Saw her son's fat face discovering he'd been burgled. Lazy toad. Deserved everything he got.

"Okay, Hugo, here we go, remember to play along with me," and at that she let out a terrified moan.

Beeny and Jango froze in their tracks, unable to move or breathe.

Pushing the heavy white door open, Evelyn asked, "Is there anybody there?" in her best shaky old woman voice. She flicked on the light switch and saw the two scallies in front of her.

"It's okay missus, just don't move and we'll be out of here." It was then that they saw the dog move from behind Evelyn's legs and heard the low growl.

"Shit Jango, she's got a dug! A bloody big Alsatian!"

Beeny, gun out of his pocket, waved it at the old woman.

"Lose the dog missus or I'll shoot him, I will, just you watch!"

"You'd better do as he says missus, that gun could go off at any time. Come on, don't be daft about this."

Evelyn, standing up straight, smirked at Beeny and Jango, no flicker of fear, and addressed them both, still holding onto her snarling dog.

"Do you think I'm some useless, old codger? My name is

Evelyn Reynolds and I'm 83 years old, but I'm not gaga, despite what my family thinks."

"Nobody said you were gaga gran, but seriously, we don't want to hurt you."

"Hey missus, the dug gets it if you make one wrong move," Beeny spat out at her trying to keep the fear from his voice.

"Come on then, just do what my mate says. We're no' wanting any trouble, we're just taking a few things. Be sensible, move the dog." Jango tried to look reasonable holding his hands out in a gesture of trust.

"I don't know who you are and I don't actually care," explained Evelyn, addressing Jango, "but I've got a plan, if you would care to listen. I've seen more of life than you ever will, you know." Evelyn looked at Beeny straight in the eye. "I got my pilot's license at twenty-three, flew solo across the Atlantic to New York where I met my husband, a wealthy investment banker. I returned to Scotland when he died ten years ago."

"I'm not interested in your life story granny! Move the dug now!" Beeny headed towards Evelyn.

"You don't scare me young man. Before I had my two children, I canoed down the Orinoco River; I've climbed Mt. Kilimanjaro and trekked to Machu Picchu long before tourists could go there on a bus. A burglar or two is nothing to me; in fact the thought of a bit of excitement is quite delicious! Living with the family as the 'aged granny' is quite suffocating and if you would put down that little toy you call a gun, I'll tell you what we are going to do. Let's have some fun!"

* * *

Evelyn led the way upstairs taking Jango and Beeny to the master bedroom.

"This is where the real loot is," announced Evelyn, "so

let's hurt the bastard and make it really count!" The tough old bird slid open the huge walk-in wardrobe lined on every side with hangers of suits and dresses organized by color, while beneath lay shelf upon shelf of shoes of every color and design.

"This boys, is what my son fritters his father's fortune on. Go look for yourself, every one has a designer label, Savile Row, made to measure, cashmere, Italian leather and as for her," Evelyn spun round to the opposite side, "straight from the catwalks of Paris and Milan! Shoes that she's never even worn once. This is what they live for, this is what my children value."

Evelyn's eyes blazed as she remembered trekking in the Himalayas, crossing the Andes and seeing the street children in Calcutta.

"Help yourself to whatever antiques you wish, but first I need you to destroy every item in here. Slash, rip, tear. Make sure everything's destroyed. Then tie me up and leave me downstairs for Roger to find on his return. Hurry, time waits for no man, as someone once said."

"Are you mad? You'll just report us to the polis as soon as we're gone. You've seen us both and you'll be able to pick us out in a line up any day," Jango exclaimed.

"No, I certainly will not. I'm a woman of my word and the reward for me will be to see the horror on my son's face when he discovers what's been done. As far as being able to identify you, I'm perfectly capable of telling the police that my attackers were two young men of Eastern European origin who spoke with heavily accented English."

Beeny and Jango stared at each other.

"Now do we have a deal?" Evelyn stuck out her hand.

"Deal!" Beeny and Jango replied together.

* * *

Back in Jango's flat the next day, as they examined the

loot spread out around their feet, the boys watched a bit of TV and drank a couple of tins.

"Did that really happen, man?"

"Aye, it did, I think anyways, bizarre old bird though!"

"*And in other news, an 83-year-old woman has had a lucky escape after being tied up during a robbery at her son's home where she lives. The robbers escaped with an unspecified amount of antiques whilst also causing thousands of pounds worth of damage to the family home. When called to the house in the early hours of this morning, the police discovered a handgun that has been identified as the weapon used in a recent hold up at a post office in Kilmarnock.*"

"That wouldn't be your gun they're talking about by any chance?"

"Aye, I think it might be..." Beeny stared down at his left sock and tried to maneuver his big toe back inside the hole it was sticking out from.

"So you actually did realize the gun was hot and the Polish guy had dumped it on the first sucker he could find? My god, Beeny, I never had you down as being as smart as that!" Jango ruffled Beeny's hair.

"Eh, well, actually...I think I just put the gun down on a shelf when we were ripping up the clothes and I...eh...just forgot to pick it up again..."

"Oh shite! You're a jammy wee dodger!"

Beeny grinned at the compliment from his mate as he popped open another tin.

"Cheers, mate."

© 2013, McDroll

CHARITY CASE
R Thomas Brown

Hap Callahan sat in his Pontiac Can Am, gazing blankly at the red seat next to him. The address on his phone matched that of the house in front of him. He'd arrived where he intended, but he still wasn't sure it was where he wanted to be. Wasn't sure if his sudden life change made sense.

He'd made what money he had chasing down extortionists. Women seeking cash from a married man after the tryst ended. Punks who found some pics on a phone or took some of their own of people too stupid to hide their actions. Hell, even the occasional sap who caught someone doing something illegal, but felt like they deserved a little payday for the effort.

When Hap came on the scene, payment wasn't likely. Oh sure, he'd bring the money, but if they took it, an ugly end was just around the corner. Not that he'd do it. No, he didn't have a taste for violence anymore. One too many ugly images in his head, and a few too many losing ends of fights. He got paid to make it happen. Paid someone else to end it.

Then, he stopped some idiots who jacked stuff from open cars. Easy job. Until he saw the pics. And the kids in them. He told himself it was just the one job. That he'd paid for justice against that asshat. Still, working for the seedy lost its luster. Enough that he was having a hard time finding people to pay him enough to ignore the sick feeling in his gut.

Then the Massey family called. He wasn't sure how they got his number, but it seemed to get there third hand from one of his other jobs. Typical. The issue was a missing boy. Not so typical. He told them to call the police. They told him they had.

They needed someone who got things done. Whatever was needed.

He could feel the desperation. And the trouble. And a bonus, too. They didn't have any money to pay. So, of course, he took the job. Hopped in the white, late seventies muscle car and headed over.

Parked. Sat. Thought. Always a dangerous thing. Taking the job was a step. To what, he wasn't quite sure. But, he was pretty damned sure he needed to get somewhere.

Hap stepped out of the car and up to the door. It opened before he could knock.

"Mr. Callahan?"

Hap nodded at the lanky man in front of him. He looked tired. And old. Not in years, but his face seemed like worry was driving a forty-year-old man to a hundred. "Mr. Massey?" They walked into the house.

"Mrs. Massey is out."

Hap didn't respond to this. "You say your boy, Zeke, is missing?"

Massey nodded.

"How long?"

"A week."

"The cops?"

"Said he probably ran away. Said they'd look, but I don't know."

"Zeke's room?"

Massey motioned for Hap to follow. The single-story house was simple, but clean. Except Zeke's room. Clothes everywhere. Bed a mess. Usual stuff. Except the pipe. The pills. The papers. The bags of weed.

"Cops see this?"

Massey shook his head. "No. We cleared it out before they came over. Didn't want to get in any trouble."

Hap nodded. Figured the cops saw enough to write it off as some druggie out on a tear. Figured he come back later. Or not. He doubted they gave much of a shit.

245

"Right. So, where would I go to get hooked up?"

"What?"

"Drugs, Massey. Where would I go around here?"

He stepped back. "I don't know."

Hap sighed. "Fine. Good luck finding Zeke." Hap turned to leave. Didn't care if the guy came clean or not.

"Fine. There's a couple of places."

Hap stopped. Wished the guy had just let him leave. "Write it down."

* * *

Getting drugs wasn't hard. Hap just needed to know where Zeke might have been looking. Massey directed him to a contact in Garland who'd hooked Zeke up with some stuff at a club.

With a little persuasion, a dealer acknowledged moving Zeke onto meth. He'd picked up a supply on the cheap from some dude out in Wise County who was trying to increase his distribution. He gave Hap the address since he figured one of the big syndicates would probably kill the guy soon anyway.

Hap sped off. Had to get there soon. He figured Zeke had probably gotten the address somehow. Hell, dealer man may have given it to him. Get as many kids hooked on the stuff as he could before the cheap maker got wiped out.

He also figured Zeke would be dead by now. If he'd gotten the drugs, he'd be back home. A mess, but back home. Not like his parents were making him stop or make any damned choices. He was gone. Probably dead.

Still, Hap wanted to be sure. And he needed to get there fast. When he heard the shotgun fire once he pulled up to the shitty house, he knew he was a little too late. Dealer man called in a warning. Protect supply and kill the jackass that roughed you up. Nice move.

It's what Hap would've told him to do.

He pulled away from the house. Didn't want any damage to the car. There weren't that many of them. A thousand or so in the whole world. Some hillbilly with a shotgun and a house full of cold medicine wasn't gonna be the end of his ride.

The dude kept yelling. Something about getting off his yard or equally old man-ish. Hard to hear over the blasts and through the accent and missing teeth. Hap walked the long way around. Still heard all the noise at the front of the house.

Out back was a mess. Dirt. Weeds. A truck on cinder blocks. Felt like home. Made Hap sick. He walked up to the back windows. Dirty house. No, filth more than dirt. Like a hoarder of slime, bugs and bacteria lived inside. Probably not far from the truth. Smelled like hell too. He'd need to get in and out pretty damn fast.

He kept walking along the back. The grime covered windows still let him see in. Dining room filled with cooking equipment. A bedroom that the old man may have slept in, but maybe not. At the end, Zeke.

Tied up in a chair. Next to some other guys. All beat to hell. Maybe burned. Tough to say. But, they were breathing. Hap stepped away. Listened. Shit. The shooting stopped. He peeked in the window to the other bedroom.

Dropped to the ground.

Shotgun blast rang out over him. Head hurt like hell. Hearing would be shot for days. He ran. Wasn't sure if the old man was behind him or not. A blast exploded a sickly oak next to him. That was an answer. Hap kept running. Didn't hear any more shots. He could see his car in the distance.

Just kept running. Hopped in and sped off. Sent a text to Massey. No need to call, he couldn't hear anyway. Text sent.

He didn't say if Zeke was alive or dead. One, he wasn't sure. Two, if he was breathing, Hap wasn't sure he still would be by the time Massey got there.

Text came back. Massey was on the way.

Hap went to get a drink. Grabbed a six-pack of Shiner at the first convenience store he found. Sat in his car and sipped. Cold. Eased the nerves. It was a shitty job. He wondered if he could get back to his old gig.

After an hour, Hap went back out to the old crap house. The old man was lying on the ground outside the broken door. No sign of Massey. Hap tucked his mouth and nose inside his shirt. Worked his way around the bugs toward the back room. The other three guys were still there.

They were yelling. Hap couldn't quite make it out through the ringing in his ears and the gags in their mouths. Still, they were dirty and bloody. No way they were coming with him. He called emergency from a shitty prepaid phone he kept in his pocket. Told them the address and that there were injuries.

He turned off the phone. He'd destroy it later and buy another prepaid piece of shit. On his way out, he spotted some cash. At least something worked out. He grabbed the pile. Hoped it wasn't covered with anything too toxic and headed out.

Back on the road, he exhaled. Work for assholes and it's waiting for idiots to come to you and dig their own graves. Try to do something nice. For free. You get shot at.

His phone rang. He wasn't sure if he wanted it to be a jerk or a charity case.

He picked it up.

"Hap here."

© 2013, R Thomas Brown

THE GREAT WHYDINI
David Cranmer

"Remember, Frank, we have very little oxygen left. So this will have to be the final run-through of your act." He paused, looking at the magician, "You sure you don't want me to go down with you again?"

"I love the way you practice your lines, Jay, even when there's no audience present." Frank Oliver eyed the brown-haired, muscle-bound assistant with a smirk. "I'll be fine."

Jay Wiedlin ignored his boss's condescension as he wrapped the showman's feet in chains and snapped the padlock in place. "Sure, whatever, but bear in mind, you don't want to live up to your stage name."

Frank cringed at the thought of the paper's headline if he drowned. Early in his career, an envious fellow conjurer had nicknamed him The Great Whydini as in "why'd he do that?" and the moniker stuck.

The magician looked at the air tank leaning up against the boat's starboard side. "Nope, you can forget about that one. It's pretty much spent, and the others are dead. So, for safety, this is the last rehearsal until tomorrow morning when I can get all the tanks refilled. Then we can hit it hard and heavy again."

"Save your breath, Jay. The Little Whydini never listens and that's why we will always be third rung," a voice sang out from behind.

Both men turned to face Angela, Whydini's wife — and Jay's lover. At forty-two, she was holding admirably onto twenty-nine with her shoulder-length blonde hair and wrinkle-free skin. Her voluptuous, tan physique had graced the current men's magazines like *Wink* and *Frolic* more than once.

She sauntered over in her band aid of a bikini and presented her husband with a key.

"Don't forget this or you will have one hell of a time."

Whydini sneered and plucked the key from her hand; their eyes met and held in recognition of the love that was long gone. The beginning of the end had been clear to both — a drunken threesome with Jay after a successful late night show. Jay's toned body and prowess had tipped the scale until wife and assistant began stealing more meaningful moments alone.

The magician turned back to the matter at hand. The boat floated above twenty feet of water on Cayuga Lake, Whydini's favorite New York retreat for testing new death-defying tricks. He slipped the key in his mouth and rhythmically swallowed it. Jay handcuffed the magician's wrists together in front of him and then helped lower his boss chained to cinder blocks overboard, letting gravity do the rest.

As Whydini plummeted through the clear blue water, he considered his dilemma with his wife. He had never been a sex hound like Angela — his career had always been his main priority, and he knew his wife was a big part of that success. The public lapped up the image of the sexy couple deeply in love with each other. He couldn't leave her; their image together was too important to his success. And yet he had been unable to keep her happy. They were just too different. As his feet landed on the rocky bottom, he realized that for better or worse, Angie and he were locked together like the chains that bound his feet.

He checked his water-resistant watch counting down the minutes. Time to retrieve the key to unlock the handcuffs and then the chains securing his feet. During the last practice, the clock had run down to the last second, so he knew he had no time to spare this rehearsal. Right now, breath-control and getting used to the weight and descent were most important.

He cleared his mind and used his throat muscles to regurgitate the key. After several sinuous waves, he felt the metal crown up into his mouth. He passed it between his lips and watched the key drift to the lake bottom.

* * *

On deck, Angie pulled Jay aside and wrapped her arms arou nd him.

"Not here." He started to pull away but she embraced harder, grabbing his crotch.

"Yes, here."

"We need to be watching in case..."

"Oh, c'mon. You have time for a blowjob."

Jay peered at the stopwatch, the seconds ticking away, and nervously looked around.

"Make it quick."

* * *

Whydini inserted the key in the lock but it wouldn't turn. He jiggled it back and forth. He tried again. Fuck! He looked up at the boat. Where was Jay? Usually his assistant's undulating silhouette could be seen draped over the side of the boat.

Dread raced through his body as he looked at the key in his hand and back to the surface. So this was her play. In twenty-two years of marriage, Angie had never made a mistake in their act. But he should have seen the signs especially when she had pushed for an increase in their insurance policy. Just in case, she had assured.

* * *

Jay pulled up his trunks and headed to the boat's edge.

"Wham bam, huh?" Angie said wiping her mouth with

her hand.

Jay vaguely made out Whydini fiddling with the lock. "He's in trouble!"

He dove overboard and in a few strokes reached the struggling magician. He went for the key but Whydini shook his head that it was no use. Jay jabbed a finger to the surface gesturing that he would be back and ascended. Damn, he thought as he neared the boat, they shouldn't have tried this without a full tank available. The concrete weights were too heavy to lift and he would have to use the winch and cable.

"What's wrong?" Angie shouted as Jay scaled the ladder.

"It's the wrong fucking key!"

"Oh my God!" She scrambled through her handbag. "The right one must be at the cottage on the dining room table."

Jay turned on the winch and swung the hook over the water. The motor rattled and sputtered until thick dark smoke plumed out.

"Shit!" He thrust a life ring and the remaining tank at Angie. "This one has a few minutes left. Get it to him. You said the key is on the table?"

She nodded, tying off the end of the lengthy rope attached to the orange ring to herself, and then hooking an arm through the oxygen tank strap. She stepped off into the water. Jay angled the motorboat to shore and sped off in the direction of the cottage.

* * *

Angie dove down several feet, put the oxygen tube in her mouth and began circling over her husband's head like a shark. She knew it would take Jay five minutes to reach the shore, five to ten minutes to search for the key that wouldn't be found followed by something to cut the chain, plus another five back. No one could hold their breath that long.

She watched Whydini yanking on the chain to create some slack to slip a foot through. In all their years of practice, he had never allowed for "backdoor" escapes. He was tied securely to the cinder blocks.

And by now, his lungs were almost out of air. As if on cue, his body arched sharply and then relaxed, adrift, like he was sleeping.

She smiled. Tampering with the winch was child's play for a woman who had spent decades with endless mechanical devices. She even took a further precaution by hiding any cutting tools in the attic crawlspace. One can never be too sure when murdering one's spouse, she mused.

Angie swam toward the back of her motionless husband, his hands outstretched in a ghostly scene. Everyone would believe she had mistakenly brought the wrong key — after all, they were the romantic couple bar none to the public. Though she would still lay it on thick, maybe even make a suicide attempt look real enough to divert any last suspicions.

She inched closer to his right side about five feet away. His eyes open but lifeless. She swallowed an extra breath in a sigh of relief that now she could live her life in peace without ever having to see another damn card trick or, the hardest part, gaze longingly at her husband while the cameras flashed.

She looked to the surface. The boat wasn't back yet. Another smirk crossed her face. She would use up the rest of the oxygen meant for her husband in the next few moments, place the tube in his mouth and then retreat to the surface to wait for Jay.

* * *

His eyes flicked on with revulsion. Whydini lunged at his wife, grabbing a handful of hair and dragging her to the lake's floor. He snatched the tube from her mouth and wrapped the slack chain around her neck by spinning in a single crocodile death roll. She kicked and clawed at him.

He was running out of time but it didn't matter. The extra weeks of practicing breath control had paid off. Angie could only hold her breath for a solid minute under calm conditions and with all her struggling she'd never make it that long.

Still, there was enough time in this final act to relish her body's convulsions and watch them subside before the lights dimmed.

About the Authors

Chris Rhatigan is the editor of *All Due Respect*. His story in the anthology *Nightfalls* was nominated for a Pushcart Prize. His novella, *The Kind of Friends Who Murder Each Other*, will be released by KUBOA Press.

Joe Clifford is the editor of *The Flash Fiction Offensive* and producer of Lip Service West, a "gritty, real, raw" reading series in Oakland, CA. His short story collection, *Choice Cuts*, is out now. His novels *Wake the Undertaker* (Snubnose Press) and *Junkie Love* (Vagabondage Press) will be published later this year. Much of Joe's writing can be found at www.joeclifford.com. He has been to jail but never prison.

Tom Hoisington is a journalist living in Eugene, OR, with his daughter.

Mike Toomey lives outside of Boston with his wife and two kids. He used to believe that writing kept him sane until he re-read the story in this anthology. He thinks "Even Sven" would make a great short film starring Dennis Franz. Let him know what you think at emptyideas@yahoo.com.

Erin Cole is a dark fiction writer from Portland, OR, the author of mystery novel *Grave Echoes* and horror collection *Of the Night*, and has work appearing in over 30 print and online publications, such as *Dark Moon Books*, *Eschatology Journal*, *Aoife's Kiss*, *All Due Respect*, *Every Day Fiction*, *Shotgun Honey*, *Pulp Metal Magazine*, and more. In 2011, her story, "The Wall of Never Doubt," won 10th place in *Writer's Digest 80th Annual Writing Competition* (Genre Short Story), and in 2009, she won honorable mention in the Kay Snow

Contest for her non-fiction essay, "My Compass." She is the proud owner of a fist-sized meteorite, a lover of spicy food, and is attracted to chaos — not by choice. Visit her cyber pad at www.erincolewrites.com

Stephen D. Rogers is the author of *Shot to Death, Three-Minute Mysteries*, and more than 700 shorter works. His website, www.StephenDRogers.com, includes a list of new and upcoming titles as well as other timely information.

Scotch Rutherford writes about dark corners between the bright lights. He's an independent actor, artist, author, and playwright. His work has appeared in *Pulp Metal Magazine, Voices from the Garage, The Flash Fiction Offensive, Darkest Before the Dawn,* and *All Due Respect.* He has recently adapted his short story, *Going South,* set for publication in *Big Pulp,* June 2013, into a one-act play, which will debut March of this year and that he will direct. This is his first anthology.

Patti Abbott is the author of the e-collection *Monkey Justice* and the forthcoming e-novel-in-stories, *Home Invasion.* More than 100 of her stories have appeared in various venues. She won a Derringer in 2009 for her flash fiction story "My Hero." Forthcoming stories will appear in *Kwik Krimes* (Otto Penzler), *Shotgun Honey,* and *Mysterical-E.* You can find her most days on her blog: pattinase.blogspot.com or outside Detroit.

Nigel Bird comes from a Dirty Old Town. He writes stories that employ the tricks of Smoke and mirrors. By day he assumes the role of being In Loco Parentis at a school in Tranent. By night he becomes Mr. Suit, a smartly dressed gangster with a short lifeline on his hand. He sends you his best, With Love And Squalor, always.

Andrez Bergen is an expat Australian writer, journalist, DJ, and ad hoc saké connoisseur who's been entrenched in Tokyo, Japan, for the past decade. He makes music as Little Nobody and ran groundbreaking Melbourne record label IF? for 15 years. He published the noir/sci-fi novel *Tobacco-Stained Mountain Goat* in 2011 through Another Sky Press and the surreal fantasy *One Hundred Years of Vicissitude* via Perfect Edge Books in 2012. He recently finished a third novel, titled *Who is Killing the Great Capes of Heropa?*, and is ploughing into #4. Bergen has published short stories through *Crime Factory, Shotgun Honey*, Snubnose Press, *Solarcide, Weird Noir* and *Big Pulp*, and worked on translating and adapting the scripts for feature films by Mamoru Oshii, Kazuchika Kise and Naoyoshi Shiotani with Production I.G. andrezbergen.wordpress.com

Benedict J Jones is a writer of short crime and horror stories, although he occasionally wanders into the worlds of Victoriana and the western. He lives in South East London and has been having his work published in the small presses since 2008 with appearances in *Out of the Gutter, Big Pulp!, Encounters Magazine, the Western Online, Delivered Magazine, Penpusher Magazine*, several anthologies and on many websites. He can be found at benedictjjones.webs.com.

Garnett Elliott lives and works in Tucson, Arizona. Recent stories have appeared in *Alfred Hitchcock's Mystery Magazine, BEAT to a PULP: Round Two, Needle Magazine, Blood and Tacos, Pulp Modern*, and *Uncle B's Drive-In Fiction*. You can follow him on Twitter @TonyAmtrak.

Alec Cizak is a writer from Indianapolis. His work has appeared in a variety of journals and anthologies. He is also the editor of the print journal *Pulp Modern*.

Christopher Grant is the editor/publisher of *A Twist Of Noir, Eaten Alive: Zombie Stories*, and *Alternate Endings*, all which can be found on the glorious Internet. He is also a writer of crime/noir and bizarro fiction.

Gary Clifton, forty years a cop, has about sixty short fiction pieces published or pending with online sites, including *Broadkill Review, Boston Literary Mag, Spinetingler, Powder Burn Flash, Out of the Gutter, Short, Fast, 'n Deadly,* and *Underground Voices.* He's been shot at, shot, stabbed, sued, misunderstood and doesn't much care if school keeps or not. Clifton has an MS from Abilene Christian University.

Jack Bates writes from his man cave in the loft of an old house north of Detroit. He writes for kids, he writes for adults, and sometimes he mashes the two to write for the darkness in all of us.

Ryan Sayles's novel *The Subtle Art of Brutality* is out through Snubnose Press. He is the editor of The Noir Affliction, a column at *Out of the Gutter.* His work appears at sites such as *Shotgun Honey, Flash Fiction Offensive, BEAT to a PULP,* and *Crime Factory.* He may be contacted at vitriolandbarbies.wordpress.com

Tom Pitts received his education firsthand on the streets of San Francisco. He remains there, writing, working, and trying to survive. His novella, *Piggyback,* is available from *Snubnose Press.* He is also co-editor at *Out of the Gutter Magazine's Flash Fiction Offensive.* Read more of his work at: tom-pitts.blogspot.com

Pete Risley lives in Columbus, Ohio. His novel *Rabid Child* was published in 2010 by New Pulp Press, and his short stories have been published in *Plots with Guns, Pulp Metal, All Due Respect,* and other venues. He's currently struggling with two in-progress novels.

CJ Edwards has been a police officer in Indianapolis, Indiana, since 2000 and is currently assigned to criminal investigations. His work has been published in *American Blue: Real Stories by Real Cops* by Varro Press, Issue #1 of *Pulp Modern*, *Needle: A Magazine of Noir*, the anthology *Indiana Crime*, and online at *Plots with Guns*, *BEAT to a PULP*, and *The Flash Fiction Offensive*. His novella "Suck" is available in a collection entitled Uncle B's *Drive In Fiction*. His blog can be found at www.fulldarkcity.com.

Jim Wilsky was born and raised in the Midwest. His debut novel, a crime fiction titled *Blood on Blood,* was released in August 2012. It is the first of a three book series. He has also had short stories featured in some of the most highly respected online magazines, such as *All Due Respect, BEAT to a PULP, Yellow Mama, Shotgun Honey, Rose & Thorn Journal, Pulp Metal,* and *Mysterical-E.*

Chris Leek lives in Cambridge, England. His work has appeared in or at *Out Of The Gutter, Shotgun Honey, All Due Respect, Spinetingler, Thrillers, Killers 'N Chillers,* and *Near To the Knuckle.* He lists his hobbies as drinking Mexican beer, smoking cigarettes and talking about himself in the third person. If he owes you money, you only have yourself to blame. nevadaroadkill.blogspot.co.uk

Richard Godwin is the author of crime novels *Mr. Glamour* and *Apostle Rising* and is a widely published crime and horror writer. *Mr. Glamour* is his second novel and was published in paperback in April 2012. It is available online at all good retailers. *Mr. Glamour* is Hannibal Lecter in Gucci. The novel is about a glamorous world obsessed with designer labels with a predator in its midst and has received great reviews. *Apostle Rising*, in which a serial killer crucifies politicians. It is also available for the first time in e-book with some juicy extras, an excerpt from *Mr. Glamour* and four deliciously dark noir stories, like the finest handmade chocolate.

Mark Joseph Kiewlak has been a published author for more than two decades. In recent years his work has appeared in *A Twist of Noir, The Back Alley, Freedom Fiction Journal, Hardboiled, Plots With Guns, Thuglit, The Bitter Oleander*, and many others. He has also written for DC Comics.

Mike Monson works as a paralegal in San Francisco and lives in Modesto, California. He started writing fiction in June of 2012 and so far his stories have appeared or are scheduled to appear in *Literary Orphans, Flash Fiction Offensive, Shotgun Honey, Yellow Mama,* and in anthologies from *Out of the Gutter* and *Near to the Knuckle*. Visit him at mikemonson.org.

Tyler Mathis writes noir fiction spanning several genres. His crime novella *Stung* appeared in *Eclectica Magazine;* his other works have been featured in *Milk Sugar Literary Journal, Short-Story.Me,* and *Death Head Grin*. He resides in northeast Pennsylvania.

Matthew C. Funk is a social media consultant, professional marketing manager, and writing mentor. He is an editor of *Needle Magazine* and a staff writer for *Planet Fury* and *Criminal Complex*. Winner of the 2010 Spinetingler Award for Best Short Story on the Web, Funk has work featured at dozens of sites and in printed volumes, indexed on his Web domain, matthewfunk.net.

McDroll's crime fiction has a nip of noir and a splattering of Scottish humour and can be found floating around in the digital world, most notably in *Shotgun Honey, All Due*

Respect, and *Near To The Knuckle.* Other stories can be found in the anthologies *Off the Record, The Lost Children, Burning Bridges,* and *True Brit Grit.* McDroll is the author of the crime novella *The Wrong Delivery* and the short story collections *Kick It Together* and *Kick It With Conviction.* Website: imeanttoreadthat.blogspot.co.uk

R Thomas Brown is the author of *Hill County.* He lives and works in north Texas with his wife and three children. You can find updates on his work at rthomasbrown.com.

David Cranmer is editor and publisher of *BEAT to a PULP* webzine beattoapulp.com/pulp.htm and books. He also writes the Cash Laramie and Gideon Miles hardboiled westerns under the pen name of Edward A. Grainger. He lives with his wife and daughter wherever work takes him.

Made in the USA
Charleston, SC
14 December 2014